Marrying Mr. Gibson

Book One,
Sons of the Spy Lord

I0545486

By Alina K. Field

Copyright © 2017 Mary J. Kozlowski
ISBN No. 978-1-944063-20-7
Havenlock Press
PO Box 1891
La Mirada, CA 90637-1891

Cover Design by Dar Albert of Wicked Smart Designs

Originally titled *The Bastard's Iberian Bride*

DEDICATION
to Betsy,
the best, biggest-hearted sister ever

She won't be forced into marriage to a nobleman's by-blow.

Paulette Heardwyn rushes to visit her dying guardian, set on learning the truth about her father and the treasure he supposedly left her. But the only man with answers takes his secrets to the grave, leaving her penniless—unless she marries his illegitimate son.

He won't be trapped into marriage by a father he's never known.

With Napoleon vanquished, an ex-soldier has plans for India. But before he can leave England, he's summoned to the deathbed of an Earl who's a spymaster, a complete stranger...and his father. And the meddlesome Earl expects him to marry the daughter of one of his spies.

Thrown together when an old enemy strikes, the would-be spouses soon realize: the Earl has set a trap that neither of them wants to resist.

Chapter One

August, 1819

The Earl of Shaldon would have glorious weather for dying.

And after so many hours in the saddle, Bink Gibson would have a sore on his arse the size of Yorkshire if he didn't reach Cransdall Hall soon.

Horizontal rays of late summer sun pierced the foliage and raised a lather on the horse's neck, and his own. He pulled his hat low, dragged a handkerchief from his pocket and mopped at the back of his neck.

Devil take the Earl. He didn't need Bink's presence for his passing. Let him die in his bed with the men who'd stood by him in life.

Bink had never had a taste for death, not even when he'd been slashing his way through the muck, and blood, and smoke of the Iberian Peninsula. And this dying...

He took a deep breath and quelled his uneasiness. God's truth, he wished he'd ignored this summons also.

His mount snorted.

"Stop your complaining," he said. "You'll have your rub-down soon, lad, in the Shaldon stables. Aye, with the finest of feed, and great aristocrat neighbors nipping at you."

While his great bloody self was led into the grand palace for what was sure to be another let-down.

A low growl emerged from his midsection. He hadn't stopped for a meal, though God only knew why not. He was in no rush for this deathbed acknowledgement, and it was well past even the town dinner hour.

Twenty-odd years ago, all hope of meeting Shaldon had been crushed by some Frog crisis on the other side of the channel. The time since had been filled with plenty of men's pleas for their mothers and laments about disappointments.

Last year had been Zebediah Gibson's, may he rot at his destination.

Bink gritted his teeth and touched a heel to his mount. Best get this over with. Best ignore the ambivalence stuffing his empty belly. Best be done and get on with his plans for India.

"*Paulette.*"

The gelding's ears twitched and Bink straightened. He'd heard it too—a feminine voice, raised in what sounded like anger.

At the bend in the road, he spotted a faded black and yellow dog cart obstructing the way like a downed bumblebee.

"*Paulette.* I'm *famished* and *sweltering*. I cannot abide another hour of this heat." A woman sprawled in the driver's perch, directing her complaints forward.

The two wheels of the cart appeared to be whole and moveable and a large cob stood peaceably in his traces. If his name was Paulette, someone had a strange sense of humor.

A rustle in the brush drew Bink's hand to his pistol.

"Sure and it's summat about here." Another female voice, this one disembodied, floated up. "'Twas that last rut made it fly off."

He eased out a breath. Nothing but women here, of course. Only the stupidest of highwaymen would lurk on the road to the Spy Lord's estate.

"Leave it," the harpy called over her shoulder. "It's sure to be broken in pieces anyway, and I'll die from hunger or this heat if I must sit here much longer."

She unfurled a fan and set a vigorous pace, while he swallowed a chuckle. A lack of food would not take her any time soon, and if the heat did, at least she'd be silent.

"We'll find it, missus," the bush woman said. "'Twon't take but a minute."

A large *harrumph* rumbled over the cob's back.

An angry mistress and her clumsy servant— well, and wouldn't he rather cross swords with the first and help out the other than stand by a bedside wringing his big stupid hands?

He cleared his throat. "May I be of assistance?"

Silence fell. The shrew's head swiveled, puffy cheeks framing an open mouth. The bushes parted and a plump, plainly clad woman popped through.

"Did you lose a trunk then?" he asked.

"*It's here.*" Another woman shouted from the trees. "Come help me."

"Wait here." His command stayed the maid. Nerves prickling, he dismounted, handed her the reins, and pushed back a veil of branches.

A few yards down the sharp slope, a woman straightened into the only beam of light filtering through the thicket.

Bink's breath hitched. Young she was, but no man who'd gone without as long as he had would miss the plump breasts or the rounded bottom under dusty skirts. No man who'd spent as much time on the Iberian Peninsula as he had would miss the eyes, dark as black olives, skin the color of the sand at La Coruña. Dark curls fought to escape her loose bonnet, and when she lifted her chin, her mouth clamped shut, but not before he'd seen the pure white of her teeth.

The air buzzed and his vision fogged. Many such girls had crossed his path during his time in hell. No matter the state of his own sorry self, his desperation had been no match for theirs. He'd come close to bedding a few—except, the Duke's proclivity for hanging men who strayed with the locals had been a powerful deterrent for any poor foot wabbler who could manage to think with the head on his shoulders.

The French command hadn't had such scruples. He'd seen a few such girls after the *chasseurs* had got through with them.

He blinked, chasing the nightmares away. "Troubles, miss?"

Her gaze narrowed and the corners of her full lips turned down. "Are we blocking the road, sir? Surely there is plenty of room for you to go round us."

A haughty bit, then, well-spoken, but from the state of that yellow cart, not an aristocrat, he'd wager. Not the older woman's servant, either. Impoverished gentry, he'd guess.

Three women in a dog cart on a road that was not a main thoroughfare. An old scold, a maid, and this snappish young miss. And no man to journey with them, during a time when England was abuzz with dangerous, unhappy laborers.

They'd be locals, surely, and when he was through with his duty, he'd give whatever man was responsible for them a piece of his mind.

"There's plenty of room for me to stop and rescue a lady in distress." He sidled down the embankment drawing closer.

The sharp chin eased higher. "I don't need rescuing."

He glanced around. "Now, where is this item you've lost and found?"

"There really is no need. My maid can help me."

"She's minding my horse."

Her eyes lifted as he neared, and her scent rose to greet him, some mixture of florals and woman. Blood-stirring it was. Far more enticing then the odor of death awaiting him at Cransdall.

"Has it fallen then into that brook below?"

"What brook?" Her frown slipped lower, and she tipped her head. "Oh, bother. No, it hasn't."

"Lucky, that. Well, then." He scanned the brush again. "Point me to it and I'll retrieve it for you."

Paulette Silva Heardwyn fisted her skirts and tried to beat down her chattering heart.

The man was as tall, and as broad, and as ruddy as some wandering Highlander from one of Scott's stories, yet there'd been no tell-tale Scots accent to his words. His speech, his grooming, even his boots, were proper and gentlemanly.

The glint in his eye was not, nor was the quiver she saw about his lips.

But, *tall*—he was that. She glanced up at the thick clutch of box tree branches, and his eyes followed hers.

"That's quite the tallest box bush I've ever seen," he said. "And is that wee brown box lodged in it yours?"

She winced. The *wee brown box* was precious to her. It had bounced from Mabel's arms onto the road, down the embankment, and into this great bloody bush that years of wind had tilted more than an arm's reach away from the slope. And, blast it all, she wasn't going to leave it.

"It's my writing case. My lap desk," she said. "I quite need it back."

"Your wee box popped out of the cart box, into the box tree, did it?"

Annoyance sparked in her, and the upturn of his lips made it flare higher. He stepped around her.

The scent of soap and horses curled around the warmth rising in her. While he gazed up at the tangle of branches, her eyes fixed on the broad shoulders rippling under dark coats.

She shook off her fluttering. He was a great bloody ox dressed up in fine clothing, this man. That was all.

"My maid was holding it." There'd been no more room in the cart's box after Paulette and Mabel's small cases and all of Mrs. Everly's trunks.

"She was careless."

"And how would you know? It wasn't her fault. We hit a great rut." A great rut that roused the dozing Mrs. Everly, knocking her into poor Mabel.

His gaze sent her skin squirming, raising the heat in her up a notch.

He wasn't handsome, exactly, not like the smith's new apprentice, or the poetically thin dancing master who came round the neighborhood for lessons, or even like Lord

Bakeley, who Mabel had ridiculously mooned over on their only visit to Cransdall a few years before.

When he smiled, he cracked a few lines around his eyes, though she'd swear this man was no more than a few years older than her own self. The sun wore on freckled skin, Mabel always said, and wasn't it true in his case. Lucky he was born male—the wrinkles only made him look rugged.

"And just how were you planning to have your maid help you get it down?"

More irritation welled in her. "I could shake the tree and Mabel could catch it."

"She might miss it entirely, or fumble it, and plop it right into the brook."

If there *was* truly a brook. "I don't see water."

"But you hear it."

Grrr. She'd only noticed the sound when he'd mentioned it.

"Or it might hit the ground and crack all to pieces." He turned his gaze back to the box. "And there's no shimmying up that tree without taking an axe to the branches." He sidled lower and reached a hand.

Her breath caught. He was only a bit short of the mark. On horseback even *she* could reach—but she wouldn't risk any horse on this slope, and certainly not Horace. And then there would be the time wasted unhitching and hitching—

"*Paulette.*" Mrs Everly's screech pierced through the thicket, bouncing off rocks, drowning the sough of the summer breeze.

Nerves itching, she looked up. The writing case was the one thing she had of the man she couldn't remember. She wouldn't lose it to a brook or her companion's impatience, or her own rush to get where she must go.

"Well?" he asked.

In spite of the heat, a shiver went through her.

She straightened her shoulders. She wouldn't lose that lap desk to fear either.

"Fine, then." She'd let him help her.

His steady gaze sent her heart pounding like the beat of a downpour. Who was he? She didn't even know his name.

He crossed his thick arms and her breath eased. The man could hold her down with one finger and do the terrible things Mrs Everly always alluded to but never truly described. Yet he hadn't really flirted. He hadn't grabbed at her. He hadn't as much as stared at her bosom.

She took a deep breath. "You could boost me."

His lips lifted into a full grin.

She took a step back, and he frowned.

"You've naught to fear, miss." His jaw tightened. "I've never hurt a woman, and I won't start with it now."

"Paulette. Leave it Paulette."

"Not even *that* woman," he muttered. He shed his gloves and coat and tossed his hat atop them.

She gasped. "I've never seen hair quite that—"

"Red. Yes." Color rose in his cheeks, but his eyes looked merry. "Now," he linked his fingers and leaned down. "Step up. I'll not need to touch more than the wee soles of your boots, though you may wish to steady a hand against my shoulder."

She swiped at a bead of sweat on her lip. "Shall you put on your gloves?"

"Have you stepped in sh...manure?"

"Of course not."

"Well then, my hands will clean up quicker than gloves." He raised an eyebrow.

She eased in a breath. She must get back Papa's case, and she must get to her destination. Both were important. Both were parts of the mystery that held the key to her future. And even if this man were to touch her improperly, what did it matter? No one would see.

What would Mama have done in her glory years?

His gaze caught her dithering and sent her blood higher.

"Well, and perhaps I can boost your maid instead."

"*My maid*?" Mabel might well drop the box all the way into the brook just to have more of this man's attention. "Right, then." Nerves jangling, she lifted the skirt of her brown traveling gown and set a foot onto hands as firm as a granite stepping stone.

"Go ahead," he said. "Put a hand to my shoulder and steady yourself."

She flexed her knee, reached for him, and he propelled her high. Her other foot groped for his cupped hands, her fingers landed in handfuls of thick hair, and she wobbled against him.

"Steady, then," he said, his voice muffled.

A gasp escaped her. He'd buried his face in her skirts at a level that sent damp heat washing through her.

"What are you doing?" she squeaked.

She wiggled and almost toppled.

A large hand clapped against her bottom. "Stop moving. I've got you."

The words vibrated through her most private parts. Heat sparked in her everywhere, turning her brain to mush.

"I see it," Mabel shouted. "Don't drop her, sir. A bit to your right and she's got it."

He shifted a foot sideways, and Paulette gasped, cupping his ears.

They were big ears, on a big, thatch-haired head.

Her heart lurched, and she wobbled again.

"Hold on," Mabel shouted. "A bit more 'tother way."

"*Quiet*, Mabel. *Blast it*, will you *stop moving*, sir?"

She bit back more oaths and caught her breath. The bank fell away to a tumble of leaves below, but just above her and a bit to the side, the wooden box nestled, looking secure.

It was not secure. She knew that. One slight nudge, one shift in her rescuer's stance, one wobble on her part, and it would slide from her hands and she would lose her father forever.

He took a step and she swayed. His hand squeezed her bottom again.

Raw heat surged through her, and she shivered. "*Stop* moving." She gritted her teeth. "And *stop* squeezing me."

"And you stop wobbling," he grumbled.

She tilted again and shrieked. "Don't drop me, *you nodcock*."

"Nodcock?" he mumbled into her skirts. "Reach for it. I've got you."

She glanced down. His legs *were* like tree trunks. His head was as thick as a boulder. He was solid.

Breath rasping, she looked around. From this better view, she could see where the slope fell off sharply. A tumble—her own or the lap desk's—would dash either to pieces.

She bit her lip, stretched her arms to their full length, slid the case from its nest, and handed it down to a grinning Mabel.

"I won't drop it again," Mabel said. "I can't speak for the gentleman and you."

His hand was still burning her backside.

"Don't worry," he mumbled.

In a heartbeat, he flipped her into his arms and set her onto her feet. She staggered and caught at a sapling.

Heavens. His hair stuck out in tufts and his neck cloth had crumpled, and as he brushed his hands, his gaze pinned her again.

Her cheeks burned. He'd locked on her eyes, not her bosom or her backside, but he might as well still be gripping her bottom the way heat poured through her—now what would he think to do?

And who was he? A gentleman, on this road that ran right by the Earl of Shaldon's estate.

He might be a villager. Or one of the Earl's men. Either way, he might cause her trouble.

She steadied herself and took the box. "Go and get the gentleman's hat and coat, Mabel." She cleared her throat. "Thank you, sir, for your help. I hope we've not held you up too long." Clutching the case, she charged up the slope.

A fine horse was tied to the back of the cart, where Mrs. Everly still sat grumbling.

"We'll be off." Paulette opened the cart's box and swapped the writing case for a satchel, setting the bag next to Mabel in back.

"But that's the bag with my medicinals," Mrs. Everly said. "If it flies off—"

"Then *you* sit in back and hold it," Paulette said.

"It's a great view from the back, missus," Mabel said grinning.

The man's scent wafted her way, his big hands untying his horse.

He smiled at her.

"Well, then," she said, moving away. "Please don't let us hold you any further."

"I'll accompany you."

The warmth in his voice promised nothing but trouble, and the last thing she needed was a meddling man poking around in her business.

"No." She walked around checking the lines and gave Horace a final stroke on his long patient nose. "We'll be on our way soon."

"Where are you headed?"

Mrs. Everly opened her mouth, and Paulette shot her a glare. "We're visiting friends." She hoisted herself into the seat. "Not a syllable," she hissed to her companions, then said as pleasantly as she could muster, "We don't require an escort, for we could easily walk to our destination if we have need."

Next to her, Mrs. Everly groaned.

"And we've already interrupted your journey," Paulette added.

He pulled his horse next to her. "I'm not in such a hurry I can't offer escort."

Her teeth chattered, even as her face burned. She *was* in a hurry, and she'd wasted a great deal of time. And she didn't know who he might know. He might know the man she was visiting. He might know Mr. Cummings, the dog cart's owner, and no friend to the man at Paulette's destination. She didn't want her journey talked of, not now. And she didn't want this man telling tales about fondling her backside.

He leveled a long look at her, eyes glittering in the sharp light like the Baltic amber earrings she'd seen on a visiting lady at services one Easter Sunday.

Perhaps their circumstances called for an introduction, but it was wiser to remain anonymous. And he hadn't offered his name either.

She held herself tight on a shiver. No, she had no need for niceties. She had serious business ahead.

He tipped his hat. "Very well, miss. I shall go ahead then, and flush out any highwaymen who are likely to bother you ladies."

"Foolish girl," Mrs. Everly said. "A gentleman's protection is not to be dismissed so readily."

"If he *is* a gentleman," Paulette said, watching his departing back. "And highwaymen won't bother three poor women like us. And what could one man do against an armed attacker?"

"That man could do something," Mabel said. "I'd wager he has a pistol somewhere or a knife stuck in one of them boots. Aye, and those hands could make great big fists. And, that jaw—he could crack chestnuts with it. The man can take a punch, and give back in kind. And strong. The way he—"

"Leave it."

Mabel's shoulders were shaking. She *would* think it was funny, but dear God—Mrs. Everly didn't need to hear the details of her mauling. The whole county would know.

She set Horace in motion.

"Did you get his name, Polly?" Mabel asked.

Mabel found something attractive in almost every man. Her maid needed to find a husband, instead of flirting with every stable boy, shop man, and farmer she met.

"He's no-one I want to know, Mabel."

"He looks prosperous enough," Mrs. Everly said. "And he did seem interested."

Mrs. Everly hadn't been much inclined to the idea of Paulette marrying, at least not until her own sister's husband had passed a few weeks before.

She'd been with Paulette as companion and chaperone since shortly after Paulette's mother's death. Shaldon's heir, Lord Bakeley, had sent his poor relation to Ferndale Cottage, in lieu of inviting her to reside at Cransdall after her husband's death.

If the lady wanted to keep the small pension Bakeley paid her, she'd stay until Paulette married. And after that...well, Mrs. Everly would have been homeless again. Except that now she'd have a home with her widowed sister.

Paulette was of age now, but she hadn't had the heart to kick the older woman out. And, not to mention, if she were to do that, she might find her own self evicted from Ferndale Cottage, since it was one of Lord Shaldon's properties.

Blast it all, she needed her own money.

"Whether he's interested is neither here nor there." She flicked the reins for Horace to move faster. "Because *I* am not."

She would reach Cransdall soon and put all thoughts of the tall stranger behind her. With any luck, she'd never see him again.

*****

Bink listened for the faint thuds and scrapes, the rattles and crunches behind him. The girl might be a shrew, but he'd go to her aid, if need be. This road was desolate, just the way the owner wanted it, and he wouldn't leave three women alone, at least not until he reached his own destination.

She had no man in her life, surely, to set off all alone like that.

Unless she was running away.

No. She might run with the maid, but not with the old windbag. He would have to ask Bakeley about her.

Soon enough a stone wall ran beside him, its layer of thick moss going grey in the dimming light. An ornate opening rose from the vegetation, the iron gates thrown open and surprisingly unguarded. The old Spy Lord truly had given up.

Two wheel ruts sliced turning lines in the damp verge. There'd been traffic along here recently. Most likely a physician had been called.

Bink halted and took a long breath. Lavender trickled into his senses. He grasped the reins with prickling hands, took deep breaths against the squeeze in his chest, and swallowed a laugh. He'd never been a swooner, not even after a battle. He was a man, a great stupid lout of one and thirty, not that bloody hopeful boy who'd passed here before, all wound up inside.

The faint rattle of wheels still reached him from much further back, out of sight. If the ladies weren't locals, there'd be an inn in the village, and if not, they could turn back and seek shelter at Cransdall. In fact, he'd send one of the grooms to make sure of it.

He tapped his mount's side and followed the wheel tracks through the opening.

The lane leveled, and when he came round a bend, lights shone from every main floor window of the long, sprawling mansion. Cransdall Hall looked as though a dance was afoot, not a dying.

Though the quiet told the true tale. The reverential hush about the place was broken only by the slap of his mount's hooves on the graveled drive. A footman stepped soundlessly out onto the porch and a groom slipped out from somewhere.

Noise broke the silence, and Bink craned his neck. A carriage was creaking up the lane. Had there been someone else behind the ladies?

He bit back an oath. Well, why not? Some other poor *bastard* had likely been summoned by Shaldon, for whatever final sorry-saying the great lord required to wedge open the pearly gates.

This other by-blow had taken the guilt offering and equipped himself with wheels.

Bink *could* have taken his employer's coach. The Earl of Hackwell would not have minded. But a man could think clearer on horseback.

Not that his mind was any less muddled now, not when it came to Shaldon. This final summons was one he hadn't been able to bring himself to ignore. And unless he was too late, he and the man would at long last meet.

And what the devil did Shaldon really want?

He waved off the groom and turned his mount toward the massive stables where he'd played with his half-brother that long-ago summer. It would buy him more time to settle his thoughts.

Except that his thoughts only stirred up more. Nothing had changed in this well-kept environ. A long row of ornate stalls stretched endlessly to house the family's famous prize-winning cattle.

Grooms rushed up quietly, as though he was the bloody master himself. He spoke just as quietly, giving instructions for his horse, and for the ladies on the road.

Moments later, a lanky young footman found him. "Mr. Gibson, Lord Bakeley says to hurry." The footman took his bag and led him to the house.

A new greenhouse graced the back garden area, but not much else had changed. An elm they'd once climbed looked larger, its limbs now beyond the reach of his longer adult arms.

Bakeley had followed him up that tree. At that age, Shaldon's heir had had a devil in him that no amount of canings could stop, possibly because Lady Shaldon promptly sacked those who didn't spare the rod to her first-born. She'd been a practical woman, tolerant of the male species, with an iron will that carried her blithely through running the Shaldon empire, and bringing the next generation to heel. His lordship himself visited when the demands of state allowed him to take time off to plant a seed, and then he was off again to save the world from the Corsican.

All that cultivation had given Shaldon two little lords and one little lady. And at least one lowly bastard, but of course Bink had come along well before her ladyship.

He followed the footman into a familiar side entrance, down a corridor, and into the grand entry hall with its marble floor and ornate wainscoting.

And caught his breath. There, in the great hall, was the woman herself, Lady Shaldon. A life-sized portrait, exquisitely crafted, brought her vibrantly to life.

Servants moved about in hushed voices, and his guide cleared his throat. He ignored the man.

The portrait must have been taken some years after his visit. She looked older, her smiling eyes plagued by some worry.

"Sir," the footman said. "Lord Bakeley—"

He nodded and turned away. He'd find time to study the portrait later. Perhaps get the name of the artist for Hackwell, who wanted his wife and infant daughter painted.

Bink followed the servant up the stairs. At the landing, he heard the grand front door open. A woman squawked, another quietly calmed her, and the servants fluttered around two figures, plucking garments from them.

Gripping the railing, he peered down.

His ladies from the lane had arrived. The dark, wee one with the plump bottom and sharp tongue took a step, and a footman moved in on her. Bink felt the tension all the way up these stairs, his hands clenching the polished wood more firmly.

She straightened her shoulders and lifted her chin, and the servant backed away. Bink let out a breath.

"I *will* see him now." The demand echoed through the hallowed hall, as though she were a daughter of the house.

"But, Polly, why not shake the dust off and freshen up first?" Her maid had emerged from the huddle of servants.

"No. I must speak with him. Before..." Her voice caught, and she cleared her throat.

Before he dies, Bink finished her thought.

Her sharp gaze moved to the staircase, her chin lifting, her scrutiny traveling up and up, sending a prickle through his spine.

She spotted him and locked gazes.

Fierce warmth uncoiled in him. Prickly, she was that. Defiant. And damned pretty.

And she most definitely had the look of the Peninsula about her.

In the course of his travels, Shaldon might've once been in Spain.

The thought washed over him like a snow shower they'd endured one Iberian winter. *Stand down, man.* This one wasn't beddable.

She was his sister.

Chapter Two

The big red-haired man at the top of the stairs finally turned away, and Paulette remembered to breathe.

"Close your mouth," Mabel whispered.

She clamped her mouth shut, praying the pounding she heard in her own ears would be inaudible to the others, or at least attributed to the quick journey and impending grief.

He was here, blast it, and who the devil was he? And why was he visiting the bedside of Lord Shaldon?

And why was she acting as silly as Mabel?

A shiver went through her. From this vantage point he loomed like a giant. And this time, he'd made a thorough inspection of her person. But he'd caught himself at the end and put back all of her clothing.

She shook her head. This was all Mabel's fault, planting the seed that had set Paulette stewing about him for the last part of the journey. Well-dressed he was, in quality cloth, with a frock coat well fitted on those shoulders which—her heart skipped another beat—were quite the most massive she'd ever seen. Even bigger than the smith's.

But no tradesman she knew of wore that sort of clothing. Perhaps he was a solicitor or surgeon. Yes, that would explain it.

She took in another sharp breath. Perhaps he was some friend of Shaldon's, someone who had served the Earl as her papa had.

The ancient housekeeper came out to greet them and soothe Mrs. Everly's grumblings.

Mrs. Everly would calm soon enough when Paulette packed her off to her sister. If travel by dog cart was offensive, well, lucky for everyone, Mrs. Everly, wasn't making the return trip.

"Paulette, you must retire." Mrs. Everly's voice finally intruded. "They'll bring a tray to your room. You must refresh yourself and change before you see his lordship. You must make a respectable—"

"No." She'd been bullied, and ignored, and talked down to enough. Lord Shaldon had not answered any one of her many letters, except to dodge and offer platitudes through some man of business. He was not allowed to go to his death without answering some questions.

She marched to the staircase, and Mrs. Everly moaned.

Footsteps scurried, and a maid, as small as herself, came up beside her.

Paulette kept walking, eying the girl. She was far too tiny to stop an unruly lady. If they wished to stop her, they would need to set the footman on her, and they wouldn't dare.

"If you will not show me the way to his lordship's chamber," she said to the maid, "I'll find it myself."

Though it had been years since her only visit, she had a memory of Cransdall's layout. All she need do was follow the halls until she stumbled over a train of hushed servants moving in and out of his lordship's sickroom.

"Yes, miss. I've no doubt you would be able to," the maid whispered. "Lord Bakeley and the doctor are with his lordship, and his other son has just arrived. His daughter has been notified but I'm not sure she'll reach here in time."

Paulette stopped. "Charles is *here*?"

She'd met Charley, Shaldon's younger son, on her disastrous visit, and like Bakeley he'd taken a brotherly pity on her. Not enough pity to write to her or to make the few hours' ride to visit her when he was in the country. The last she'd heard, Charley was in Egypt, or Paris, or Vienna, or some other exciting environ following in his father's footsteps.

The maid's eyes went wide and her pale cheeks bloomed pink, a wholly English rosiness that Paulette could never hope to achieve.

The girl ducked her head, probably realizing she had overstepped, imparting information that was too much like gossip.

"Miss, I'm new here. I don't know the brother's name, but he's just gone up the stairs ahead of us."

Paulette's skin buzzed. The man she'd met on the road had just gone up the stairs. The flaming-haired giant who'd ogled her was not one of Shaldon's operatives, nor was he a solicitor, or physician, or a respectable gentleman. He was Shaldon's son, but not a son she'd ever heard about.

He must be, he had to be, a by-blow.

She felt her face heat and then a niggling chill swept through her. Perhaps Shaldon had others. Perhaps...

No. No, no, no. She was the beloved daughter of Paul and Sela Heardwyn. She picked up her skirts and continued on.

*****

The footman delivered Bink to the sickroom door and vanished. Before he could knock, the door flew open.

James Everly, Viscount Bakeley, eldest legitimate son and heir of the Earl of Shaldon, nodded back at him. A grin split his face, quickly squashed into a somber expression. "Hello, brother," he said.

That flashing grin was the Bakeley he'd known the summer he'd spent at Cransdall so many years ago.

Bakeley, the man, had grown into his mother's son—stable, a good steward of the vast family holdings and wealth, a conventional lord. Not a sneaking, swindling, lying spy. Boring, almost. They'd run into each other in London months earlier, re-establishing the thin fraternal tie. Not so thin that Bakeley hadn't hinted at some frustration with Shaldon since the Earl's return to Cransdall.

Bakeley had managed the estate since his mother's untimely death years earlier, and he'd done a damn fine job of it from what Bink could see. During their chats, Bakeley had mentioned some investments that had soured, some bad years due to weather. And of course, the troubles of the post-war economy. Shaldon, who'd spent his life letting others manage his riches while he managed the world, thought the estate should be doing better.

Of the many emotions roiling in Bakeley right now, one had to be relief that the badgering would soon end.

He pounded Bink's shoulder. "You're still bigger than me."

"And I can still take you, if you keep pounding on me."

He launched a soft jab at Bink's other shoulder. "We'll have a mill when this is over, what say you?"

A murmur of voices in the background brought Bakeley up. "Right then. This is a dreadful business. Shall we go in?"

Bink's empty stomach churned. "I've come this far."

Bakeley ushered him through a dressing room and into a bedroom with its grand canopied tester and ornate hangings. A thin, soberly-dressed man—a physician probably—hovered nearby. On the other side of the bed a solidly built manservant fussed with the bedclothes. The window curtains were drawn against the dusk, and candles spread uncertain circles of light.

Nerves rebelling, Bink fought for a breath, the air in the room thick from the warmth of an unnecessary fire and the tension of slow dying.

He stepped up to the bed.

A pair of dark eyes under grizzled hair followed his movements. Nothing else in the man moved—well, except for the upturn of his lips.

Bedclothes rustled and a hand emerged, yellowing flesh clinging to big bones. He still managed an aura of strength and command.

"Come closer."

The voice was firmer than Bink would have expected. Even in his dying this man radiated power.

Bink's feet seemed frozen in place, his spine locked upright.

"Edward," the sick man said.

Edward. Edward Bink Gibson was the name on his baptismal register, yet it was like some other man being summoned.

He took in another deep breath. This was something to be got through, like the death of an anonymous soldier a man stumbled across in the smoke, the survivor tied to the dying, invisibly, intimately, even without the knowing that came with fighting shoulder to shoulder, or swilling from the same rum pot, or sharing a meal.

Bink moved closer. The man held his gaze, intelligence shining through the fog of what must be pain. His sallow skin had been freshly shaved, his hair combed.

"You summoned me," Bink said.

"Indeed. Blast this bed." Those words slurred, and the laugh that followed ended on a spluttering cough. "You're a fine fellow."

"A fine fellow you had to meet before you died?"

He rattled out another laugh. "No. A fine son. And we've met, boy. On the Peninsula." The fingers lifted. "I had to see Addy's boy for myself. Took off and enlisted. Too stubborn to ask me to buy a commission. You made me proud, boy."

A coughing fit brought the manservant to his side and gave Bink time to sort through the pictures careening around in his jumbled brain. No Earl of Shaldon had crossed his path—or that of his commander, Major Beauverde, the current Lord Hackwell—he was sure.

The man was lying, like all spies lied; just like he'd lied when Bink was a boy, promising to meet him that long ago summer.

"He needs to rest," the physician whispered.

"Damn you, I'll have an eternity of that." The garbled cry came with another cough. "I could not tell you, Edward." He lifted his head a fraction. "Don't you remember? You took a *padre* across the *montanhas,*" he said, adopting a heavy accent.

Bink squeezed his brows together. Not possible. The priest had seemed a smaller man, an older man. A Portuguese man.

And yet...

He moved closer. The dark intelligent eyes. The bushy brows. The gruff arrogance.

His head filled with memories, his thoughts sailing out of the closed stuffy room into a shepherd's hut. Beauverde had saved his sorry arse from a possible hanging, packing him up on a mid-winter escort where freezing his balls off had been more of a danger than any Frog-eater.

There'd been nothing of humility in that maddening priest. He'd singled Bink out for his hair and goaded him to admit his Irish. He'd pushed and prodded and tried to shame him—unsuccessfully—to make a good confession, not accepting the truth that Bink wasn't Catholic.

Bink slid a branch of candles closer. The face was drawn, jaundiced, lips pressed thin, yet the eyes twinkled with flecks of copper, a glimmer of his own.

A chuckle rumbled up and Bink swallowed it back. Well, he'd known about the Earl, hadn't he? Shaldon had been no diplomat. He was a spy.

"Bloody hell," Bink muttered.

Shaldon's dry cracked lips turned up. "You made me proud, my son."

His chest eased, a weight lifting. *You made me proud*, instead of *you're a sinner, and fool, and a disappointment*. Zebediah Gibson, the man who'd played father to Bink, had left the world declaring him a failure, the bad mix of English aristocrat and Irish slut, the boy with no skills but his fists, who'd left to kill men in a hideous war. Zebediah had blamed it on the call of blood, the summer spent at Cransdall before Bink went off to the worldly school Lady Shaldon had paid for.

"I've heard you're working for Hackwell. Not that you'd need it, but you'll be provided for," Shaldon said.

Bink opened his mouth to decline any bequest, but voices at the door distracted him and a flurry of skirts rushed to the bedside. The scent of flowers wafted up, and he looked down on a mass of springy dark hair, a straight nose, full lips and a bosom.

The lady from the road had invaded the sickroom in all her road dust, with a slick of tempting perspiration making her shine.

He shook off the unbrotherly thoughts.

Bakeley crowded next to her, and Shaldon's head tilted.

"My lord," she said. "Sir."

Bakeley put a hand to her arm. "I'm sorry, Father—"

Shaldon's fingers danced up again. "Paulette?" His voice sounded like oiled gravel, but his eyes lit. "Is it you?"

Paulette. The girl, not the horse. Gripping her bottom had driven that name from his memory.

"My lovely dear. Grown into a beauty. Good you're here."

"I've written you many letters, my lord." She clenched her hands. "And when Mrs. Everly received news of your illness, I knew I must come."

Shaldon slid a glance over to Bakeley. "You will explain."

"Yes, Father." Bakeley shot Bink a look, accompanied by a quirk of the lips that could have been an incipient frown or a squelched smirk.

The skin on Bink's neck rippled. This was the strangest dying he'd ever attended.

"Lord Shaldon." The lady poked an elbow at Bink, trying to nudge her way closer to Shaldon. "Sir, I beg you, I must ask you, I must talk to you about my father."

Shaldon moaned loudly, his eyes fluttering shut, his mouth falling slack.

Bink gave way for the physician who shoved in and reached for the sick man's wrist. Bakeley had the lady's elbow and was steering her away from the bed.

"He cannot...Bakeley, he *must* speak to me," she said, trying to pull away.

Bakeley shushed her, and Bink could see the lift of her shoulders as she drew her back up.

"His pulse is weak," the doctor said. "I should like to examine him. Kincaid, you will assist me."

The manservant, Kincaid, sent them a stern, unservile look, the kind Bink had deployed often himself in the service of Hackwell. He nodded to the man, one servant to another.

"I'll send word when he comes to." Kincaid said.

The lady's face hardened. Bakeley tucked her hand on his arm and clamped his own firmly over hers.

"Very well. Brother, Paulette, I can see the road dust on both of you. Please come and refresh yourselves."

"I will gladly stay and help," she said.

"Kincaid would not let you near him. We'll discuss his bequests. He won't mind, and they're unlikely to change."

Paulette tugged at her hand trapped under Bakeley's. "But—"

Something in the red-haired man's throat rumbled and stopped her train of thought.

Danger, his eyes flashed, at Bakeley, not her. He turned on his heel and walked to the door, exactly as if they were expected to follow him, as though he were the older brother and the heir to the earldom, and not some gentleman's bastard.

Bakeley nudged her. She cast a last look at Shaldon, and wondered if he was feigning a swoon. She'd seen it done by girls at the village assembly.

But no. Surely not. Though Mrs. Everly had attempted to shield her from the mysteries of dying, Mabel had no such scruples. Going in and out of a swoon seemed to fit. And Mabel had said they might not make it in time.

To be so close...tears welled and Paulette squeezed them back.

"Shall I carry you then?" Bakeley asked, sounding bored. "Are you fainting, my dear?"

Her cheeks burned. She straightened her spine and allowed herself to be led out. "I am not your dear," she whispered. "Your father is dying. Your demeanor is entirely inappropriate."

"I am grieving in my own way."

She gritted her teeth. "It's so unfair. I've tried and tried to speak to him." Her voice broke and she gulped in air. "I *need* him to answer some questions. I *need* him to tell me the truth."

Shaldon's bastard had waited still as a statue by the door to the corridor. "The truth from Lord Shaldon?" he said. "You might as well hope to get wine from a milk cow."

The flatness in his tone spiked her irritation. "How would I know? I've only had a chance to speak to him once, years ago, when I was so young I barely remember."

"That's one more chance than Bink has had," Bakeley said.

"Bink?"

The big man fixed his gaze on her. "That would be me, miss."

What a ridiculous name for a man playing a gentleman.

Bakeley whisked them along to a drawing room, ordered refreshments, and closed the door. "Now."

He still gripped her hand. She tried to pull away, but he clamped tighter.

"Introductions. Paulette Heardwyn, meet Edward Bink Gibson. Mr. Gibson is my half-brother, and his lordship's eldest son."

"That we know of." Mr. Gibson studied her, all his earlier warmth gone. "Pleased to meet you, Miss Heardwyn." He turned to Bakeley. "Is Miss Heardwyn a younger relation?"

The hair on her neck quivered. Shaldon was *not* her father.

"Heavens, no."

Even if she could doubt Bakeley's words, his loud laugh reassured her.

"Absolutely not. Paulette's father was one of our father's men who died in service." Bakeley dropped her hand and went to a cabinet, setting out glasses and a bottle of brandy. "Father settled Paulette and her mother onto one of his properties."

"I am right here, Bakeley."

"Sorry, my dear."

His manners, the few times they'd met, had always been a tad condescending, but never as atrocious as this. Possibly he was deeply affected by his father's imminent death, stuffing down his grief to the point of appearing unfeeling and callous. But she doubted it.

There was no accounting for the ways of these English lords.

"Here." He passed her a glass of brandy and gave one to his brother. "You'll be needing something stronger today."

She sniffed the glass. Their man of all work, Mama's former compatriot, Jock, had let her share his ill-gotten brandy, and she'd quite liked it.

She could not be totally out of charity with Bakeley if he was including her in something stronger than tea. She took a sip and let the warm liquid roll through her.

"Father is Paulette's principle guardian. Or was, since she has reached her majority."

Yet she was still not in control of her life. "Now he's the principle trustee of my inheritance, at least until I reach the age of five-and-twenty." *Or if I marry an approved suitor, which I will not do.* She took a hardier sip.

"I believe he will dispense with that duty much sooner," Bakeley said. "By dying."

The thought sent a little flurry through her. She didn't know the other two trustees—only their names. Her inheritance had been less than modest, the allowance granted her enough to keep Mabel. Enough for a genteel life in the country in one of Lord Shaldon's genteel cottages.

It would never be enough for a life of adventure and travel, which she would dearly love to experience, or a husband, which, truth be told, she would gladly do without.

And it would never be enough to search out the treasure Jock said her father had left her, not without Shaldon's help.

Unless, perhaps, Shaldon's will really did include her. What had Bakeley meant about a bequest? Would it be vulgar to ask directly, while the Earl lay dying so nearby?

"Out with it, Bakeley," the big man said. "Say what you want to say and be done."

She sent him a grateful nod, and he raised an eyebrow, making her heart tumble.

He'd read her mind, blast it. Jock had told her a good spy was inscrutable. Her mother certainly had been, spending the last years of her life as a humble country widow, reserved and distant, even to her own daughter.

She must try harder to squash her passion and impatience.

Servants bustled in with refreshments and then quietly left.

"Paulette, shall I fix you a plate?" Bakeley asked. "Will you take tea also?"

Her hands twitched and she gripped the glass. Bakeley's solicitousness was an annoying stall. "I'd much rather you refill my brandy glass."

"I'll do it." Mr. Gibson moved close and loomed over her, the shadow he cast making her skin tingle. When he lifted her glass away without touching her, she caught her breath, and with it that whiff of horses, and leather, and him.

Drat the man.

"Won't you sit down, miss?" He pointed at the sofa and went to the brandy bottle.

She settled herself onto a straight-backed chair at a round table.

"You'd best take a chair also, Bink." Bakeley put down the plate he'd loaded up with meats and cheese for her. "For what you are about to hear, you will want to be seated."

Bink's skin prickled and he cast a hard look at Bakeley. His brother's jaw had gone firm and he wasn't smirking now.

"Bad news, then? I believe I'll remain standing." He topped off the lady's glass and his own.

"Yes, well." Bakeley grabbed the bottle, poured another drink, downed it, and frowned at the glass. "Our father left you hanging twenty years ago, but he left us all hanging, Bink. Now at the end, he's taking an *active* hand. You've no idea the favor Bonaparte did for us. Gave Shaldon something to manage—someone to manage— besides us." He began to pace and stopped in front of Bink. "And there are only four of us, dear brother. No other by-blows lurking about."

Bakeley was in an uncharacteristic lather. Whatever the bad news, this show went some ways in making up for it. "Your mother managed to leash him then, even from far away?"

The young lady's eyes flared with interest, he thought, not missish shock. This one was no soft bit of fluff.

Bakeley shuddered. "Perhaps." He opened his mouth, looked at the lady and pressed his lips tight.

"He cared not to have another child out of wedlock?" the lady asked.

Bakeley cleared his throat.

"By-blows are a great nuisance for a man with a conscience," Bink said.

"Did his lordship have a conscience?" She rose from the chair. "He seems to have one now, if he's leaving you a bequest. Or perhaps that's just his pride. You're from his bloodline."

Yes, like one of his stallions. "I'd guess in Shaldon's case, his lady's pride was the determinate."

Her eyes took on a dreamy cast, softening her face and making her look even younger. "He loved her."

Bink's heart did a flip. Perhaps there *was* some tenderness in this tough little bird.

"It was an arranged marriage." Bakeley refilled his own glass. "From her grandfather's commercial interests, she brought a fortune—an enormous fortune—to the union. Mother was set to marry Father's older brother until Uncle took a fall and cracked his skull. They had to call Father back from Ireland to take on the title. She knew him a week before deciding she could tolerate him, and they were married as soon as the banns could be called. And I came along some eight months later."

"And they lived happily ever after."

Bink squashed a smile. The lady's sardonic tone had returned, thank goodness. He'd hate to think he'd misjudged her.

Bakeley reached for the bottle again, and her lips turned down in a frown. "I should like to hear what you have to say, Bakeley, before you have many more glasses of that."

Bakeley set down his glass, walked to the cold fireplace, and rested a hand on the mantel.

It was such a fine piece of drama, even Miss Heardwyn noticed. She sent Bink an eye-roll.

"Well it must be bad," Bink muttered.

Bakeley turned. His mouth worked as if his lips were struggling with some great piece of gristle. His hands slipped behind his back, a soldier at parade rest.

"Yes, well. You are each to receive a small sum as an inheritance. Not much. Not enough for any real independence. However, if you meet certain conditions, you are to receive a great deal of cash, and the title to the house and acreage acquired for you, worth four thousand a year, with the potential for more if you manage well."

Bakeley's gaze skittered from Bink to Miss Heardwyn, as he tugged at his neck cloth.

The lady gave Bink a pointed look. She tilted her head and he saw the pulse at her neck, a curl bouncing against it. Her lips parted and then pressed closed. She lifted her eyebrows.

She was begging him to ask.

Talking about money was vulgar. *Let the bastard do it.*

Well, why not? "I've no need for his lordship's money," Bink said. "Give my small sum to Miss Heardwyn, and you'd best end the suspense and tell her the conditions she must meet to receive that property and income."

Her eyes flared. "Shaldon wouldn't give me a property. I'm sure it's meant for you, Mr. Gibson."

"No," Bakeley said.

She went very still, yet Bink could feel the tension rolling from her. Could it be she was poorer than she looked? Her dress was finer than Lady Hackwell's had been when she was merely a wealthy spinster, yet he knew Lady Hackwell had been an odd one. More ladies overspent on dresses to keep up appearances than dressed down.

"Bakeley, tell her what she needs to do to receive her property."

Bakeley's jaw moved and he took a deep breath. "It's not meant to be *her* property. It's meant to be *yours*, as in both of yours, upon meeting his condition."

Bink's blood pounded through his ears on the way to his feet. The Earl's gleaming gaze when Miss Heardwyn appeared, Bakeley's nerves, the Earl's swoon—undoubtedly faked, like a cutpurse's accomplice distracting a mark. Something here was amiss.

Bakeley's aristocratic brow glistened with beads of sweat, and in spite of his tension, humor glimmered in his eyes. He cleared his throat and said, "His lordship wishes for the two of you to marry."

Chapter Three

No. No. No. Paulette's vision clouded. She locked her knees and stared through pinpoints at the fireplace poker, and somehow managed to stay erect.

Shaldon wanted her to marry his *by-blow*. His *bastard*.

It was true, she was no prize, in either beauty, breeding, or dowry, but she'd had respectable offers. The vicar, whose wife had died leaving five children, had asked her to marry him. And a prosperous yeoman from an ancient, well-known family had been so unaccountably smitten, he'd promised to hire a full-time cook for her.

Her vision cleared and she looked around. Bakeley's brow had creased. Mr. Gibson's eyes— his eyes bore into hers and she knew the moment they went from feral to concerned, sending her insides quaking.

Shaldon's by-blow wasn't a pretty man, nor as handsome as Bakeley, but when she looked closely she could see the resemblance in the brothers, in the line of the jaw, the length of the nose, and the curl of the lips. Strength and danger had its own allure. Jock had warned her to be alert for this kind of peril.

She sensed he might not be unwilling to take Shaldon's bait, and fought for a breath to set him straight.

"Miss Heardwyn," he said, before she could speak, "even with a smallish portion, your intelligence and beauty will bring you a better man than the Earl of Shaldon's bastard."

She huffed out a laugh. Her intelligence? Her beauty? A dark little shrew, a teacher had once called her. Her options had been a desperate vicar and a love-struck farmer. Most gentlemen didn't like such as she. Men wanted fair skin, golden hair, and blue eyes.

Biting her lip, she studied him. His speech had taken on a northern cast almost as bad as that of Mr. Cummings, or the man Kincaid, and his mouth quirked like he wanted to laugh.

He was mocking her.

"You're turning me down then?" she asked.

"I will never marry."

Her chest tightened. "That has been my intention also."

Bakeley moved closer. "It's a good arrangement. Your work for Hackwell has taught you how to manage an estate."

His work? *His work*?

He must have seen her shock. "I am steward to the Earl of Hackwell. I served him in the army, as a sergeant."

"Yes. Paulette, Mr. Gibson will manage your property well. And you'll have your own home. You'll have enough money to gad about traveling, as you once expressed a wish to do. Perhaps you may even have a Season."

"A *Season*?" she cried. Married to a land steward, there'd be no Season. It hadn't ever been truly possible, but the thought of closing and locking that door forever depressed her.

"Bakeley, she'd have no entry into society, not on my arm."

Bakeley took a step closer. "Lord Hackwell and I—"

"Bakeley." Mr. Gibson put up his hand. "Leave us."

When the door closed, Bink loaded a plate and sat opposite Miss Heardwyn. Paulette.

"We may as well eat," he said.

Her mouth firmed, and her lips paled, and she would not meet his eyes.

"I am sorry for this, Miss Heardwyn. Shaldon cannot leave off from his meddling and spying, even unto death, but we must not let it bring us down. We'll find a way through this."

A sob escaped her and she blinked rapidly and took several breaths, before reaching for the plate Bakeley had prepared for her.

"One small bite," Bink said.

She nibbled a piece of cheese, poor wee cornered mouse.

"You'll have my portion," he said. "I'll see to it. And I'm sure Bakeley won't put you out of your home."

A strangled sound escaped her as she swallowed, and he tried to remember the state of his handkerchief.

Ah no, he'd used it on the road, like a regular lout. A true gentleman wouldn't have sweated.

"To have shelter and regular food and a maid is no small thing for a woman alone," he said.

The plate hit the table with a firm smack and her eyes flashed. "You have no idea," she said, her voice cracking.

Iberian temper. He'd seen a flash of it on the road.

His nerves prickled, interest unfurling. Her breasts moved with each breath, and he vaguely wondered if she was corseted under the dusty gown. "I don't, miss," he said blandly.

She jumped to her feet. "You've traveled. You have a position and a purpose. You have a f-family."

Her face had flushed and the skin at her neck stretched tight over a jumping vein. She clenched and unclenched her fists, her anger—her passion—palpable.

His own heartbeat raced to match hers. This was a handful of woman, and wouldn't he like to...No. This was no time for a tupping. The lack of family had her genuinely afraid. For himself, he'd dealt with that lack years ago, and she was right, as a man, he'd had more chances to make his own way. But it wasn't impossible for her, and he needed to set her straight.

He set his plate aside and leaned back into the plush upholstery. "Family? What, you mean Bakeley? Steven Beauverde, Lord Hackwell, is more of a brother to me. I served him in the war. When he inherited I came back as his valet. I nicked him so many times shaving he had to make me his steward."

"From soldier to valet to steward. An earl's son? You expect me to believe that?"

"It's the truth."

She waved a hand. "No lord would make his valet his steward."

It was what he'd thought also when Hackwell had suggested it. "No lord in his right mind. God's truth, I had to be taught the job." He stood. "As did his lordship. He was the second son. Unlike Bakeley, he wasn't trained from birth to manage."

"Bakeley is a second son."

He made himself laugh, wondering if she'd meant to take a jab at the bastard. If so, she'd have to do better.

"His lordship and I learned though, we did. And do you know who our teacher was? Miss Annabelle Harris, she who is now Lady Hackwell. We learned from a woman."

She sighed. "If you are trying to woo me—"

"No."

A tremor went through her. "Then what is your point?"

What was his point? He studied her and watched her color rise again. "You'll find your purpose, Miss Heardwyn. Shaldon won't leave you penniless, and if Bakeley puts you out of your home, you must write to...to Lady Hackwell. I'll speak to her and see you provided for." She stiffened and he put up a hand. "Without matrimony, and in no way improperly. I have the ear of Lord and Lady Hackwell." And once he'd found his fortune in India, he would have money to send to a poor spinster.

She pressed her lips firmly and stomped to the door.

"Miss Heardwyn?"

Her hand paused on the latch.

"What *is* your purpose? What is it you want to do?"

Her shoulders dropped and she hurried out of the room.

Moments later, Bakeley popped back in.

"Ye Gods, with that one you'll earn your inheritance."

"We're not wedding. Put it out of your mind. But tell me more about her."

"You'll marry when you see that property. If you can stand living with—"

"No. To hell with the property." He was past thinking about English estates. He'd put up all of his savings to secure a spot with the East India Company. A man might breathe and fight and find his fortune in a place like India.

Bakeley poured more brandy. "Very well. She does have an interesting background. Her father was one of our father's spies."

"Yes, I gathered that much. Her mother was Spanish?"

He shrugged. "Or Portuguese. I don't really know. The grandparents came to Cornwall in the last century. I know she's settled in a cozy little cottage in the next county, and she's about to be unsettled from it."

"How so?"

"The property has been sold to one of her neighbors who's been coveting it. Paulette will have to move, as soon as our father leaves this world. Those were the terms of the sale."

Bink braced a hand on the fireplace mantel and leaned into it. There should be a special place in hell for men who displaced orphans and widows. "He's pushing her out? How can he do that?"

Bakeley shrugged. "He wants it his way. Why not marry her, Bink? She can live fashionably in London, and you can go your own way. Last we talked, you were looking into India. Or do you have another Mrs. Gibson in your sights?"

God's blood, he'd forgot about mentioning India to Bakeley.

"Why not marry her? Why *not*, Bakeley? I won't marry for money, that's why not."

"Father did. I hear Hackwell did also. Or are you saying Hackwell loves his wife?"

Bink poured himself another finger of brandy. From what he knew, both Shaldon's and

Hackwell's marriages were for money *and* love, and both men had been damn lucky to find both.

"Oh. I know what it is. You thought you'd slipped once and for all out of the paternal noose. You don't want to slip it back on."

Bink laughed and downed his drink. "I'll go and wash this road dust from me."

"I'll come along and play your valet."

"I'll still not marry."

Bakeley clapped his shoulder. "Yes, yes. We'll see."

When Paulette arrived at her room, she was relieved to find only Mabel there. The maid quickly pocketed the paper she was studying.

"Another political tract?" Paulette asked.

"Aye. At the inn where we stopped, I was given it. How is his Lordship?"

"He was conscious, and then when I tried to talk to him he was not. What are the servants saying?"

"He won't last the night one says, and another whispers he's too mean to die. Though that one I wouldn't put stock in, a young bounder of a footman with a wandering eye. Handsome he is, but you'll stay away from him, Polly."

With Shaldon trying to marry her off to his by-blow, the footman would be the least of her troubles.

The maid poured some water into a basin. "Come and wash. The water will soothe you. I'll ring for some supper, and we'll get you into your nightclothes. Mrs. Everly has taken to her bed and with so many maids to cluck about her, we won't see her complaining face for the next few days. Praise the Lord."

"Mabel," Paulette chided. She should say more. Though Mabel had been her nurse since before she could remember, she shouldn't tolerate disrespect of Mrs. Everly, who was after all yet another woman dependent on others for a home.

She tucked her loose hair behind her ears, and dipped her fingers into the basin. "Can you not open a window, Mabel? It's stuffy in here."

Mabel's skirts swished, and Paulette ducked her face closer to the water. A cool breeze whipped in, wrapping her in the scent of Cransdall's lavender fields and easing her tension.

She glanced at the upholstered sofa and rubbed her eyes. Perhaps just a moment's rest while Mabel readied her gown. "Mabel, help me out of this and bring me the new gown. I'm going back to the sick room."

The smell, Bink decided, was all wrong.

He twitched on the hard-back chair pulled next to the bed, and watched the supposed valet, Kincaid, bend his big frame over the mattress to stuff another pillow under Shaldon's head.

Bink had been around death, both the stuttering kind and the mercifully quick, and this was all wrong. This sickroom smelled of tobacco and boot polish, like the Earl had paused for a smoke between coughing spells while his valet buffed his slippers.

Not this valet, though. Kincaid was no more of a valet than he himself had been to Hackwell.

The old man lay in the center of the big bed, only his shoulders, neck and head visible.

If he was faking, he'd starved himself for this role. The eyes and cheeks had sunken in, and the counterpane draped a lean body.

But then again, Bink had never truly seen the Earl undisguised. Perhaps in his natural state he was a tall, broad-shouldered whippet.

"Leave us," Shaldon said.

Bink twitched again and squashed the compulsion to obey.

That command hadn't been addressed to him. And anyway, he'd been summoned to this midnight meeting and he bloody well wasn't going to be dismissed before it even started.

The manservant headed for the door.

"Hold there, Kincaid," Bink said.

The man kept going.

Bink jumped to his feet. "I said hold. You're not leaving me alone with a sick man."

"You'll have things to discuss with—"

"Aye. And I imagine you know all about them already. Or, if you don't, who's to worry? He wouldn't have you by his deathbed if he didn't trust you."

When Kincaid went to stand at the foot of the bed, Bink's breath eased. He'd stood by dying men, friends and strangers too, but none so strange as this man who, if his mother's deathbed confession to a child of eight could be believed, was his flesh and blood.

"I loved your mother," Shaldon said without preamble, his voice firm.

Bink's heart pounded, the words landing like a nine-pounder filled with case shot. He took a steadying breath and said, "Yet you couldn't marry her."

"No."

The tone was matter-of-fact. Not pandering, not filled with pathos or regret, just brutally honest.

A man could take brutal honesty and deal with it—it was the lying that took the world down around you.

Bink knew snippets of Shaldon and Addy's story, told after her death through the scratched and twisted lens of his mother's husband, Zebediah Gibson.

The man he'd believed was his father, until Zebediah had thrashed Addy to a lingering death. Love had never been a theme of Gibson's stories.

"I'm sorry I wasn't there to save her."

Shaldon's words were firm and filled with an anger that rang true and echoed his own.

He beat back the memories. Zebediah, the little weasel, had spoken out against the violence of war, but when his mercantile travels brought him home, he'd never spared the rod on any man, woman or child under his fist. To Bink's everlasting shame, he hadn't been able to save his mother. He'd barely been able to save himself.

At least, not until he'd started growing a man's height and muscle, and Zebediah released him to Lady Shaldon's custody.

"Paulette needs help."

Shaldon's words tore him out of the past, rattling him again.

This was but more managing. At her husband's behest, Lady Shaldon had removed Bink from an evangelical tyrant and put him in the care of a headmaster with an even bigger stick, trying to make a gentleman of him. He'd run away from that mess, and he'd see himself out of this one.

"Heardwyn had something. Held by the trust. Don't know," he rasped out. "Evidence. Money. Don't know. You can save her," Shaldon said.

The Earl's sharp gaze drilled into Bink, sifting through his reaction, weighing, analyzing, calculating. The honest man had died, and the bloody spy resurrected, as manipulative as the best sharker.

"Bakeley can save her, or your man here, Kincaid."

The old man's lips thinned. "Needs a soldier. And you're a good one." A coughing fit followed, and the sick man began to wheeze, sucking in sharp, noisy breaths.

Kincaid hurried around and raised him up. "Get the doctor," he ordered.

Bink yanked the door and summoned the physician, who was deep in conversation with Bakeley. He stepped out and both men went in and shut the door on him.

He rubbed at his aching head. A few hours of sleep and he could be on his way. He'd met the Earl. Now he should pull up camp, head back to Greencastle, wrap up his plans for India.

But damned if he didn't want to know more. He spotted a fresh bottle on the sideboard and poured a drink.

Shaldon claimed to have loved his mother, and what the blazes did that mean?

Bink had seen all sorts of the love men could feel for women, everything from a need for a plump arse to besotted servitude. Only Hackwell and his lady seemed to have achieved a genuine respect and friendship along with that bloody need to be in each other's pockets all of the time.

It wasn't anything he could understand. He'd only ever experienced that first kind of love.

The corridor door opened and Miss Heardwyn—Paulette—paused in the threshold, a candle held high.

And the question he should have asked slapped him—*who* would she need a soldier to save her from? For if a strong arm was needed, the danger was certainly a who, and not a what.

His gaze slid down her body and took in a frock that outlined her curves. Her hair had been combed and pinned, but a few wild curls strayed over her forehead.

She'd need saving from lusty men, that was a fact.

She searched the room and her gaze landed on him.

"Come in," he said.

She closed the door behind her.

"Did you get some rest?" he asked.

Her mouth moved in a grimace. "Yes, but I didn't plan to. I meant to come up sooner. Is he still...is he sleeping?"

"He wasn't a few moments ago. The doctor is with him."

"Good." She crossed to the door and raised her hand to knock.

Before her knuckles hit the oak panel, Bakeley opened the door, his face grim.

"It's over," he said. "He's gone."

Chapter Four

Paulette made the journey from the sick room to her bedchamber in silence, her emotions more frayed by the presence of an escort. Mr. Gibson had simply taken her hand and wrapped it over his arm, and brought her along, reassuring her he would give her his portion of Shaldon's bequest and she would find someone better than him to take as a husband.

Her jaw ached from clenching it, and a storm raged behind her eyes. She wasn't grieving though.

She was angry.

She mustered a "good night" and closed the door on Mr. Gibson.

Bloody men. Bloody arrogant aristocrats, and their insufferable retainers. Her father had perforce abandoned her, to spy for their bloody war. Her guardians had ignored her. Her vicar had needed a mother for his children and a woman to warm his bed, and her yeoman—well, he'd had to let go that cook and a maid when the year without summer ruined his crops.

Even dear Jock, who'd been her friend and tutor, her only link to her mother and father's true lives, even he had taken a blow to the head and couldn't remember Papa's final message to her.

Soft snoring came through the dressing room door, where Mabel slept on a cot. Paulette walked to the fireplace and rested her forehead against the cool wood, counting to twenty as her mother had taught her to do.

She had a temper like her Spanish great grandmamma, her mother said. Bashing something—the china shepherd on the mantel, the vase full of flowers, her forehead—would solve nothing.

She must *think*. There was a treasure, Jock said, but if Shaldon knew where it was, he'd taken the answer to his death.

Oh, she'd cornered Bakeley just now, fishing for answers, but all she'd discovered was that the trust documents were held by a solicitor named Tellingford in London.

That was, at least, some news.

And then Bakeley had insisted she must stay at Cransdall until he got hold of the other trustees, and promised to send for all of her things from Ferndale Cottage.

He *expected* her to stay at Cransdall. Well, they would see about *that*.

Her lap desk sat on a chest, beckoning her.

She pulled it down, examining it again for the millionth time. Intricately carved and smoothly dovetailed, it was a child-sized case that traveled well, her father's own work. She traced her fingers over the carvings, imagining him in some foreign country, listening while he installed paneling, worked an intricate relief, or fitted the boards of a floor in an enemy's palace. Perhaps Bonaparte's himself. Papa had had many skills, her mother said. Being a reliable father hadn't been one of them.

But he'd loved her, she *knew* he'd loved her. He'd sent her this lap desk and with it a silly poem she'd once thought must signify something, something Jock had forgotten, her mother had denied, and that she herself had never been able to work out.

Because the poem means nothing, Paulette.

She swiped at her eyes and hugged the carved wood to her chest, stretching out on the sofa. Squirreled away in a hiding place at home was enough money to take her to London. She'd return the dog cart and put Horace and Mabel in the vicar's care, and be on her way.

On the morning of the funeral, Bink found Paulette already in the breakfast room sipping tea.

"You're up early," he said.

She barely glanced up from the paper she was reading, and he was relieved to note that today, as yesterday, there were no tell-tale signs of weeping.

"As are you, Mr. Gibson."

They hadn't spoken since the rushed reading of the will the day before. Bakeley had gone through the document with them, though he'd paid little heed to the portions allotted to his siblings and Shaldon's retainers. The bulk of the estate went to the heir, as was usual.

What had caught his ear and drawn the lady's sharp attention was the scant description of the property Shaldon intended for them, Little Norwick, an estate not five miles from Hackwell's Greencastle. The size of the property and the condition of the dwelling, he didn't know. Unoccupied since the last lessor moved out, he'd never taken notice of the true owner's name.

Well, now he knew.

A footman poured him a cup and went off to find fresh toast for him, leaving him alone with Paulette.

The dark intensity, the moodiness—he still did not wish to be leg-shackled to her, but he couldn't help feeling sympathy for her.

"There's a filly I have my eye on purchasing for Lady Hackwell. I'm taking her out this morning before the funeral. I'd invite you to ride along, but you'd accuse me of wooing you."

"I would not be good company." She stood, bringing him to his feet, and pushed the newssheet his way. "You may wish to read this. This is from a few days ago. There is much about the trouble in Manchester."

Bink frowned. Hackwell's estate might be in the path of the soldiers likely to be sent, and any of the troublemakers coming from London. Until this unrest was settled, or until he got word of his ship sailing, his place was there. "You needn't worry. There may be those coming from the north to attend, but Cransdall will be safe."

"And what of you, Mr. Gibson? Will you stay here and be safe? Or will you risk travel?"

"Those going are less likely to be a danger than those returning home, if the militia is called in and it goes sour."

She raised her brows. "You believe it will go badly for the workers?"

"The brute force of battle-hardened men against unarmed workers? Yes."

"And the roads will be dangerous." Her brow furrowed and she bit her lip. "But yet you'll travel them."

"It's different for a man."

"Of course it is."

He sighed and clamped a hand over hers. "Stay, miss. It's a fact I'm bigger and stronger than most men and women and I've the experience of battle."

The spark in her eye told him he'd hit a nerve. Worry threaded through him. She was planning something.

"You'll be safe here, Miss Heardwyn. You must stay."

She lowered her gaze and nodded. "I'll leave you to your breakfast, Mr. Gibson."

"Until later, Miss Heardwyn."

He watched her exit the room, shoulders slumped as if she'd been beaten, and hated himself for having to be part of the world that was caging her.

The funeral of the Earl of Shaldon was as furtive as his life had been, barely wrinkling the life of the village around him, just as he'd wanted, Bakeley claimed. Only Kincaid, the butler and a few older stablemen joined them for the brief service and internment in the family crypt.

Bink still felt numb, like the day after a battle. The hurried visit, the vexing meeting, and the rushed funeral had him reeling.

There'd be time on his journey to sort through the facts. He had the funeral meal to get through— one last chance to speak with Paulette about the arrangements for the bequest he was passing to her—and then he'd leave.

On the short walk from the church to the house, the servants hurried ahead of them. "Well, Bakeley, or, I suppose I should call you Shaldon— no more surprises? Nothing else crawling out of the Earl's dark corners?"

They reached the front drive, and Bakeley stopped. "Won't you stay a bit longer? I can summon our sister home from Lincolnshire. She's no longer a squealing brat." He cleared his throat. "And you could get to know Paulette a bit more.

She's not a bad sort. We had her out for a visit a few years ago, and had a new marquess sniffing about after her."

"Well, there you go," Bink said casually, belying the ache in his jaw. A marquess sniffing about after a girl with no dowry wasn't good.

But she wasn't his problem.

Bakeley shook his head. "No. How the devil the man wound up on the guest list, I don't know. I was one insult away from a duel, if I happened to be the dueling sort. Paulette would be worth the combat, but a boot to the arse would be more fitting for Agruen."

Bink's pulse quickened. "Agruen?"

"You know the man?"

"I know the name." He willed his hands to unfist and walked on, forcing Bakeley to catch up.

"Yes, well, Paulette was convinced he'd taken some ring of hers. Got him alone to accuse him, stupid girl, and I came along in the nick of time. He's a bad piece of work, but there are plenty more out there like him. The girl needs a protector."

"She'll be at Cransdall. You protect her."

"And do you think I'll be able to keep her here once she puts a few shillings together. She needs a husband, Bink."

"You're a fair way to being just like your father," Bink said. "Find her somebody else to marry." Because if Agruen came within ten feet of a woman under Bink's protection, he'd have far worse than a boot coming at him.

Later, while they waited in the drawing room for the ladies, Bink and Bakeley nursed another drink.

"I had a thought," Bakeley said. "Kincaid needs a situation. You need a valet."

Bing groaned loudly. First a wife, then a valet. Both Earls of Shaldon—the old and the new—were pains in the arse. "Stewards don't have valets."

"Every explorer has his faithful manservant. Every sahib his—"

"Pension the man off, for God's sake. And did not your father leave him a settlement?"

"Our father."

"Which art in heaven?"

They both chuckled. Zebediah would have beaten him for such irreverence, but he had a feeling the old earl was laughing along with them from wherever he'd gone after leaving this earthly plane.

"He did leave him a small amount, but Kincaid only looks old. He's much too young for a pension. What's to be done with him?" Bakeley mused.

"What's to be done with Miss Heardwyn? Perhaps *they* should marry."

Bakeley tossed back a drink and sighed. "Cummings is probably inventorying the house goods at Ferndale Cottage now. Can I not prevail upon you to partake of wedded bliss? All of my problems solved: Miss Heardwyn will be your wife, Kincaid will be your valet, and you'll finally be the gentleman you were born to be. Ah, and Mrs. Everly."

Bink opened his mouth to say a very firm *no*, when the lady in question interrupted them.

She planted her hands on her ample hips. "She's not here yet? Forever late, that one, though I've told her over and over again she must be mindful of punctuality. And if she's not late, then she's too early, and sometimes leaving without me. Shall I send a servant up to knock on her door?"

"I'll do it," Bink said. Anything to get away from this harpy.

"You know where her room is?" Mrs. Everly's eyebrows spiked into points.

Behind her back, Bakeley grinned.

"I escorted her back to her chamber the night Shaldon died." He heard her sharp intake of breath as he closed the door.

If Bakeley threw Miss Heardwyn out, Bink would somehow find her and her maid a home. But Mrs. Everly was not coming with them.

He met the housekeeper in the corridor and asked her to check on Miss Heardwyn.

"But Mr. Gibson, she's left already. I thought you did know, as you breakfasted with her. She's gone this morning, and her maid with her. When the staff went to bring fresh linens, her room had been cleared, and I sent a man to check at the stables. One of the boys said they'd hitched the cart up themselves and left much too early for to be going to the funeral. Did she not say anything to his Lordship?"

"I believe not. Did she tell anyone where she was going?"

"I don't know. Her home, I'd imagine. Where else?"

Where else indeed? Her home that was no longer her home. What had Bakeley said? The buyer would be taking an inventory already.

Chapter Five

The next day, Paulette was in the shed tending to Horace when she heard the rustle of horses and the rumble of wheels in the lane.

Mr. Cummings was dismounting. Behind him, his factotum climbed down from the box of an open wagon.

On a Sabbath, and before breakfast...it must have to do with the dog cart, which she was planning on returning on the morrow. She wiped her hands on her apron and went to greet them.

"I'm so very sorry, Mr. Cummings. My visit lasted longer than I expected, and I just arrived home very late last night. I'll bring your cart back to you today after services. Will you come have some tea? Mabel is making a pot."

"You dinna tell me the truth of your visit, did you, miss?" His hard eyes pierced her, and he moved too close, forcing her back a step.

"It was no lie. I was visiting an, er, acquaintance."

"Lord Shaldon."

His factotum, a thin rangy man, spat into the dirt at his side.

Cummings laughed, and she could see the gaps where he had teeth missing.

She took another step back. "I will return the dog cart today." She turned, and a hand clamped on her arm.

"Why are you here?" she asked, willing her voice not to shake.

"Why are *you* here?" His smile didn't reach his eyes. "Didna the Earl tell you before he kicked up his heels?"

Blood thrummed in her ears. *Tell me what?* Cummings knew Shaldon was dead, and his eyes glittered as she had not seen them do before, except when he'd managed to turn a family out of their home, or watched a mother sell her child into servitude to pay a debt to him.

When his eyes ceased their glittering and began to glow, her heart shrank within her. Mr. Cummings had always been the crotchety tight-fisted neighbor, gentry, but not really gentlemanly. He was at least twenty years older than her, and she'd never seen this particular light in his eyes. Not once.

She clenched her fists. To hell with what Cummings thought Shaldon had told her—she needed to make him leave.

Easing in a breath, she fought for composure. "Yes, I spoke with the Earl briefly. Now, as you're a gentleman, Mr. Cummings, please let go of my arm. I want to go in to my breakfast."

"Do you now?"

"Yes, and you are welcome to join me, though my table is humble as I don't often have guests."

"Guests? But you don't own this house."

Her heart sickened. Shaldon had not left her the house, nor had he said anything of her continuing to live here. "Of course not. It belongs to the Shaldon estate."

"No. It belongs to me."

Coldness slammed her, and she felt the blood drain from her head.

He owned the house? How could that be? No. No, he was mistaken, or trying to take advantage of the Earl's death. She would write to Bakeley. Bakeley would set him straight.

She drew herself up. "You certainly do not. This house belongs to the Earl of Shaldon."

"The Earl's dead. He sold it to me weeks ago, possession to take place upon his burial, which was yesterday."

A weight pressed against her pounding heart and the chill numbed her hands beyond feeling. This could not be. And yet…It would fit. Shaldon, the wicked man, wanted to arrange things his way. This was his not-so-gentle shove into a marriage of his arranging.

"I will need to take an inventory," Cummings said.

"And I will need to see a document." She turned on her heel.

"Stop right there." His hand gripped her again.

"What's to do?" Mabel had turned the corner of the house and was advancing, her thick butcher's knife in her hand. "Good morning, Mr. Cummings. Did you stop to pay your respects on the way to services? I'm just cutting a piece of the ham I put up." Her voice pleasant, she pointed the sharp tip at him. "Has Mrs. Cummings fed you your breakfast? Och, I see not, considering the way you're gripping my miss's arm."

Cummings pulled his hand away and wiped it with the other. "That will be my ham. I might as well eat some of it."

As Bink passed the small church, worshippers spilled out and mingled, most of them turning to watch him. He pulled up his horse and called over a young boy.

"Which is the way to Ferndale Cottage?" he asked.

All conversation at the church stopped, and the boy's mouth gaped.

Bink searched the crowd for a particular reaction. If Mr. Cummings was among them, he should shove his way through the crowd of mostly ladies right about now.

"You are looking for Ferndale Cottage?" It was the vicar who plowed through, a harried-looking man of middle years.

"I am," Bink said.

"It is not right, sir," the vicar said. "It is the Sabbath. Your employer—"

His employer? He sat up straighter and searched the crowd, his heart pumping harder. Cummings had set upon her already, this day.

"Cummings is not my employer. I'm here on behalf of Lord Shaldon. Where is Cummings? I would speak with him."

"He took his man and a wagon this morning and—"

Bink pointed at a lane leading east. "This way, Vicar?"

"Yes. A mile or so."

Bink was already spurring his horse.

Outside the village the lane was not so well maintained. Shallow muddy tracks showed a wagon had passed here. That it had not passed again heavily laden meant he might be in time.

When he rounded a bend, he saw that he was not. Two women, laden like the refugees he'd seen in Spain, trod along, trying to find purchase in the muck at the side of the road. Paulette's skirts had a band of mud a foot thick, and the burdens she bore were surely too heavy.

"Miss Heardwyn," he called, quickly dismounting.

She ducked her head, and when he reached her, turned away.

"Oh sir," Mabel said. "That Cummings—"

"Mabel." Miss Heardwyn spoke tersely, her voice gravelly.

"He's evicted you?"

The young lady nodded without looking at him.

"Yes, and taken everything, even the ham my Miss bought with her money. He's left us a few shifts and a change of clothing and not even our horse to carry them out."

"Mabel." The lady's chin came up and he saw tear tracks on her dust-spattered face.

Something twisted inside him. Miss Heardwyn—Paulette—would end up on the streets somewhere, if not in London, then York, or Manchester.

His insides roared, and he all but strained himself to speak gently. "We'll see about that. Let me help you." He tugged at the lady's parcels until she released them, and tied them onto his horse.

Her hands fisted and she looked away while he took the maid's burdens also. Anger rippled off Miss Heardwyn, but it was overlaid with grief, and astonishment, and an icy kind of fear.

He'd seen this before, women and children wide-eyed, stunned, hungry, cold. Homeless.

But now you can do something about it, man. He was not under orders now, not really. His business at home would just have to wait. Hackwell would understand, and if he didn't, his lady most certainly would.

"We're going back and getting what's yours." He circled his hands at her so-tiny waist and hauled her up onto his horse.

"What—" she gasped and clung to the horse's mane.

Her long skirts rode up, revealing a nicely turned ankle and calf, and the anger inside him stirred to something more feral.

That comely ankle and calf could be his, to look at, to touch. He had only to press her a bit. He inwardly shook himself.

"Hold on, miss."

He swung the maid up next, eliciting a shriek.

"Quiet now, Miss Mabel. You'll startle the horse." Though he'd doubt much would shake this doddering old eunuch. When his own mount had stumbled in last night's violent rain, this gelding had been the only saddle-horse left at the inn where they'd sought help. "He's a sweet enough goer. If you'll pull up your skirts you may sit astride with more comfort, and no one's the wiser. We'll take you down before anyone can see."

The maid hiked up her skirt and scooted around her mistress's grumping.

"Are we going back then?" Miss Heardwyn's voice, now that she'd found it, was laced with danger.

"Aye." Bink took the gelding's reins and led him off.

"And then what, Mr. Gibson?" Her voice trembled with suppressed fury.

He looked straight ahead, through the overhanging trees hedging the fields.

Then I shall introduce Mr. Cummings to my fists.

"We'll get your things, then."

The horse stumbled and Mabel gasped again.

"Don't worry ladies. Just hold on."

There was nothing untoward about Mr. Gibson's touch when he lifted Paulette down from the mount, yet the strength of his hands seared her and incited a burn in her cheeks.

She bent and straightened her skirts, and more blood rushed, making her dizzy. Mabel gasped when the horse side-stepped and prattled about being too heavy. Mr. Gibson grunted—Mabel was no light-weight—and muttered a polite reassurance.

When she'd straightened herself and had the opportunity to look, Mr. Gibson was frowning.

No. Not frowning. Frowning implied some minor disturbance. A deep line creased his set-in-stone forehead, running between his eyes like a water-carved cliff she'd once seen in an illustration, and tension radiated off him like the rays off the sun, sending some of its heat her way.

Mabel was right—he *was* a handsome man. He bent and checked the horse over, the tight curve of his buttocks inspiring more blushes, and she imagined his back muscles bunching and moving under his tightly fitted jacket as he tested the girth and the leather.

He went to a bag strapped to the saddle and pulled out a pistol.

Her heart soared with hope, even as she knew she was on the brink of something unknowable. She wanted her home back, and yet she didn't. The future was a black yawning hole, but with any luck, Mr. Gibson would shoot Mr. Cummings and she'd have that tiny bit of reckoning.

"Surely it won't come to pistols, sir," Mabel said in a small voice.

"No, surely it won't," he said carefully. "But one can never be absolutely sure with a thief. Are you ready, ladies?"

Dismay overtook her in the small yard. Her lap desk sat haphazardly in the wagon, leaning against a crate. Cummings' man had yanked it from her, and when she'd slapped him, well...

She took a breath. Cummings had raised a hand to her. *That*, she would never forget. That, she would find a way to avenge.

Two other men, farmers who leased from Mr. Cummings, met her eyes and looked away quickly.

Mr. Gibson handed the reins to Mabel. "Where is Cummings?" he asked.

Their gaze slid toward the door. Cummings stepped out, coatless and hatless, his bristled grey hair pulled tight across sunken temples into a queue.

He launched himself across the green toward Paulette. "I told you to leave."

Mr. Gibson stepped in front of her. "Hold there. Miss Heardwyn is not leaving without her belongings."

Cummings' stinging gaze flicked from her to Mr. Gibson, and a shrewd smile turned his lips up. "Who be you?"

"My name is Gibson, and I speak for the Earl of Shaldon."

The factotum appeared behind him and spat into the dirt.

"Who was buried yesterday," Cummings said.

Paulette sidestepped her champion. "And succeeded by his son. And that is my lap desk. It was a gift from my father and it is rightfully mine."

Let Cummings try to hit her with Gibson by her side.

"You think so." Cummings drew closer. "I don't know who your man here is, Paulette, but this cottage and all its contents are mine, as of yesterday."

"He told you who he is. And you've offered no proof of ownership," she said.

"I don't need to show you proof."

"Yes. You must. Otherwise what you're doing is theft." She looked at the men loading the wagon and the factotum. "And you men are complicit. If there is no proper bill of sale, I'll bring charges against all of you." She crossed her fingers under her skirts. "I'm not without means."

Cummings laughed. "I see. You have your big fancy-man here—"

Cummings' head popped back, the impact of a large fist toppling him backwards into his man.

"A right good one," Mabel said from behind her. "Land him another, Mr. Gibson."

Mr. Gibson brushed his hands together. "I have a copy of the document. I'll share it with you later, Miss Heardwyn. For now, I need you to instruct these men which items you wish them to remove from the cart."

"I'll bring charges against you," Cummings spluttered, his man helping him up. "You assaulted me."

"And you impugned this lady's honor."

That deep line appeared again creasing his brow.

"And mine, Cummings. But very well, send your man for the magistrate. I'll share my documents with him, and bring charges against you. Theft. On a scale large enough to have you transported." He nodded at the workers. "And them as well."

The men looked at each other, their countenances going grim, but at a look from Cummings, they hunched closer.

She feared for Mr. Gibson's safety. Surely he couldn't take on the two farmers, Mr. Cummings, and the squirrely factotum. His pistol would have only one round.

She stepped up next to him and fisted her hands.

The creaking of wheels in the lane drew everyone's attention.

The men on the box of an open wagon she recognized—Lord Shaldon's manservant held the reins, and next to him on the box was the vicar. "Sorry for the delay, sir," the manservant said. "The man of God wanted to come along."

A rush of relief mingled with a profound embarrassment as she greeted the vicar. He'd found a new mother for his ever-increasing brood, and they'd remained friends, yet he was probably pitying her.

The vicar nodded a greeting to the two laborers. "Are you evicting Paulette on the Sabbath, Cummings?" he asked in the sonorous tone he used for his sermons.

"Good of you to finally make it, Kincaid." Mr. Gibson introduced himself to the Vicar and said, "Cummings was indeed throwing Miss Heardwyn into the road and taking her possessions, even down to her clothing, I believe. Although what a man would do with a young lady's clothing I have no idea." He cast a glance her way. "Though he's only a bit taller than you, Miss Heardwyn. Perhaps the dresses will fit."

She covered a laugh, and Cummings spluttered. "See here—"

"Now. Let's make a short Sabbath job of this. Miss Heardwyn. Tell Lord Shaldon's man what is yours and have your maid pack your things.

Kincaid, make sure everything is properly loaded."

"My pots. And the ham." Mabel walked past them, stopped, and turned. "And Horace."

Paulette's heart swelled. Cummings was a harsh master, even to dumb beasts. It was parting with Horace that had started her tears.

"Horace is mine." Cummings cried.

Mr. Gibson raised an eyebrow.

She forced down another giggle threatening to rise as a great weight was lifted. "He's my horse. My *Horace*. It was a great joke when I named him, you see? He was a gift from Bakeley on my eighteenth birthday. He and a gig I, er, no longer have."

She had overturned it, attempting to get Horace to move a little faster on unsuitable terrain. Mr. Gibson did not need to know that story.

And yet he seemed to read her mind. His face softened and humor glimmered golden in his eyes. "Not the great beast that brought you to Cransdall Hall?"

Her heart floated higher. She nodded and pressed her lips together. She did not want to smile, not in front of Cummings.

He signaled to one of the men. "Get the lady's horse."

Before Cummings could grumble, more rattling wheels sounded as two riders in Cransdall livery preceded a post-chaise with its postilion riding one of a pair of greys.

The bright afternoon sun hit Paulette squarely in the eyes.

"Where are we going, Polly," Mabel asked. "Did he say?"

She'd been wondering the same thing. "I don't know."

They'd turned west when they should have turned north if they'd been headed back to Cransdall, and she'd not had a chance at either of the inns where they'd changed horses to talk to Mr. Gibson. He'd sent the groom to hurry them along at each stop.

Well. That wouldn't work at the next one. He *would* speak with her there.

She saw the clump of pretty buildings nestled in a valley and knew this must be an inn. It looked to be grander than the last two, the stables forming three sides of a square around it.

When the post-chaise drew up in front of the door, one of Shaldon's grooms appeared at the side, tipping his hat and extending a hand.

The half-timbered building rose to three well-maintained stories. "What is this place?" Paulette asked.

"I don't know the name, miss, but the mail coach comes through, and the Edinburgh coach, and I heard Mr. Gibson say it's the only inn in ten miles without bed bugs."

Her foot landed in a puddle. "Blast it," she said. She still wore her gown with its fringe of mud. "Watch your step, Mabel."

She glanced back and saw an inn servant unstrap her valise. A stableman led the chaise off, and the wagon, piled with her trunks and small bits of furniture, followed behind with Horace tied to the back.

Alarm coursed through her. No bed bugs. He meant for them to stay the night here in this great, likely high-priced, establishment. "Where is Mr. Gibson?"

"I don't know, miss."

"You don't know much," she snapped.

She closed her eyes and took a breath. It was not his fault. He was only a groom.

But when she opened her eyes, he was smiling. He was missing a tooth, and was, she realized, quite a bit older than her first estimation. Another redhead, only this one had the lean lines of a hunting hound.

"It's what me mum always says, miss, but I've told you true. I'm to lead you inside to a private dining room and stay with you like a footman until you're settled and safe and your tea is brought in."

"Those are very specific instructions."

"Yes, miss."

"From Mr Gibson?"

"No, miss. From Mr. Kincaid."

Her heart sank just a little, and she chided herself.

Mabel caught up with them. "Johnny—"

"Johnny?"

"Well, it's his name." Mabel studied the cobblestone entry. "I'll look after my miss, Johnny, and you can go find your dinner."

"I allow as I can, Miss Mabel, but I haven't lasted this long doing what I can instead of what I've been told to do. And me seeing Mr. Gibson talking to Mr. Kincaid, afore Mr. Kincaid talked to me."

Paulette's heart beat a little faster.

Mabel opened her mouth, preparing for one of her speeches, like when she'd been Paulette's nursemaid eons ago. Her plump cheeks went rosier than usual and her lips trembled somewhere between a smile and a scolding.

Johnny's eyes twinkled, focused solely on the maid.

A groan found its way up her throat. She'd seen one or two of Mabel's romances over the years. They'd come to naught, as would this, if the maid planned to stay with her.

"We'll not have an argument on the steps of this inn, Mabel. Johnny, deliver us into the parlor and then go and find Mr. Gibson. I must speak to him immediately."

Paulette surveyed the room while an inn servant poured tea. The paneled walls gleamed with a fresh oiling, and the aged stone floor had been scrubbed to a dull finish without a speck of the road dust and mud from outside. No fire burned in the well-swept hearth, but the day had been warm.

The maid closed the door and Mabel passed her a cup. "Drink up, then, Polly," Mabel said. "And don't you be worrying. Mr. Gibson will see to the accounting, I'm sure."

"I'm not worrying," she lied.

With Cummings distracted by Mr. Gibson and his men, she'd recovered her bit of money and stowed it away in a pocket.

Cummings' man had looked for money. She'd seen him pawing through drawers and testing the floorboards, but not the panels along the wall of the kitchen. Oh, he'd checked the shelves and lifted the lid on every jar, but he couldn't spring a panel loose if he didn't know the spring was there.

She had money, but it must be stretched. She needed to see the solicitor in London, and perhaps meet with her trustees if they were in town.

And if she could find the lord who'd made her first visit to Cransdall so miserable, well, she didn't need to be a lady of fashion to take back what was hers.

She swallowed a sigh. Cransdall was not a lucky place for her, not the first time she'd been there, nor this second. There would not be a third. She'd track down Lord Agruen and recover her mother's ring, and somehow she'd find the treasure Jock said her father had left her. Lord Shaldon—both lords, old and new—were irrelevant to her now. Neither would stand in her way.

Only one stumbling block remained, and he would be joining her soon.

Kincaid grunted through Bink's instructions about securing Miss Heardwyn's goods, making it ever more clear to Bink the man was not an upper crust batman at all. Whatever his role for Lord Shaldon, it had been much more than washing his smalls and scraping off his beard.

Whatever grief Kincaid felt for his master's death, he was keeping it in. Probably, if he'd been abroad with the spymaster, he'd seen enough to take dying in stride.

The older of the two grooms from Cransdall trotted up. "She's wishing to speak to you, Mr. Gibson," he said.

"Is she now?"

"Aye. She and her jolly maid have sat down to tea, and there's a third cup awaiting you, sir."

He'd delivered that information straight-faced.

"Have we met before?" Bink asked. "Johnny, is it?"

Johnny grinned. "You were a boy, and I was but a little more than one meself. I never seen the young lord smile so much as when you were there, then and now, truth to be told. He said I'm to stay with you as long as you wish."

Bakeley had settled him with another dependent. At this rate he'd have all of Little Norwick staffed for the lady. If they were to marry.

The other groom, a freckle-faced youth, was arranging straw for his resting place to take the first watch over the wagon.

Johnny noticed his glance. "Ewan, there, is me nephew. A good fellow. He'll serve you right also."

Bink laughed. Bakeley was having him on. In Bink's present state, he didn't need a valet and two grooms. Or a wife, for that matter. Bakeley, or rather, this new incarnation of Lord Shaldon, was applying the weight of a *fait accompli.*

And to hell with that. He'd diverted them to this inn for a good night's rest, and tomorrow he was returning them to Cransdall.

When he entered the parlor, Paulette looked up, and then jumped up, rattling the plates at her elbow.

A crumb clung to the corner of her mouth, sending a jolt through him.

If he licked it away, he could taste her.

He managed a greeting, tore his gaze away and surveyed the room. He'd stopped here once with Lady Hackwell and the children. It was as tidy now as it had been then. "I trust you are comfortable," he added.

"Mr. Gibson..." She swallowed.

"And the food was palatable."

She nodded, wringing the napkin in her hands.

"I can see it was." He poked at the corner of his mouth and watched as her color rose and she dabbed at herself.

He squashed the urge to smile and pulled out a chair. "Johnny did say there was a third cup here and I see there's a third plate also. May I eat while we talk?"

"Of course." She seated herself.

The maid, who had moved off to the side, bobbed a curtsey. "I'll just go and check on our things."

"No." Bink waved her to a settee near the fireplace. "Please sit, Mabel."

"Yes, Mabel. Do not leave us. You may count on her discretion, Mr. Gibson."

He'd already seen that the maid and the lady were thick as thieves. She'd been Miss Heardwyn's nursemaid, Bakeley had said.

So far, Bink had heard no whispering among the staff about Shaldon's plans for a wedding, and he didn't wish to. Still he'd prefer that kind of gossip to rumors he'd compromised the lady in the inn's private dining room. That rumor would certainly result in the wedding neither one of them wanted.

But he would certainly enjoy the compromising. The thought brought forth an image he quickly pushed down.

Miss Heardwyn's cheeks still glowed, as though she'd poked around in his brain. She was not completely uninterested, he'd wager—another speculation that sent heat sizzling in him.

Stand down, Gibson. All the talk of a marriage was working on the both of them. Well, on him anyway. He hadn't had a woman in, he didn't know how long. The squalor of London and the misbegotten children Lady Hackwell tended had turned him off the professionals. And though he'd had plenty of come-hither looks, he'd avoided entanglements with local widows. It seemed best, as the lord of the manor's steward, to be prudent, or else for the price of a tumble he'd find himself leg-shackled.

And it was best to be prudent dealing with this sort of woman also. He loaded up his plate with cold meats and vegetables and a thick slice of bread. "What did you wish to discuss?"

"Where are you taking us?"

"For tonight, I've arranged rooms here."

Miss Heardwyn squinted and pressed her lips together.

A tap at the door brought the innkeeper's smiling, buxom maid with a flagon of ale and a pint tankard. Bink thanked her for the drink, and silently, for the interruption, and started speaking before the door shut on the wench, before the lady across from him could stop glaring at her and untie her tongue.

"I know we haven't gone far, Miss Heardwyn, but it is, if you will remember, the Sabbath, and in spite of it, we've all had a hard day's labor. The servants are entitled to a rest. Kincaid and the men will watch over your wagon. Nothing will go missing."

She studied her teacup and worried at her lush lower lip with those perfect white teeth. She was a beauty, was Miss Heardwyn, much more to his taste than the flaxen-haired serving wench, and in other circumstances...

"As to the cost." She cleared her throat.

"You are not to worry, miss. I've said you will have any monies Shaldon has left me, and I mean it. I will bear the cost tonight, and tomorrow we'll make the arrangements with Bakeley for the rest."

Her gaze shot up, eyes flashing. She did not want to be in his debt.

Or... she did not want to return to Cransdall.

She stood and walked to the fireplace. The room had gone warm, and he debated opening one of the casement windows a tad wider.

"Mabel, wait outside please," the lady said, her back to the both of them.

Bink eased out of his chair. "Leave the door open, Mabel. You may stand outside and eavesdrop but don't allow anyone else to listen."

The maid's lips quivered as she curtsied and hurried out.

He turned back to the lady. "Is this where you tell me you will not return to Cransdall?"

Paulette's breath caught. Mr. Gibson had moved up next to her with a great deal of stealth, close enough to lay hands on her if he wished.

His big body radiated warmth and suffused her with his scent. Even after a hard day of riding, the man-scent was subtle, no stronger than her farmer's had been on a Sunday morning, dressed in his best. But the yeoman farmer had repelled her. There was nothing repellant about Mr. Gibson.

She reached for some calm, trying to still her heart. She was shorter than most women, true, but even if she'd been tall for a woman, he would still tower over her. He spread one enormous hand against the mantel and leaned into it, sending her heart fluttering into her throat.

She coughed to clear it. She must not let him think her weak. "Returning to Cransdall is out of the question for me. If you take me there, I will never be able to leave."

Quiet followed, the long silence making her wonder if he'd actually heard.

"Where do you want to go?" he asked.

This inn was on the main road, the groom had said. She might have enough money to get to London, and then a bit more for her keep once she arrived. For a few days, anyway. Once she located the solicitor and one of her trustees, she would be provided for, surely.

She would not tell him those plans.

"What of your belongings we rescued today?" he asked, before she could speak.

Grrr. He was tricky, this one. She had not thought that far ahead. "They will be safe at Cransdall, surely. Kincaid and the grooms can take them back. You can return to your home."

"And you—"

"You are not my keeper, Mr. Gibson."

He studied her for a too-long moment, sending warmth up her cheeks. She would not look away. She would not give him the satisfaction.

"I'll ask you to sleep on it, and we'll talk again at breakfast." He reached one long finger up and swept a lock of hair behind her ear.

His touch jolted her, too delicate for the man. She could feel her breath rising and falling like a bellows-blown fire, all deliciously lit up within her, with a promise of something she couldn't fathom.

She'd scoffed at Mrs. Everly's warnings about men. After all, her farmer had actually kissed her and she'd never felt this. And it was...*wonderful*.

Humor glinted in his eyes, bringing her back to earth. "Until breakfast then," he said, and was gone.

Mabel popped back in. "Our room is ready." She rustled about, gathering their things, and appeared at her side. "What is it, Polly? You've gone all pink and sweaty." She inhaled sharply. "Did he kiss you?"

"*No.*"

"Oh, too bad, that. I'd warrant the man knows how to properly kiss."

"And how would you know a proper kiss, Mabel?" She put on a stern face. "And what about Johnny?"

Mabel's guilty look completely undid her. She laughed. "I'm still *not* going to marry him."

She'd shared Shaldon's plan with her maid, swearing her to secrecy.

"You would have a home. Little Norwick, Johnny said it is. It sounds lovely."

Paulette caught her breath. "You *told* him. You promised not to gossip." Now all the servants knew Shaldon's plan for them to marry.

"No." Mabel shook her head. "He just knew. And no one was gossiping. He just mentioned it when we talked."

"Really? Well, yes, Mabel. And I could live at this Little Norwick croft, in a thatched, dirt-floor cottage with a man who was forced into marriage—he does not want it either, you know. And what a life that would be."

Mabel bit her lip. "He'd not bequeath you a mere cottage, Polly."

"And how do we know that? I can't trust Shaldon, not after he sold my home out from under me."

"So we're back to Cransdall. And then what?"

The innkeeper's girl who had flirted with Mr. Gibson appeared, wanting to clear the table.

She wouldn't risk having whatever they said reported back to him.

"If our room is ready, let us go up."

Paulette slept in fits and dozes, the hustle and bustle of the inn, so unlike her quiet bed in the country, jostling her awake most of the night. Well before dawn she lit a candle, nudged Mabel, and quietly dressed.

There would be room on the coach going south, the innkeeper had promised Mabel the night before.

Paulette sat in the small public parlor, a cup of tea going cold, a blank piece of notepaper mocking her.

At this hour, the local ale-drinkers were all home and rising to care for their animals. The room was quiet, the morning fair. Mr. Gibson had been unwilling to travel at night. He would still be abed.

She set her pencil to the paper.

Dear Mr. Gibson,

She propped her chin in her free hand. Perhaps *Dear* was too strong. Perhaps she should have omitted it and just begun with his name.

It was too late now. If she rubbed it out it would leave a dark mark.

I thank you for your kind offer to escort me to Cransdall.

She looked up at the naked antlers racked above the fireplace, someone's dead trophy. And how had the innkeeper obtained that? Some rich man had made a gift of it probably, not out of kindness, but because he'd grown tired of the prize.

Mr. Gibson wasn't escorting her out of kindness, either. He wanted to dump her on Bakeley.

And—had he actually said *he* was going to Cransdall? Or was he merely sending her in Kincaid's care?

You are absolved of all concerns for my care, nor do I wish to receive any financial considerations which might necessarily create an appearance of indebtedness to you.

She lifted her pencil. That sounded a bit insulting. He'd been a bastard for all of his life and forced to work for a living. None of that was his fault. She had no wish to offend him.

Not because it is you, but because I have lived in obligation and obedience for all of my life and am quite tired of it.

Quite so bloody tired. While tossing and turning during the night, she'd had a chance to speculate on the amount of her trust and her inheritance. Once she'd disposed of her business with the solicitor, surely she and Mabel could live quite simply in the country. Not in her own village, where Mr. Cummings ruled, but elsewhere.

She would give up the idea of a Season in London, which had always been a fairy dream, much like her thoughts about taking up her mother and father's trade. She could teach drawing, and music, and French to the children of tradesmen and the local gentry. She and Mabel would have a garden and chickens. They would not starve, and in the quiet moments, she would try to get back what was hers from Agruen and figure out her father's mystery.

She jabbed her pencil at the gnarled table. She was settling, damn it. Damn it, she would find a way to find the life that should be hers, once she worked out what that was.

A raised voice came from the kitchen and she tilted her head. From here, she might not hear the mail coach horn. She must hurry and finish this.

I am going to London to seek out my trustee, and my parents' solicitor. I have received an accounting from the innkeeper and will pay you back as soon as I have arranged all my affairs, which shall be very soon, I believe since the amount is not so great as I had anticipated.

She took a sip of her tea and frowned. It had gone lukewarm.

And she did not know how to end this.

A distant horn sounded, and her heart beat faster. She hurriedly set her pencil to the paper.

Sincerely,
Paulette Silva Heardwyn

Mabel rushed in with Paulette's spencer, and she folded the note, wrote Mr. Gibson's name on it, and handed it to the man on duty.

A servant picked up their bags and led them out through the heavy oak door.

The air, fresh with the morning dew, carried the scent of horses and leather. Lantern lights bounced off the bright yellow coach, painted quite like the dog cart, quite like a bumblebee ready to flit away. Her heart lifted.

Ostlers jostled a new team into place, readying the coach to leave within minutes, and in the shadows near them a man lingered, watching them work.

She extracted her ticket from her reticule and approached.

The man turned and her heart fell. It was Mr. Gibson.

Chapter Seven

She looked lovely in the shimmering light, hair loosely knotted and ready to fall at the slightest touch, lips pressed together just daring a man to attempt to breach them.

Bink took her bags from the footman.

"You're ready to go then?"

She balked like a surly burro. He let her have room, but he blocked her access to the mail coach.

"I'll have these stowed on your wagon. We'll have time for breakfast before it's readied."

"I'm leaving on this coach." Her voice trembled, and she cleared her throat. "Kindly give them back to the servant."

Bink moved nearer. "No, Paulette," he said softly. He was close enough to see fire building in her eyes. He'd seen a few grand Spanish tantrums before. This one wouldn't stop him.

Still, he didn't want to embarrass the girl.

"I've purchased the tickets. I *will* go," she hissed.

"The agent will give back your money. I'll see to it."

"I am not going to Cransdall. I am going to London."

London. All the folk thought London held the key to everything. He, however, had seen the real London in the weeks he'd spent helping Hackwell search for his missing nephew. "Why London?"

"That is my affair." She pressed her lips together and inhaled loudly. "One of my trustees is there."

"One of them is on the Continent, I'm told."

Her head snapped up and her eyes widened momentarily before compressing into a scowl.

"Nor is the other likely to be in town this time of year."

"Curse you, and curse Bakeley." She stamped her foot. "I will *not* go to Cransdall. You have no *authority* over me. You must give me my bags and move. The horses are harnessed. The coachman is taking his seat. Please." She put out a hand and tried to push him away.

The group of men had turned to watch, and some laughed.

"You lot mind your business," Bink said.

He shifted the bags to one hand and reached for her arm. She was trembling.

He would not see her humiliated. Nor would she travel to London in a public coach with only her maid.

"Stay now, lass. Don't fret. If you must go to London, I will take you there."

That evening, Bink knew he was in for it when his mount trotted into the stable yard at Greencastle. Hackwell's stalwart horse, Chester, was here, and her ladyship's new traveling carriage also. And from the number of strange cattle, they'd brought guests.

Devil take it, he'd only meant to stop the night here on the way to London—or longer if he could persuade the lady to stay, but Hackwell had come home early from the house party in Hertfordshire where he'd been politicking to get a new Poor Law in place. The man had taken to his Parliamentary duties like he'd taken to soldiering, every bill a battle campaign requiring a good deal of hobnobbing, usually with Lady Hackwell at his side. That sort of campaigning could never include Bink.

However, when Hackwell visited the rookeries, Bink went along. Even before their marriage, Lady Hackwell had been a strong voice for the denizens of those London neighborhoods.

Helping the poorest of the bastards was a worthy cause, and Bink would have liked to do more than just serve as a guard to the two or three of whichever lords Hackwell coaxed into going, trying to force some compassion into their coddled hearts.

As he dismounted, the head groom of Greencastle hobbled up to take the reins, exchanging greetings.

"When did his lordship return?" Bink asked the elderly man, keeping his tone matter-of-fact.

"Came back late on Saturday. Mary sent for 'em as Master Rob took a fever, and the babe was a'sniffling."

Hackwell's four-year-old nephew and their baby girl had been hardy enough the day Bink had left.

"How are they now?"

The groom chuckled. "Fit and full of it, he and the babe both, Mary says." He frowned. "His lordship was asking questions."

Bink patted his horse and waited, giving the old man his best stone face.

"Ach," the old man said, surrendering. "Which horse did Mr. Gibson take? What did Mr. Gibson say about his travel? Might've wanted to know where you went, but he didn't ask it outright."

He unstrapped his bag. "There'll be a post chaise and a wagon along any minute. See to them. I'll have Mrs. Bradley sort out the new guests."

Below stairs, the servants were immersed in preparations for dinner. Bink found the housekeeper and issued instructions, then went to the set of rooms not far from the servants' hall, the lodging and office of the steward. His exalted domain.

He steeled himself and pushed open the door.

Hackwell lounged in the sitting room chair, dressed impeccably for dinner, yet still managing to look disheveled, and with the same wicked gleam that had fired in him before a battle.

"Gibson." He stretched his long legs within tripping distance. "So good of you to return."

Bink growled a greeting and tossed his bag on the only other chair. "Ye came back early, milord."

"This is my home." His eyes narrowed. "And where have you been?"

He gritted his teeth. A steward was a grand bloody servant, but still a servant after all. "A personal matter, milord."

A dinner gong sounded distantly. Hackwell ignored it.

He'd best get a drink into both of them before Hackwell uncoiled his bloody questions. Bink went to a cabinet and poured out two brandies. He debated reminding his lordship of his dinner hour, and decided against it. It was not for the likes of him to tell the Earl of Hackwell to get himself up to the eating room—well, not tonight, anyway.

"I had a letter this morning, Gibson. From the new Earl of Shaldon. It seems the old earl died and you attended the funeral."

He sloshed a little more drink into his own glass and handed the other over to Hackwell.

Hackwell's hand closed on the glass, and his gaze locked on Bink's. "You devil, why didn't you tell me?"

"Tell you what, milord? That I'm an earl's bastard? I wasn't raised in that great house. I dunna think it signifies."

Hackwell rose, clinked glasses and downed his drink. "As to that, I always knew you were not what you made yourself out to be. And you may dispense with the Paddy accent." Hackwell poured himself another finger of brandy. "I see I do not have to condole with you on your father's death, though I also see you are feeling something. Right now I can't tell what it is besides irritation with me. Irritation that I've found you out. Here's to you, Edward Bink Everly." Hackwell drained his glass and set it down. "And hell, man, I'm not talking about you keeping the secret of your parentage. I'm raising my father's and my brother's by-blows—you know I don't give a damn about that." A wicked grin spread over his face. "What I'm talking about is your impending nuptials."

Hot liquid coursed down the wrong pipe and Bink choked, his face flaming, while he sought to bottle the ire threatening to burst.

Bakeley. Bakeley had shared information as if it were fact, as if he could bloody well step into the Spy Lord's shoes and run another man's life.

Not this man. He set his glass down carefully. "No."

"No?" Hackwell's eyes narrowed. "I understood it to be your father's wish, this marriage. His ward, is she?"

"Wishes and facts are not the same thing."

"So the new Earl of Shaldon...your brother...is mistaken?"

"He most certainly is."

"I see." He walked around the low table. Scratched his head. Stopped in front of Bink. "If that is so, tell me then, Gibson, why did the parish read the first banns yesterday?"

Bink swore a stream of oaths.

"Such language, Mr. Gibson." Lady Hackwell swept into the room.

"Bink has had a shock, my dear."

She looked at Bink quizzically. "I ran into Mrs. Bradley and she told me about your guest. And I believe *her* chaise has just arrived. And Mrs. Bradley and I have decided to move *her* into the yellow chamber near my rooms. I'm afraid there were too many male guests near the room you selected for her. Though I know you didn't know about our visitors. Steven has brought along some possible votes."

His face heated up again. "You will know best, your Ladyship."

She looked a question to her husband, and he shrugged.

"Bink says he has no wish to marry. I believe he may wish to stay in my employment as steward, rather than run his own estate and stand for the Commons as my political ally."

Standing for Commons? That was a wrinkle. They'd never discussed any such thing.

He cursed—inwardly this time, in deference to Lady Hackwell. Hackwell's mention of the

Commons was just a ploy. Just more aristocratic managing.

Hackwell blocked the way to Bink's inner chamber, and her Ladyship, her dinner gown flowing over the new heir growing inside her, made an imposing barrier to the corridor door.

A bead of sweat chose that moment to slide down his neck, and he took a step to the window and opened it.

He'd had enough. He'd served enough. "This is as good a time as any to mention, I'm taking a post in India. I've already put up the money. With Maharashtra destroyed last year—"

Hackwell made a noise low in the back of his throat.

His wife laid a hand on her husband's arm. "Oh, Bink. Dear, Bink. You are free to go to India, or China or the Americas, if that is what you wish. You are free, but you are also part of our family, and like a brother to Steven, and an uncle to the boys and our daughter, and your leaving will never be what any of us wish." She beamed him a smile, radiating the calm she'd applied to the houseful of misbegotten urchins she'd taken in before her marriage. "To have you take your place in a great house with a wife and children, and to ally with Steven in helping the poor, oh...well, we must find our happiness where we will."

She patted Hackwell's arm, and he laid a hand over hers, the affection between them unmistakable. Hackwell had come to embrace his new life only because he'd found happiness with her. It was not something Bink ever expected to find for himself, not while he was too poor to be naught but a hired man.

A memory of his mother flashed through his mind.

No. 'Twas not only the money at issue. A wife needed care, protection.

She smiled and rubbed her stomach. "I believe I shall tell the cook dinner will be delayed. As I said, Steven has brought some important guests home with us. You will join us at dinner, Mr. Gibson." She dropped a kiss on her husband's cheek. "And I'm going right now to make your Miss Heardwyn welcome."

Paulette was unprepared for the phalanx of staff that practically levitated her into the great house, up the stairs and across the threshold of a glowing, golden room. Someone had opened a window, and the breeze blowing in carried with it the fragrance of grass and a hint of the rain that had followed them for part of their journey.

A bathing tub had been set up, and a team of young housemaids were already filling it.

While Mabel helped her with her spencer and bonnet, the grey-haired housekeeper directed the footmen and grooms. They settled her trunks onto the carpet, and a tea tray on the table in front of the windows.

A tall, dark-haired woman in an elegant, wine-colored gown was the last to sweep in. All the staff curtsied or bowed, and she smiled, her gaze landing on Paulette.

Who curtsied also.

"Miss Heardwyn." The tall lady advanced on Paulette, bringing with her the essence of lavender, her dress rustling over a swollen belly.

No wonder she seemed to glow.

She inclined her head and her smile warmed more. "I'm Lady Hackwell. You are most welcome here. And this is your maid?" She looked at Mabel and smiled. Mabel dropped in another awkward curtsy, tongue-tied.

"This is Mabel, er, Brown, my lady."

Mabel flushed. In this great house, she must transform from maid-of-all-work to lady's maid and go by her surname.

"Well, Mabel Brown, Mrs. Bradley will see to your dinner and lodging. No doubt you will want to help Miss Heardwyn settle in first and prepare for dinner."

"I—"

"Oh please, you must join us, Miss Heardwyn. Mrs. Bradley, see that she has what she needs to get ready."

Paulette let out a breath. "I'm afraid I may not have an appropriate dinner dress."

Lady Hackwell's eyes swept over her. "Dressed just as you are would be appropriate in our home, Miss Heardwyn. We do have a few guests, but no one so high in the instep they would worry about a pretty young woman's gown after a long day of travel." She took Paulette's hand and squeezed it. "We are dining tonight with one other lady, and three of my husband's parliamentary associates. We are all out of balance. Do join us." The door shut on the last male servant, and Mrs. Bradley ushered all but one maid out of the room.

Her ladyship beckoned the maid. "Jenny, come and get me when Miss Heardwyn is ready so she and I can go down together. I will be in the nursery." She squeezed Paulette's hand once more, and left.

"Oh, she was very nice," Mabel whispered.

The young servant smiled. "'Elp you with your baff, miss?"

"Excuse me?" *Help you with your bath.* "Oh. Yes. Jenny, is it?"

The girl nodded.

"Shall I shake out the blue dress, Pol...miss?" Mabel asked. "Or do you wish to wear the brown for mourning Lord Shaldon?"

The blue dress was her finest, though it had been made over from one of her mother's for her visit to Cransdall years earlier.

She wouldn't wear her newest dress, the brown she'd made last spring from Mrs. Everly's left-over yardage. Nor would she mourn for Lord Shaldon, the insufferable man.

"The blue will have to do." She reached around, fumbling for her gown's ties, and Mabel came over to help.

Mabel was right—Lady Hackwell was all friendliness and welcome. This chamber was just as warm and cheerful, all of it shining bright and spanking clean. It needed an abundance of servants to keep a place of this sort.

She took in a breath. And to have such a finely-clad steward. Hackwell must be quite wealthy. Mr. Gibson didn't wish to leave, so perhaps he knew something about the Earl's promised Little Norwick. It wouldn't be as grand as this. Perhaps no grander than Ferndale Cottage.

And perhaps he wished to remain because Lord Hackwell was as congenial as his lady.

Yes, indeed, Mr. Gibson's situation here was good. No wonder he didn't want to trade this for a living that perhaps needed more care than four thousand a year could provide.

While Mabel slipped out of the room to press the blue gown, Jenny helped Paulette settle into the bone-soothing water.

"Shall I brush out yer 'air, miss?"

"Yes, thank you, Jenny." She closed her eyes and gritted her teeth for the hair pulling to come, but the girl's first strokes were gentle, tentative.

"Just give it a good tug," Paulette said. "Else we'll be here all night with my rat's nest."

"No, miss, yer curls are lovely."

"And require firmness. Don't worry, Mabel bashes me every night with that brush all the while complaining how heavy it is."

Jenny chuckled. "'Tis a lovely hairbrush."

"My mother's." Another thing rescued by Mr. Gibson.

"Lucky you are to 'ave it," Jenny said.

The hint of wistfulness made Paulette turn. "Jenny, your accent is not from this area, is it?"

The girl's hand paused. "I'm from town, miss."

"From London? However did you wind up in the country?"

"Her ladyship. She 'elped me. There are a bunch of us 'ere she 'elped, though I been with her the longest, almost a year now."

"She hired you?"

"Not right off. She found me and brought me home. She was Miss 'Arris then. And then Lady Cathmore took me to the house in Sussex."

"You worked for Lady Cathmore?"

"No, miss. It were...was..." She cleared her throat. "The house in Sussex is an orphan home or such as are like orphans, miss, one with good food and no beatings. Both their ladyships run it."

She picked up the toweling and helped Paulette to stand. "Miss 'Arris had a houseful of us, but when her friend Miss Montagu married Lord Cathmore, he made her move all of us to the country."

"From London to the country? Did you like that?"

"Well, I liked living with Miss 'Arris sure enough, and I liked the country too. Both places the food was better than what the pieman could sell and much more regular, and she made sure we had lessons."

"Not as exciting as the city."

"I'd trade a clean bed and regular meals for that excitement any day, miss."

Paulette met Lady Hackwell at the stair landing and they descended together.

"How lovely you look," Lady Hackwell said.

Her face heated. Only Mabel bothered with compliments. No one else ever noticed her, except to criticize.

She nodded her thanks. "Jenny told me about your home for orphans."

"She's one of our successes."

"She's a very good girl. Are both of her parents deceased?"

They had reached the last stair. Lady Hackwell took Paulette's hand and tucked it in the crook of her elbow, sending a rush of warmth to her eyes. The unexpected intimacy felt almost maternal, not that Paulette's mother had been much of an example of tenderness.

"They are both living, as far as we know. Her father was transported a few years ago, and her mother... cannot provide a home."

Paulette thought of her vicar, who did so much for the poor, to the detriment of his own family at times. Shame pricked her warmly. His inclination to doing without had been another reason for turning him down. "The parish cannot help her?"

"My dear, London is awash with the poor, far more than any parish can provide for. It's one of the reasons our guests are here," she whispered.

"My husband is trying to convince members of parliament to do something constructive for a change." She pushed open a grand door. "We are here," she announced.

All conversation stopped, while the gentlemen rose. Paulette's cheeks flamed. All of them were richly dressed for this country dinner.

"Are the children well?" a woman asked.

"Yes, and thank you for waiting." Lady Hackwell apologized, taking the blame that should have been Paulette's. It had been, after all, her bathing and changing that had delayed dinner. A splash of color drew her eyes to the woman who'd spoken, a fashionably-dressed matron who looked to be Mrs. Everly's age.

But as her gaze roamed the room it froze on a pair of arresting brown eyes, sending her heart into a relieved flutter.

Mr. Gibson was here, dressed for dinner. Dressed like the son of an earl. He towered over all the other gentlemen, even the very tall Lord Hackwell, who greeted her as cordially as his wife had.

She barely registered the rest of the names— Lord Shurley, Lord and Lady Tepping, and a fair-haired boy of about twelve or perhaps older, Lord Hackwell's brother, Thomas.

Perhaps this *would* be a less formal affair.

Lord Hackwell took her arm and turned her to where Mr. Gibson had joined a new arrival, a man with his back to her whose dark hair was streaked with grey. She saw the man's head move and Mr. Gibson's eyes flare.

And then he turned, and Paulette's stomach sank. This man she knew.

Chapter Eight

L ord Agruen.
Mr. Gibson said something to Agruen, inciting the sardonic smile that signaled Agruen was up to no good.

The abominable trickster. The malignant teller of tales. The thief.

So she would not have to go to London to find *him*. She could take up her unfinished business right here.

Lord Hackwell led her over to him, into the cloud of his nauseating odor, part perfume, part something noxious.

"Miss Heardwyn, so happy to see you again," Agruen said. "The lady and I have met at Cransdall, as a matter of fact. And I understand the old man finally keeled over. My condolences on the loss of your guardian, Miss Heardwyn."

"Ah, there is Grey," Lord Hackwell said.

A man tottered in on a cane he was far too young to need. Where one of his arms should have been, his sleeve had been folded and pinned.

"Gibson," Lord Hackwell said.

Mr. Gibson set his feet moving. He swung by the boy, Thomas, and urged him over to assist the maimed man.

Agruen's low chuckle unnerved her. "Hackwell. Dinner with your steward, a child, and the child's crippled tutor? One would think we were in America."

Lord Hackwell smiled. "Grey, a *hero* of Waterloo, is missing an arm and part of a foot, but his brain is a lively one, and his hearing is perfect. And I must say, Agruen, all of our male guests are the direct progeny of exalted earls, well, except for Grey. And, of course, yourself. We shall give you credit though for being the grandson of a marquess. Will you excuse me?" He bowed to Paulette and walked off.

Agruen chuckled. "Well, I've been put in my place." His gaze swept over her. "But the progeny of earls? I smell juicy gossip, Miss Heardwyn. You must fill me in."

She wouldn't give him the satisfaction. "Was your father a younger son, then?" He was of course, and she knew it. He'd mentioned it during one of their walks in the garden at Cransdall. Both his uncle and his cousin had fortuitously died, bequeathing him the marquisate. His wife had died also, soon after receiving her coronet and bestowing her dowry.

His look became shrewd. "I suppose Shaldon has settled some money upon you?"

A chill went up her spine. Agruen's wife was gone and he might be seeking a replacement, and surely a big purse would be required. "I am still as poor as a church mouse. Come, everyone is going into dinner."

Bink looked down at the berries ladled with sauce on his plate. He really had no appetite. Listening to Agruen converse with his hostess and Lord Tepping had reminded him how tedious polite conversation was, all gloves-on one-upmanship. Worse had been the tense, silent interplay between Agruen and Paulette. Agruen was looking for an opening to attack, and just as assuredly, Paulette was parrying him without saying a word.

That business Bakeley had talked about was still between them.

"You look glum," Thomas whispered. "Do you not like her then?"

Bink cast the boy a quelling look. "How is your Latin coming along?"

Thomas's lips went through a series of movements that in other circumstances would have made Bink laugh. They finally settled into a disgusted line.

Across the table from Bink, Grey watched his charge with a neutral expression, finally catching the boy's eye.

"I am doing well, sir," Thomas said.

Miss Heardwyn, seated across from Thomas, leaned forward. "Do you enjoy it?"

To her left, Agruen sniggered. "Who could possibly enjoy Latin, right, boy? Miss Heardwyn, if you had been educated, you would know that."

The ass. Seating Paulette next to Agruen was not a good thing. The man had all but insulted her when she'd entered the room earlier. He'd been very close to getting a taste of Bink's knuckles.

Now Miss Heardwyn colored deeply. Her eyes flashed a warning of Iberian retribution and she dropped her gaze, drawing a shade on the war going on inside her.

Lady Hackwell's chat with Lord Tepping went quiet.

Was Paulette educated? Like most genteel ladies, probably not. He'd been running so hard from the idea of marrying her, he'd also avoided all routine polite conversation. He knew a lot about her circumstances, but very little about her.

Certainly she acted the lady. Someone had trained her that much.

"I am enjoying Latin, Miss," Thomas said, and Bink felt a rush of pride in the boy. "Thank you for asking. Captain Grey makes it ever so interesting. We are studying *The Gallic Wars* by Julius Caesar."

Agruen smiled sardonically. "I say, Miss Heardwyn, I have been set in my place once again tonight by a Beauverde."

She raised her eyes and sent Thomas a half-smile.

Bink's heart lifted. "I myself would have enjoyed Latin and Greek more if it hadn't been taught with such liberal administrations of the cane."

That won him a smile of his own, one he couldn't help returning.

"You see, Ensign Beauverde," Grey said, "you are fortunate to have a one-armed tutor who applies his cane to a more practical use."

Thomas's lips quirked. Grey had conferred rank on the boy the day he moved into the Hackwell household. Grey wasn't smiling, but humor lurked under the thick layer of matter-of-factness.

Bink had found Grey through a network of wounded ex-soldiers, moldering in London. The bookish fifth or sixth younger son of a baron, he'd been a sensible, steady officer with a reputation for fairness, and a knack for turning his unit of Wellington's scum of the earth into a fighting force. He was the perfect man to take a boy from the streets and turn him into a gentleman.

"I suppose you ladies had governesses who were as restrained as Grey here?" Agruen asked, raising an eyebrow.

Bink went still. The man would not let it alone. Now he was also picking at his unfashionable hostess, who arguably had the poorest pedigreed blood lines of anyone at this table after Paulette.

At the far end of the table, Hackwell still conversed amiably with Lady Tepping and Shurley. Grey, always adept and alert, stepped in to keep their conversation diverting.

"I had music and dance and art teachers," Lady Hackwell said, "and oh yes, for a while I went into the village to study French with an émigré. But no governess."

Agruen's lip had curled up. "And yet you managed to become an accomplished lady."

The bloody ass. The ironic tone sent Bink's blood boiling.

"I also had no governess." Miss Heardwyn smiled at Lady Hackwell. "Only, as you say, the usual teachers. I was fortunate to learn French from my mother."

"Only French?" Agruen's dark eyes pinned her. "Wasn't your mother Spanish?"

She cocked her head and examined Agruen, and Bink felt another surge of pride. She'd recovered her composure and was dueling with all of her guards up.

"My mother and father were English, as you well know."

Agruen set down his fork. "Oh dear. Have I offended you?"

Bink found his voice. "Are you close friends with Bakeley, Agruen?"

"I beg your pardon?" Agruen blinked.

"Your visit to Cransdall. You said you and Miss Heardwyn became acquainted there."

That eyebrow shot up again. "Why yes, we did. It was—"

"Four years ago. The summer of Waterloo," Miss Heardwyn said.

"Actually, I was there to see Shaldon, but the Earl was detained elsewhere. I'd never met the son. Are *you* close friends with Bakeley, *Sergeant* Gibson?"

The question rippled down the table silencing everyone. Bink forced his lips into a smile, and locked eyes with the ass.

They'd met a decade ago in Spain, and who could forget it? Agruen had been Josiah Dickson then, attaching himself to the army, tagging along as some kind of government operative, as useless as a tea kettle with no fire.

Various answers rumbled through him. He'd kept his secrets, damn it.

But the truth would take Agruen's attention off Paulette. "No. Bakeley and I are not close friends at all. We are half-brothers."

"Mr. Gibson is Lord Bakeley's—or now Lord Shaldon's older brother." Miss Heardwyn's eyes glittered.

Agruen gazed at her for a long moment, then he looked hard at Bink and smiled broadly. "I see. And you escorted the lady from Cransdall."

Anger spiked in Bink. That quickly the man had turned his assault back to include the lady, and his devious mind had already deduced an expected relationship between them.

Lady Hackwell set down her napkin. "Of course Mr. Gibson escorted the lady. You smile, Lord Agruen, but heavens, there is no scandal in it. Miss Heardwyn was to be our guest, and it only made sense for Mr. Gibson, who is an honorable man, to accompany her when he returned from his father's funeral. Especially now, with the rumors of trouble among the weavers, I would not have a young woman travel alone. Would you?" She pushed back her chair and stood.

Bink got to his feet giving a smugly smiling Thomas a prod.

"Steven, we will excuse ourselves. Lady Tepping, Miss Heardwyn, shall we withdraw and leave the gentlemen to their manly discussions?"

Paulette's eyes glittered. "And we will talk later," she told Agruen.

He watched her glide out, erect and proud and radiating passion. By God, she was a fine woman.

When he sat down, he noticed Agruen grinning at him.

Deep lines etched the ass's forehead, and Bink wondered if they were from scowling over the gaming tables. Agruen's skin wore the yellow pallor that came with drink, a bilious liver, and probably the pox. As tall as Hackwell, he'd gone soft since his days in the Peninsula, shabby under those fine clothes—a dissolute, despicable ass who'd acquired his title by the lucky deaths of others.

A memory flashed, turning Bink's stomach.

And Agruen was dangerous. If Paulette wanted to talk to him, she would not do it alone.

Paulette settled herself in a chair in the drawing room, praying Lord Hackwell's regard for his wife would bring the gentlemen out sooner. Now that she'd survived dinner and broached the need for conversation with Agruen, she wanted to speak to him before she lost her nerve.

Lady Hackwell poured tea and passed it around.

"Agruen is an ass," Lady Tepping said.

Paulette choked and set down the cup.

Lady Hackwell passed her a fresh napkin. "And his is a vote Steven and Lord Tepping need."

"Yes, along with Shurley's, and I'm not certain Lord Hackwell and I had greater luck at our end of the table. Shurley, however, is at least a gentleman."

Paulette had not heard the conversation at Lord Hackwell's end. And, too busy steeling herself against Agruen, she'd barely heard Lady Hackwell's small talk. "But you did not discuss a parliamentary bill." *Did they?*

"No we did not. That will come later." Lady Hackwell sighed. "While they are shooting birds, or perhaps even now over brandy. If the gentlemen do not get to it, we will bring it up before the visit ends. I fear I am not meek enough for some of the aristocracy."

"It is all the cause of you lacking a *governess* or an *education*." Lady Tepping smiled and then laughed, and Lady Hackwell joined in giggling.

The feather in Lady Tepping's headpiece trembled, and Lady Hackwell put a hand to her belly.

"Come, Miss Heardwyn," Lady Tepping said. "You may laugh with us. You are in good company here. Tell us about the travel—how were the roads from Cransdall? Did you encounter roving bands of thugs?"

Paulette described her journey in the vaguest of terms, omitting her eviction and Mr. Gibson's rescue. The ladies, if they sensed there was more, refrained from probing. Lady Tepping shared news from letters she'd received about the discontent among workers.

"That is all I know about the fears of an uprising," Lady Tepping said. "But I do have one interesting *on dit.* Anglesey is to be made a full general. I wonder what Wellington has to say?"

"Lord Wellington?" Paulette asked. "Are they political enemies? I'm sorry, I'm woefully ignorant."

"This relates more to gossip than to politics," Lady Hackwell said.

"The juiciest, most entertaining of gossip. You must let me explain." Lady Tepping launched into the story of the Marquess of Anglesey's affair with Lord Wellington's former sister-in-law, their Scottish divorces and remarriage to each other. "Scotland, you see, is more lenient about divorce. Except that now our courts have decided they will no longer recognize those Scottish divorces unless the couple originally married in Scotland."

"So the trips to Gretna Green will pay off if the couple is unhappy later. Perhaps I should have demanded Lord Hackwell take me there."

"If they marry in Scotland they may divorce?" Paulette asked.

"Why, yes."

She must have looked shocked because Lady Tepping added, "Not for no reason of course. One must have the usual charge of adultery or some such, and witnesses can always be found to testify to whatever charge works best. I've made a study of it and threatened Lord Tepping on one or two occasions. We were married in Edinburgh, you know."

Paulette's heart took it in. This was shocking and novel. Watching her mother rot in the country, she'd always thought of marriage as an impossible snare.

"My dear," Lady Hackwell said "Lady Tepping is having us on. There are no two people so firmly hitched as she and her husband, except for me and mine of course."

Both ladies were still laughing when the men joined them.

Agruen slunk into the room, his oily smile in place as Lord Hackwell spoke to him. Paulette sat straighter in her chair. She would need to muster all of her wits, all of her composure, and, perhaps, all of the skills Jock had tried to teach her.

Bink circulated within the room, following Paulette who was unobtrusively trying to speak to Agruen.

The ass coerced her to play the piano, grabbing a music sheet from the pile, a new popular song. She stumbled through the piece, hitting sour notes here and there.

Agruen moved to the other side of the room, watching, and when the song ended, started out for the bench where she sat.

"Go and turn pages for her, Thomas," Bink said. After helping his tutor to his room, Thomas had been allowed to return to the drawing room.

Thomas looked at him quizzically and saluted. "I'll report back, sir."

Bink grinned, watching the boy's meandering path to the piano. Thomas and Agruen reached Paulette at the same time.

She made room for the boy on the bench.

He'd spurted up in the past months, catching up to his Beauverde height. Something he said to Paulette made her smile, the warmth of it reaching all the way to Bink and making him chuckle. Watch out, Hackwell—Thomas would have no trouble with the ladies.

Aye, and wouldn't he like to have that smile cast upon himself?

Agruen said something to make the smile slip. She flipped pages of music, her lips moving. The chatting and scowling went on until finally she began to play quite ably a dark, sad, melody.

The room quietened, everyone listening, and at the end applauding. She played two more songs of her own choosing, and the party broke off soon afterwards. Thomas hovered nearby her as she said her good nights, and walked out with her.

When the guests and Lady Hackwell went up, Hackwell pulled Bink aside.

He steeled himself for the questioning about Paulette. It had been a whirlwind since his arrival, and he'd had little time to think. He needed to clear any immediate estate business and decide what to do with her.

And Lady Hackwell was the person to talk to about Paulette, not her husband. If anyone knew what to do with an orphaned young lady of very little means, it would be Annabelle Harris. But with this damnable party here, finding the moment would be difficult.

"Free up your afternoon tomorrow, Gibson. I'm going to need you."

"For the shooting?" Bink asked. "I have letters to catch up on."

"We'll shoot in the morning. Better you're not there. That fool Agruen is likely to blow up a gun. Damned dangerous business with one like him. No, Bella and Lady Tepping will handle this bunch in the afternoon. You and I have…estate business."

"I see. Something I need to prepare for?"

"Not at all. Only be dressed for a ride. Can you see to the locking up?"

"Aye, milord."

Hackwell smiled and clapped him on the back. "You're a damned stubborn man, Bink Gibson. But a good one."

He was in the same sitting room chair Hackwell had occupied earlier, nursing a whisky, when Thomas arrived.

One candle lit the room dimly. The house had gone quiet. Thomas had likely waited for the nursemaid to drowse before sneaking out. Paulette should be abed now, too, in some virginal white nightrail, her dark hair spreading over the pillow.

He shook off that thought and threw back his drink. If the boy was here, he had something to say. "Well?"

"He stole something of hers."

A ring, Bakeley had said. Bink waited.

"Leastways that would be my guess from the way she talked to him and he talked back. He's a shady bugger. I don't like him."

"What was it he stole?"

He wrinkled his nose. "Somethin' of her mother's I'd warrant."

"What exactly did they say?"

Thomas eyed the bottle of whisky on the shelf.

"If you'd conceded to letting your brother send you off to school you'd be quaffing that under the stairs with a bunch of lordly brats. Not here though. Not yet. It'll stunt your growth. What was said?"

Thomas flung himself into a chair, grumbling. "I couldn't hear all, what with one ladyship talking my arm off and the other ladyship telling me to go to bed."

He would have to talk directly to Paulette in the morning. Before he attacked the stack of mail.

"All right. At least you got Miss Heardwyn all tucked in. Now it's me telling you to go to bed."

"She's not tucked in."

"No?"

"That's why it took me so long to get down here. From what was said, I had this feeling like, and I waited around in the corridor. Your lady is in the library and he's there too."

Chapter Nine

Paulette pushed through the library door and held her candle higher. Other than her own little pool of light, the room was shadowed. She could not see more than a few feet in front of her.

That sickening perfume swirled in the drafty room. Agruen was here somewhere, sitting in the dark, waiting to spook her.

Perhaps she should have gone ahead and met in the kitchens as he'd wanted, but somehow the library seemed safer.

Drawing too close to him would be foolish. Everyone else was abed. There was no Lord Bakeley here to come around the corner and rescue her.

So she must rescue herself, and she'd come armed for it.

She felt her way to the wall and circled around, spotting a candelabra on a table, and lighting the candles with her own.

That was better. She set down her candlestick. Warm light showed a high shelf filled with leather bound volumes. In other circumstances, she would love to explore them.

The curtains were drawn over a nearby window, and she opened them, casting a scant pool of light from a waning moon.

A low chuckle nearby made her hair stand.

"You are undoing all my dark work." The voice was a growl, but easily recognizable as Agruen's.

Paulette scuttled back to the light, knocking into a chair, the clatter reverberating through the room.

Agruen moved out of the darkness, his neck cloth loose over a flopping shirt. The scent of stale alcohol mixed with his overpowering cologne and a smell like a ripening privy. It had not been so powerful during that interminable dinner.

She caught her breath and steadied it. "Do not approach closer. I am not here for a tryst, Agruen. You have something of mine, and I want it back."

He laughed and took an intimidating step. "You are accusing me of theft?"

"You took a ring of mine. Don't try to deny it. A maid saw it in your chambers at Cransdall. You must give it back."

"Must I?" He stepped up to the table and she went to the other side. The candle flame flashed in front of him, like the fires of hell.

"It was my mother's."

Not that Mama had valued it. Paulette had found it after her mother died, a strange, lopsided ring too large for small fingers. She'd worn it around her neck on a chain, wondering about the mystery of it, wondering if it had aught to do with the treasure.

"It could have no meaning to you," she said.

Except as a means of tormenting a girl without friends.

She squeezed her lips shut. She might be friendless, but she was not without resources. Her hand slipped through the slit in her skirt and eased the knife higher in its sheath.

In spite of Jock's tutoring, a strong man could take it from her, Mabel had warned her once.

Agruen would not be so strong. He was drunk, dissipated, weak. And disgusting.

"You look like hell, Agruen, and you smell like death."

His lips pulled back in a ghastly sneer. "That ring of your mother's is part of a puzzle ring, lovely Paulette. Did you know that?"

The skin on her back rippled and her hand shook around the blade handle. She eased in another breath.

She hadn't known, but a puzzle made sense. The design had an off-center design like the curved fingers and thumb of a hand. "Of course," she said.

"And did you not wonder where the other piece was?"

"How could I if I didn't know there was another piece?" She put up a hand. "Come no closer."

He snickered. "*I* have its match, little Paulette. That's why I took your ring. I'm going to solve the puzzle."

Her heart quickened. The puzzle. The treasure. The puzzle of where the treasure was hidden.

How could this ass have the other half of her mother's ring? Where did he get it? And how long had he had it? If the ring had an answer, he must have found it by now.

He laughed darkly. "Close your mouth, Paulette. I can see the question on your pretty face. I got my part of this puzzle from another *whore.*"

Heat surged into her cheeks.

Composure, Paulette. Unman your opponent with your calm.

Jock's words failed to compose her. She eased in a breath. "My mother was *not* a whore."

She was a spy.

"Was she not? Yet she had the other half of a whore's ring."

Her next breath was deeper. "No. The whore had *her* other half, if there even was a whore. And I want it back. In fact, you've had years to solve the puzzle. You might as well give me both pieces."

He circled the table and gripped her arm. She tried to wrench away, but he stayed fixed, his hand firm. Panic built in her.

Just like with Cummings, she had underestimated this man's strength.

"What have you got there, Paulette, under your skirt?"

His chuckle sent fear raging through her and breath whooshed out of her. Before she could catch it back for a scream, Agruen went flying back into the darkness with loud thuds and grunts.

"Are you all right, then, miss?" Thomas appeared at her side.

She quivered and shook, but praise God, the boy didn't notice, and didn't really expect her to speak. He was riveted upon the dark action beyond the light.

"Lay off," Agruen yelled. "What are you doing?"

"What were *you* doing to the lady?"

Her heart skipped a beat. This last growl had issued from Mr. Gibson.

He'd come to her rescue. Her heart swelled and clanged against her breastbone.

And then plummeted. He'd known about this meeting.

Heat rose in her and she snagged Thomas's sleeve. "You followed me."

The boy's gaze jerked to her. He blinked.

Gad, she could take lessons in lying from this boy. Her anger died, a laugh bubbling up. Yes, he'd followed her, and thank God for it.

Agruen came into the light, his body jerked up unnaturally, his shirt stretching his neck higher.

Mr. Gibson was behind him.

The door opened and more light suffused the room.

Paulette's cheeks heated again. Damn it all, she'd been a fool. She'd walked into another of Agruen's traps, only this one would turn into a fine spectacle and end with her being sent away again with another keeper like Mrs. Everly. Only now she had no home to go to except perhaps Cransdall.

And she wasn't going there.

Dressed only in a belted banyan, Lord Hackwell stepped closer, a candle held high. "What's afoot, Gibson?" he asked, calmly.

Mr. Gibson released Agruen and wiped his hands together. "Just helping his lordship here to his feet." His voice was steady. There was even a trace of humor.

He was covering for her.

She blinked. He and Thomas had come in together. He'd set the boy to look after her.

He wanted to protect her, but he didn't *want* her.

She cleared her throat. "I...had trouble sleeping. I came in for a book."

Agruen refastened his waistcoat. "Indeed. And I happened to be in here." He looked up, his evil grin back in place. "And I say, Hackwell, I will not marry her, if that is what she was planning."

She gasped. "*How dare you.*"

"Indeed, you will not marry the young lady," Mr. Gibson said, all humor gone.

"Are you well, Miss Heardwyn?" Hackwell asked.

She nodded. "Yes."

"Gibson," Hackwell said, "see to the lady." He looked hard at Agruen. "As long as you're here, Agruen, let's have another dram of whisky. Or do you prefer brandy? I've a fine bottle here somewhere." He nodded at Mr. Gibson and led the other man into the shadows.

Mr. Gibson's large hand swallowed hers, sending his strength coursing through her and, now that the threat was gone, settling her trembling.

Bakeley hadn't taken her hand when he rescued her in the garden at Cransdall four years ago. But then, she hadn't realized it was a rescue until later.

"Thomas, off to bed," Mr. Gibson said.

"But—"

She couldn't see the look Mr. Gibson gave the boy, but it moved him along. Thomas wished her a good night and crept away into the dark corridor.

"Close the door on your way out, Gibson," Lord Hackwell called.

Mr. Gibson picked up her candle and led her out of the room. "Come along. As I recall, you enjoyed the brandy at Cransdall. You could use a spot of it tonight."

*****

The lady's quaking urged Bink to hold more than her tiny chilled hand. A damned dangerous slope, that, with a snare at the bottom, but one he was having trouble resisting.

He let go of Paulette's hand and wrapped an arm around her, and fought the urge to let his hand slip further, down to the backside he'd had a handful of the day they'd first met.

She was slight, but not fragile. She hadn't changed out of the gown she'd worn at dinner, and from this angle he could see that handsome bosom, kissed by the dark curls escaping from the pins at the back of her head. Willowy, she was, but womanly also.

Desire uncurled in him and his shaft stirred. Aye, Shaldon had laid him a clever trap.

"Thomas told you where I was," she said, breathless.

"Yes."

"Why were you there?"

"I was eavesdropping," he said, keeping his voice mild.

She inhaled sharply.

"I wanted to see what you had to discuss with Agruen, as you so obviously found him disagreeable earlier."

Her body stiffened. They had reached his quarters, and he opened the door and urged her in.

She locked her knees and dug in the heels of the feminine slippers peeking from under her skirt. "Where are you taking me?"

"This is my sitting room."

"My reputation—"

"Paulette. You were willing to meet Agruen privately tonight. Do you fear me more?"

She swallowed. Sighed. "Perhaps you are the greater danger, Mr. Gibson." Her shoulders moved with another sigh and she walked through the open door.

His breath caught, desire rising. Like a fool, he followed her in.

He lit candles until the room was bright enough for him to see the tiniest of beauty marks on one of her cheeks and then crossed the room and opened a window, letting in a fresh breeze that rippled through the flames, the light dancing over her skin. Bink turned away and poured the drinks and tried to quell the yearning to touch her.

She had seated herself in the straight-backed chair the housekeeper usually occupied when she came to discuss accounts. He handed her a glass and sat opposite her.

She twirled the amber liquid. "I love the look of this in a fine crystal glass. It's so lovely the way it sparkles in the candlelight."

More stirring within him. The lass had depths. And courage. And intelligence. She was not a shrew, or a hysteric. She had seen through his plan to save her embarrassment and played right along.

"*You* are lovely," he blurted.

Her head jerked up, and a devil within him made him pitch his voice lower. "Could you but see yourself now, *you* are sparkling in the candlelight."

She scooted to the edge of her seat, ready to bolt, he'd warrant.

"Stay, lass. I won't leave this chair." *Unless you wish it.* Desire percolated within him and beat in his ears. For too long he'd had only the administrations of his own hand.

He gave himself an imperceptible shake. And it must stay that way. They had matters to discuss. "So the Marquess of Agruen is a thief. I'm not surprised. When he was a mere Mr. Josiah Dickson, I came very close to thrashing the cur in Spain."

Paulette's mouth dropped open and her countenance darkened. "I would that you had."

His pulse drummed harder and an ache came along with the pictures in his head. He pinched the bridge of his nose and tried to dispel the memory. A woman beaten half to death. Bink beating the man Dickson named as the culprit. Then, weeks later, Dickson on top of a girl barely old enough to bleed.

Bloody liar. Bloody rapist. Bink had been pulled off Dickson, well before getting justice.

"He has a ring that was my mother's." Her low voice brought him back from his shadows. "I want it back. And, as you probably heard, there's a second ring, part of a puzzle—"

"I've seen such, with a third part, a heart."

She blinked and chewed on her lip.

"You would like to know where he got the other part."

She clenched her hands. "My mother was not a-a whore."

He leaned forward and rested his elbows on his knees. "To a man like Agruen, all women are whores. The lady who had that other half of the ring was not likely a whore either."

She nodded, picked up her glass, and took a drink.

"Let me help you. Will you tell me why it's so important?"

She set the glass down carefully and lifted her eyes.

Ah. She was crafting a lie.

"It was something of hers, is all, and I have so little. I found it among her things when she died."

"It seems a small thing. Are there no other jewels?"

"A few trinkets. A few items of clothing. One letter she kept from my father."

Her gaze slid away and she bit her lip, as if mentioning the letter had been a mistake. It must be important.

"Did she not leave you that wee knife you have hidden under your skirt?"

Her eyes went wide.

"Or is it a wee pistol?"

Her lips firmed and he waited.

"It is a dagger." The frown she sent him was mulish. "And it was hers. As was this dress, though I made it over a few years ago. You're thinking it is dreadfully old-fashioned."

Men don't notice much below the bodice and yours is very fine indeed. "I didn't pay heed to the fashion of the dress, only that it is very becoming. May I see your blade?"

She inserted a hand into a slit in her skirt and drew out a five-inch blade, sharpened to a gleaming point. She flipped it around and presented it to him.

And his breath caught at the trust she was showing. He cupped his hands under hers without removing the blade. A shiver went through her and he noted her hands were still cold.

"You are chilled. Shall I close the window?"

She shook her head. "What do you think? What kind of knife is this?"

He took it gently from her and turned it over. A Celtic knot looped through the hasp of the squat blade. "This is a dirk. Scottish. It's a lovely blade. Looks to be well-balanced." He touched a finger to the edge. "Very sharp. You are carrying it sheathed?"

"Yes."

"May I see the sheath?"

Even in the candlelight, he could tell she was coloring deeply. "It is fastened to my leg."

Visions assaulted him again—Paulette, lifting her skirts, those trim ankles, a garter high on firm thighs. Stubborn need surged into his loins. He leaned back and rested one ankle on the opposite knee. It was impolite, but expedient. "I would like to see the sheath some time also, if you would permit. Did your mother carry this?"

"I don't know. Maybe. It's another thing I found among her things when she died. She must have. This dress has several pockets and slits. And...there are pistols also."

"She did not talk about the knife and pistols?"

"No."

Her grandparents came from the peninsula, Bakeley had said. Her mother had weapons squirreled away. She'd told Agruen her mother was British. Her father had been one of Shaldon's men.

Was her mother a spy also? "And what of this puzzle Agruen plans to solve?"

She shook her head and looked away. "I don't know."

That might or might not be true. He tried a different tack. "What is your plan?"

"As I told you, I'm going to London. I'm going to speak with a solicitor named Tellingford, and my trustees if I can find them. And I did plan to find Agruen. I want my mother's ring back." She frowned. "Perhaps he has it with him."

Why a man would carry such a ring on a hunting trip, Bink couldn't imagine, but he kept the thought to himself.

He saw her frown transform into hard determination. His nerves came to attention. "Leave that bit of searching to me."

She inched a little closer on the edge of her seat. "Truly?"

Truly, and how, he did not know, for the man surely had a valet with him. Hackwell would keep the villain in thrall for a while, discussing his parliamentary scheme, and in view of Paulette's pestering and Hackwell's politicking, Agruen would likely leave in the morning.

But then, the man *was* good at assaulting women and running away.

Bink stood. "Come, lass. Let us get you back to your room." He took her hand and drew her up. Light as a lamb, she was. Tucking her hand in the crook of his arm, he blew out the candles. He could do without light if he was going to go searching.

In the darkness, she seemed to draw closer, smelling like flowers and good soap. She fitted snugly against him, her hip bumping his, her hand gripping his arm as they climbed the stairs. Need swelled again in him, sending an ache through his loins.

He could have this. He could have the woman, the estate, and the settled life so easily. All it would take would be a bit of seduction, and he'd had practice at that. He knew how it was done.

Though he had never seduced an innocent. The widows and opera dancers he'd taken had played the game too.

And he was going to India.

"Can you see in the dark?" Her low murmur vibrated along his upper arm and into his chest, sending a new ripple through him.

They had reached her door. He slipped her hand away and leaned closer. "Yes and I'll be on the lookout for a wee lass moving about in these halls."

Her soft chuckle smelled like sweet brandy. His hands found their way around her waist.

"Will you please stay in your room, Paulette?"

"You'll help me?" she whispered.

"Yes."

The touch of her lips was like a hot brand. In the dark, she'd landed the kiss on his neck.

Oh, aye, he could see in the dark. He found her mouth and pressed his lips onto hers, wanting to taste, trying to be gentle.

Chapter Ten

Paulette's heart sparked with a hot rush of blood. His lips, his hands—she felt herself falling, wanting, pressing closer. His tongue touched her lips and she parted for him, letting him in. And his hands, oh his hands, they were touching her bottom like they had that first day, sending the fire into her center.

She felt the ripple of muscle in his shoulders and slid her hands higher, fingering the hair at his neck. She'd started all this, aiming for his cheek and kissing his neck, where the hard pulse under soft skin had driven her wild. She pressed herself closer and matched what he did, twining her tongue with his.

His hands gripped her harder and levered her up, pushing at her skirts until her warm female part smashed against something quite hard, and shocked pleasure surged through her. This was...He was...

She squeaked as he shuffled them over and her back touched the wall. His hands smoothed her legs, and cool air swirled. He brought her closer, tighter, his hard place rubbing up more shivers of pleasure.

Soft kisses moved over her cheek, down her neck and her bosom, and further, over the edge of her bodice. He took her nipple through layers of fabric and suckled.

She felt the jolt all the way to her privates, a hot, coursing lava melting her inside. She heard panting, hers, and a low grumble, his.

And the creak of a door latch.

Mr. Gibson froze, and the next moment she was standing and he was putting her dress in order.

She blinked. Her eyes had adjusted, but there was still not enough light to truly see, and no light had poured from an open bedchamber door.

There'd been no need to stop. No one would have seen them.

"To bed with you, love," he said, his voice shaky. He pressed his lips to hers briefly. "Leave everything to me."

When her bedchamber door closed on him, she leaned against it and hugged herself.

If anyone had peered out of one of the bedchambers, they would have seen nothing. It was too dark. She was achy and itchy, and all warm inside. They could have kept on.

Still...it had been her second compromising situation of the evening. Mr. Gibson had rescued her from Agruen—who surely would have tried to assault her—only to take liberties with her himself, liberties that if discovered would result in her being locked up in that small hut Shaldon had planned for them, with a man who would hate her for trapping him into marriage.

And she didn't want that. Though she wouldn't mind being kissed by Mr. Gibson again, because he certainly knew what he was about.

She touched the wet spot on her bodice and felt the tight bud he had created through the fabric.

And he had called her *love*.

"I'm right sorry, Polly," Mabel whispered nearby. "It was me opening the door."

She closed her eyes. "Relight the candle, Mabel."

Mabel shuffled about. "Oh my, he is a strong one."

"Let it be, Mabel."

The tinder sparked and started to glow, and the candle wick flamed, revealing Mabel's broad grin. The maid came closer with the light and looked her over.

"If he tumbles you, you must make him marry you. You could do much with four thousand a year."

She should never have told Mabel about the bequest. "Just help me out of this."

Mabel stripped the dress off of her and looked at the bodice. "I'm not sure that wet spot won't stain." She was still grinning. "You've been gone quite a while. Their ladyships went off to bed ages ago."

"And how do you know? Where were you, hmm? Out in the stables perhaps."

Mabel smiled again, and then laughed.

"It's not funny, Mabel. You must be careful of your reputation also. And perhaps you could see about that stain. I'll need that dress for London."

"Oh, aye."

Mabel's blithe manner rankled. "Perhaps I should send you back to Mrs. Everly."

Mabel put her hands on her hips. "You ungrateful miss, bite your tongue. Besides, I wasn't doing anything much beyond talking, and only briefly. And I'm not sure but with all the visiting staff there won't be some goings on in this house, and that poor housekeeper tearing her hair out. Not as I'd mind you having a visit from Mr. Gibson, but I've had a cot set up to stay with you here."

A scratching at the door brought Jenny. "Is there aught else tonight, miss?" she asked.

Paulette reached for the blue dress, draped over a chair. "I've a spot where I, er, spilled something."

"We should see how it dries," Mabel said. "In the morning—"

"No." Jenny crossed the room and took the gown, studying it. "The housekeeper says attack stains afore they set. I'll just take it down now and sponge it and 'twill be dry by morning perhaps."

And she could travel to London with one decent dress in her bag.

"Thank you, Jenny," Paulette said. "But don't linger about."

Mabel closed the door on the girl and turned the key in the lock. "She's a good girl, and I warrant, I'm tired, as must you be after sitting up all last night waiting for the London coach. Now to bed, and dream about that big fine man."

Paulette waved off the teasing, sensing Mabel's worry. Her maid had got wind of Lord Agruen's presence.

"You must also be careful, Mabel."

"Aye. I will be. And so must you."

She hadn't been careful tonight. No—she hadn't been smart. Agruen was not a man to take on alone, perhaps not even by Mr. Gibson.

Bink eased the door of Agruen's bedchamber open a crack. A dim light showed from within, and he heard the faintest of rustles in the dark corner.

An Argand lamp stood on a table, the wick turned down low.

"Excuse me, yer lawdship," he said gruffly. No response. A valet would surely respond. "Is anyone here?"

The hair on the back of his neck stirred. Someone was here, but not Agruen or his servant.

Anger surged through him. Bink Gibson could sniff out a thief at thirty paces. He did not employ thieves. If a thief was present, he or she must be one of the visitors' servants.

He stepped in and closed the door. "Who is here? Come out."

Thomas crawled out from under the bed, and Bink's breath eased. "Bloody hell," he huffed.

"Shhh." Thomas put his finger to his mouth. "We have to hurry."

Fifteen minutes later, he deposited Thomas in the nursery, threatening to lock him in, and headed below stairs. He took the steps quietly and turned down a corridor. The housekeeper's sitting room door clicked open. Mrs. Bradley stood wrapped in a dressing gown, her hair covered in a white cap, a candle in hand.

"Mr. Gibson. Thank heavens. I heard something." She took in a sharp breath. "There. Do you hear it, too?"

A faint thud came from the kitchens.

His skin rippled again. This night was like his time on the Peninsula—one bloody up after one bloody down.

He reached for her candle. "Let's have a look. Stay behind me, ma'am."

The servants' hall was empty, as it should be at this late hour, everyone abed above stairs.

A muffled cry came from further on. The laundry room door was unaccountably closed. He ran and flung it open.

A man craned his neck their way and froze, breeches down, shirt straggling, arse bare to all the world.

The housekeeper screamed. A girl was stretched on the mangle table, writhing, breasts exposed and legs bared to her hips. A gag muffled her frantic cries.

Bink shoved the candle at the housekeeper and jumped the small space, seizing the man's collar, and tossing him back into a worktable with a loud *oof*. The man staggered, his breeches tangling with his legs, loose and flopping like his flagging prick.

Bink tossed laundry to the housekeeper. "Cover her, then get his lordship. He's in the library."

The man jerked and metal flashed. Bink dodged, just in time, a scream cutting the air. He grabbed the wrist with the knife, swept a sharp kick to a bared knee, and twisted the man round with a crack that released the knife and brought him down on his face.

He pressed a foot into the man's kidneys and jerked the arm he still held.

"Leave off, you ox," the man groaned.

Leave off? Bink clenched his teeth, his heart racing.

The voice was unfamiliar. This was not one of his men, not one of the Greencastle servants, or the ones from Cransdall either.

He ground his foot harder. It didn't take much imagination to know which of the visitors he belonged to.

Images of Spain, of blood, of a woman, and then later a girl, sent his heart raging. The master might escape justice, but his man wouldn't.

A whimper from the table brought Bink back, and he glanced up. A panting Mrs. Bradley was pulling at the girl's bindings. She grabbed a blue garment and covered the girl with it.

The room dimmed and his chest squeezed. That was Paulette's blue dress, the one he'd just pawed, not an hour ago, in the corridor outside her room.

Paulette.

He leaned in as the girl sat up, and breath whooshed back into his lungs.

It was Jenny, one of Lady Hackwell's Longview girls. Not Paulette.

He dropped the arm and lifted his foot away, and hoisted the man up.

"Now there's a sight." Agruen growled from the doorway. "You've done it now, Spellen. If that flaccid thing dangling in front is your cock, no wonder you had to tie the girl up."

Bink's blood roared.

Before he could lash out, Hackwell pushed into the room, his gaze sweeping over the scene.

"Take care of her," he said to the red-faced housekeeper. Then he turned his eyes on the villain. "Fasten your trousers."

Bink checked Agruen's man for weapons before letting him fumble with his breeches and fall. Nothing broken, nothing bruised, that Bink could see. Too bad.

Hackwell tossed a length of washing line. "Bind him. And then lock him up and set a guard."

The girl's gag had come off and her whimpering turned to quiet sobbing. She latched onto the housekeeper and planted her face in the woman's bosom.

"The charge will be rape," Hackwell said.

"Bloody bitch kicked me," Spellen spluttered. "I never got in. And anyway she wanted it. She agreed to meet me here."

Jenny's head came up. "You lie," she shouted.

"And you gagged her and tied her?" Bink growled.

"She wanted it."

Agruen pushed forward. "Oh, come now, Hackwell, haven't you ever heard of this game? Many women like to be tied up. Some men too."

Bink pulled Spellen's arms to his back, making him gasp again. "Well then, we'll make it nice and tight so your man here enjoys it."

Mabel's arrival with a cup of chocolate woke Paulette. The sun shone brightly through the open curtains and shimmered off the yellow walls.

She shoved back the covers and took a sip. Chocolate was a rare treat. "Oh, this is divine. But it's so late. Why didn't you wake me?"

"You were up half the night and finally sleeping so soundly."

"I must find—." She bit off the next words, *Mr. Gibson*.

"He's ridden for the magistrate."

She climbed from the bed juggling her cup. Perhaps he'd found the ring and would charge Agruen with theft. "Why? What happened?"

"Well, no one is saying much, but they're all a-whispering, and one of the maids is still abed, but no one is allowed to talk to her except the housekeeper. They're saying she's sick."

"Have you seen Jenny? What does she say?"

"That good girl you had running all night with your laundry and such? I've not seen her either. But I heard whispers Lord Agruen's valet is *locked up* in a *stout shed* back beyond the stables, with two of the footmen keeping watch."

Paulette's heart quickened and she gripped the cup tighter. His valet was locked up, and a maid abed. One didn't have to have a governess to deduce the connection.

A dagger to the man's privates would be the proper solution.

Mabel reached for her cup, a strand of hair peeping from under her cap. She must have had a long visit to the stables to wheedle her news.

"That was a very long whisper, I'd say. I wonder where you heard it."

Mabel shrugged.

"Well, then," Paulette said, "Where's Agruen?"

"Johnny said he's out with the other lords shooting."

"And where's Thomas?"

"Thomas?"

"Lord Hackwell's brother. Did you not see him last night? A tall boy?"

"Why, in the nursery, I suppose."

Paulette poured another cup of chocolate, and drank it down, her stomach growling. Perhaps there would still be some cold toast and bacon set out. Perhaps Lady Hackwell was in the breakfast room. Perhaps she would tell her what happened to the maid.

And perhaps she would also know when Mr. Gibson was to return.

She must try to find out without sounding too interested.

Lady Hackwell appeared for breakfast a little after Paulette. When Paulette inquired about the ill maid, Lady Hackwell sent the footman for more tea and coffee and bade him close the door. She slid her plate near Paulette's and drew closer.

"Lord Agruen's valet assaulted one of my maids last night." Her voice shook and her fist tightened around her knife.

Paulette's skin crawled. It was as bad as she had thought. The valet *would* be as vile as the master.

"I would be pleased if you would not mention this to anyone for the girl's sake. We are still sorting out the facts."

Had it been unwelcome?

"Mr. Gibson and the housekeeper discovered them. It was quite unpleasant."

She pictured Agruen's valet sneaking into the women's quarters. "Oh, the poor girl."

"Yes."

"Was she one of yours? I mean, was she from your home in Sussex?"

"Yes. It is easy enough for a girl to succumb to a pretty face and a smooth manner." She spread jam on her toast, the knife shaking. "But not this girl, I think, and not in these circumstances."

Not Jenny then. The saucy, pretty girl looked to have a bit of the flirt in her. She and Mabel had quite liked her. "What will happen to her?" She'd been rescued from Agruen twice. Perhaps she could hire the girl away from the whispers and the condemnation likely to follow.

Not that she needed another maid. She could barely afford to keep Mabel.

Lady Hackwell patted her hand. "Do not worry. We do not rescue them to throw them away again after one mishap." The door latch creaked. "I'd be pleased if you would keep this private," she whispered.

"Of course," Paulette said.

"Do you ride, my dear?"

"Well, I have a horse and I used to have a cart that I drove by myself, but riding, well, not often." Only a few times in fact, when she'd straddled Horace bareback. The one time Mabel caught her, the maid had come close to an apoplexy. She set down her fork. "Actually, to be honest, one couldn't say that I ride at all."

Lady Hackwell laughed. "It's time you started. Leave everything to me. If you do not mind a riding habit that's a bit made over, well, I know just the horse for you. We'll have you on Moonglow, the gentlest boy in our stables."

"I believe the gentlest boy in your stables at present must be my Horace, whom Mr. Gibson rescued for me." Paulette smiled. "Though he has never had a saddle strapped to him, so perhaps you are right." Her cheeks heated. "Horace, I mean. In any case, it is ever so nice of you to offer, but I'm not sure I'll be with you for very much longer."

Lady Hackwell studied her without blinking, and her smile grew warmer. "My dear, I'm talking about this afternoon. My husband wants to take you round. Thomas will go with you—you were ever so kind to him last night, I'm afraid he's ready to have you stay forever. And of course, we'll send a groom along. I'd go myself except that this one—" she patted her stomach, "has started to make his or her presence known. But I have no doubt you'll do well."

It was Johnny, Mabel's beau, who boosted her onto a yellow gelding and coached her on how to keep her seat and manage the horse. The heavy skirt of the sapphire blue riding garb was a devil to work with, but once arranged, it anchored her to the saddle.

Three maids had swarmed her after her breakfast, carrying the dress, tucking and pinning. They'd come back an hour later with the altered gown, and Lady Hackwell had insisted she keep it.

None of the maids had been Jenny, which seemed a bit odd. The girl had been so helpful the night before, yet...she'd not brought the soiled gown back from the laundry. She would need to have Mabel check on it.

Johnny released her and she circled the yard and brought the horse to a halt.

"That's right, miss," Johnny said. "You have the hang of it. Sure and you never rode before?"

She laughed and patted the horse's neck. "Never with a saddle. And never aside. But don't tell anyone that, Johnny."

He pounded his heart and promised. She liked Mabel's conquest.

"Are you coming with us today?" she asked.

"Not as I know, miss."

Riding had her nerves jumping, and riding with Hackwell—well, he seemed a kind enough man, and certainly his wife thought so, but Mrs. Everly's whining voice started up in her head. *Unless he's your husband, never be alone with a titled gentleman.* And didn't her experience with Agruen prove that?

Her face warmed. And then, there was the untitled gentleman who'd kissed her last night.

"Master Thomas will be along to help you, needs be," Johnny said, smiling.

Ach, Mabel's new man beamed a quite handsome smile. She wished she could keep him, for Mabel's sake. "Well, then, I'll count on Thomas hanging back to help me while his lordship rides ahead."

Male voices drew her attention. Lord Hackwell and Mr. Gibson strode toward the stables, both in riding attire. Her heart lifted, and then a memory of the previous night's kiss swept through her, and a furious heat overtook her.

Chapter Eleven

A few deep breaths restored Paulette's good sense. With Mr. Gibson along, she would be safe from his lordship. And with his lordship along, she would be safe from Mr. Gibson.

And she must know whether he'd found her mother's ring.

She lifted her hand in a greeting.

"Excellent," Lord Hackwell cried. "You *do* ride, Miss Heardwyn. You there, where are our mounts?"

Johnny doffed his cap and trotted into the stable.

"I need a word with Miss Heardwyn," Mr. Gibson said.

His lordship looked from him to her, laughed, and walked in after Johnny.

Mr. Gibson patted her horse's neck. "It wasn't there."

Her skin buzzed at his nearness and she tried to steady her voice. "Thank you. I heard about what happened last night."

"Yes, well, the valet was below stairs, and the coast was clear, as they say." He frowned and seemed to study the horse's mane.

"We do not need to go riding today if there is business with the legal authorities."

"He insists we both go. Were you told where we are going?"

"Only a ride around the estate, I thought."

He lifted his gaze and she saw humor there under layers of fatigue. The poor man had been up half the night and had already had a morning of hard riding. "An infernal, managing busybody is Lord Hackwell. He insists we visit Little Norwick."

A tremble passed through her. Little Norwick was the cottage bequeathed to the proposed Mr. and Mrs. Gibson. The croft that was to be her prison.

Panic threatened to bloom. Perhaps they would lock her up there today. She had no means of escape—a horse she didn't really know how to ride, no money and no loyal servants with her. She might be stuck there, as she'd been at Ferndale Cottage.

His large hand engulfed hers. "We will visit and come back. Do not be afraid. No one will force your hand, least of all Hackwell. His lady would thrash him senseless if he tried."

She gulped air and tried to calm herself. "Of course. It's...it's so near here?"

"A few miles as the crow flies. Quite a bit farther by roads. We'll be crossing fields, which is why we're not going by carriage."

"Have you been there?"

"I've seen the edge of the property but never the house."

A short while later, her worry had been replaced by exhilaration. Thomas rode alongside her at times, and at others, while they carefully skirted around crops soon to be harvested, behind her, the two men ahead, with Mr. Gibson leading the way through gates.

They pulled up in an overgrown field. "The house should be up there," Mr. Gibson pointed. "That hedge was the property line and this is the

back approach. These fields should have been let."
He frowned.

"Your brother was negligent," Lord Hackwell
said.

"More like his father had the run of it and
didn't bother with such details." Mr. Gibson
prodded his mount and rode off.

"You mean your father," Lord Hackwell called,
laughing.

Mr. Gibson's back went straighter and he kept
going.

"There's only trees," Thomas said.

And a tangle of them at that. The house must
be small indeed.

Lord Hackwell chuckled. "Yes, well, the next
residents will have some work to do on these
details." Hackwell spurred his horse and went
after Mr. Gibson.

"We'd best follow, I suppose," Paulette said.
But when she looked back, Thomas was not
moving. The boy had been sullen all morning.

She caught his eye and pulled a face at him.
"What's wrong with you today?"

His mouth turned down further.

"You didn't want to come, did you?"

"I wanted to see Jenny, and they wouldn't let
me."

"Jenny..." The hair on her neck prickled. She
turned Moonglow around and moved him closer.
"Jenny?"

Her breath caught. *The valet was below stairs
and the coast was clear.*

She'd sent Jenny down to the laundry.

She reached out for Thomas, and Moonglow
shied.

"Damn it," she cried, grasping handfuls of
mane to keep from toppling.

Thomas reached for her reins and held Moonglow steady while she righted herself, face burning.

When she looked, the boy's mood had shifted.

"Well, I'm new to this," she said, and he grunted like a twelve-year-old scoundrel. She took a deep breath. "Jenny was the one attacked by Agruen's valet."

"Yes," he said.

"And no one would tell me. But everyone else knows, or will know before the day is out."

He bit his lip. "They'll send her away."

"No, Lady Hackwell won't do that, will she?"

"For her own good, the nursery maid said. They'll find her a new place far away, else she'll always be that girl who spread her legs."

"*What*?" Paulette exclaimed.

He shrugged. "Every rank swell as visits will be bothering her. It's not fair."

No, it wasn't. But much in life wasn't, and didn't she know it. And if Jenny found herself carrying a child...egad, it would make the poor girl's life even harder.

"Your brother will not be so cruel as to send her away," she said.

Only, she didn't know that to be true, did she? Lord Hackwell seemed kind, but he might think sending the girl away was kinder.

"And Mr. Gibson will make sure she's looked after," she said.

The boy shook his head. "He'll be in India."

"*India*?"

"Yes. I'm not supposed to know, but I heard Steven whispering about it."

Mr. Gibson was leaving for India. He might as well be disappearing from the face of the earth.

Moonglow chose that moment to explore some vegetation. "Blast it, Thomas. Help me here. And do not worry about Jenny. She is coming with me."

Jenny, and Johnny, and Mabel—and how the devil she would feed them was anyone's guess.

Of course, there was the treasure that Jock always spoke of, and maybe it was real if Agruen was after it. Or maybe it wasn't.

Thomas helped get Moonglow under control, and she looked around at the tangle of trees, shrubs, and weeds.

Little Norwick needed work, but it was real. And it could be hers. All it would take was a wedding.

They caught up with Lord Hackwell and Mr. Gibson and picked their way over the open field to a small path wide enough to accommodate a cart. At the top of the tree-thickened rise, a roof came into view.

Several roofs—a village of roofs, at different heights and angles, topping walls and wings and wide swathes of diamond-paned windows.

"Cor,"Thomas cried, "It's bigger than our house, Steven."

Lord Hackwell turned in his saddle and flashed a grin that took in both her and Mr. Gibson next to her. She felt herself coloring. Mr. Gibson displayed no emotion, making him look...grim.

Her heart plummeted yet one more time this day. Mr. Gibson was feeling pressure, more so than she. For her, this house would be a kind of freedom, at least for a while and with enough money and the three servants she could bring with her.

For him, it would be a large, weighty anchor.

She could not do that to him, could she? He wanted to go to India, which would leave her managing all by herself. None of her servants would know how to take on the full load. Johnny could handle the one horse, Jenny the cleaning of a few rooms, and Mabel could cook, and that was a start. For the rest of it, she could hire a steward.

But supposing...

How did it work, the management of an estate like this? The home farm fields would have to be cleared. For that, workers were needed, and money to pay them.

Mr. Gibson had learned from Lady Hackwell, he said. Perhaps Lady Hackwell could tutor her.

Once her business in London was settled, he could be off to India.

And...perhaps, if what Lady Tepping had said was true, there was a way she could set him all the way free.

They drew closer and she could see gaps in the roof where shingles were missing, windows covered with boards, and paint hanging in strips.

As they passed a fenced kitchen garden, a hare darted out through the gateless entry sending her mount shying and shaking.

In seconds, Mr. Gibson was there, reaching for Moonglow's bridle.

That same serious mood preoccupied him.

"I'm fine." Her voice trembled and she cleared her throat. "Though this is the second time in the last quarter hour I've almost slipped off. Perhaps Moonglow and I need a rest from each other."

His lip quirked. "You've done well."

"Yes. Well enough for the first time in a blasted side saddle." His smile sent her heart dancing. He was truly a kind man, with a good sense of humor.

And a good kisser. They could do more of that before he sailed off for India.

Another flutter went through her, and she shook it off. "This is a great pile, is it not? When do you suppose we will come to the Little Norwick hut?"

His smile widened and he added a chuckle. "From the look of the outside, the floors may have indeed crumbled back to dirt. We shall soon see."

"We're going inside?"

"Oh yes. Never does anything halfway, does Steven Lord Hackwell. The caretaker is meeting us." He glanced her way, concern in his eyes. "Do you not wish to see it?"

Her deep blush touched a nerve in him. They hadn't talked about that kiss the night before.

Kiss, nothing. He'd almost ravished her in the corridor, only a glimmer better than that scoundrel Spellen. Except of course, Paulette had not been tied up and she'd been a full participant.

But he had tied her in knots with kisses.

No, he'd seduced her, almost, and the end would have been the same, only instead of his head in a noose like Agruen's valet could expect, he'd have his leg in a shackle and this great house to take on.

Would it be so bad?

"I confess, I'm curious."

Her voice brought him around. Curious. That was it. She'd been curious last night, yes, that had been part of it, not just the great power of his kissing or this pull between them. Would she act thus with another man because she was curious? Certainly, she hadn't with Agruen.

She kicked her mount and trotted off behind Thomas.

He shook off the tendrils of jealousy. Of course there'd be other men who could stir her. And it was not for him to tie down this sprite who wanted so much to experience life.

Inside the manor was not so bad, at least not by Gibson standards. Old-fashioned, yes, it was, with its ornate carvings and gilded décor. Faded, yes—the draperies were patterned with diamond shapes bleached by the sun. And when the Holland cloth covers came off in clouds of dust, the upholstery was worn in places also.

"This must have been a favorite chair." Paulette stared down at the huge wingback, its cushions sagging, the arms threadbare. She glanced at him, eyes glittering. "For a man as large as yourself."

Hackwell hovered nearby. "Miss Heardwyn is right. Try it out, Gibson."

He bit his lip. "Let's get on with this."

Below stairs was next, a tour of the service areas and kitchen, and his steward's mind ticked through the amenities. A Rumsfeld stove had been installed and a water closet added. The butler's pantry still held a complete dinner service.

The caretaker noticed his interest. "The house conveyed with all the furnishings, dishes, and linens, many relatively new and in good repair."

"And they are still here," Hackwell said.

"I could have wished for the funds to make more repairs, but I've kept a good eye on the place."

Indeed he had. Perhaps he could recruit the caretaker to manage Hackwell's properties when he himself left for India.

The second and third floors were next, with more parlors, and a generous number of bedchambers. An airing, a thorough cleaning, and the bedrooms would do as they were for a few more years.

The caretaker led him up a smaller flight of stairs. "There are servants' chambers above in the attic, and this floor is the schoolroom and nursery."

His head buzzed as he surveyed the sunlit room. It was much like the nursery at Cransdall, with more beds crowded in. Five child-sized cots, two cribs and an assortment of furniture and toys occupied the large open room. Paulette's eyes brightened and she pressed her hands at her waist, her lips together. When their eyes met, hers shimmered. "It was a large family, I suppose. I've never seen anything like it."

She colored deeply and looked away.

Desire sparked in him again. "Indeed. And very jolly, by the look of those worn out hobby horses. Raced them, I'd warrant."

A smile lit her face. "How many children—" Her gasp made him turn.

Hackwell, Thomas, and the caretaker were gone. He ducked into the corridor and heard them moving around upstairs.

Excitement thrummed in him. He was alone with a woman who he'd heartily kissed less than twenty-four hours ago. Alone in a bedchamber of sorts, talking about how many children might fill it.

Damned managing Hackwell. Paulette should not be in here alone with him.

She ducked her chin, looked everywhere but at him, and finally stepped to an open door leading off from the nursery. He followed her.

This was another bedchamber, for the nursery maids, probably, with a bed big enough to accommodate two.

Paulette sat down upon it. His heart beat a staccato.

She leapt up, paced to the window, peered through the wavy glass.

When she turned, she'd set her mouth and clasped her hands in front of her.

"Mr. Gibson, you do not wish to marry. You wish to go to India. Is that correct?"

Her voice shook, the trembling lighting up the air around him. He moved a step closer. "That was the plan, yes."

Was the plan. He could see that word *was* triggering some strong emotion in her.

"I know I've been adamant about going to London, which I still will do. I must see...well, not for social reasons. I know I'll never be part of the *ton*, but to be able to take care of my business, and perhaps visit a famous place or two, and shop..."

She gazed at a spot on the wall and cleared her throat. "I have a proposal, Mr. Gibson. It will serve us both and answer to Bakeley once and for all."

Chapter Twelve

She crossed the distance between them and lifted her chin. Only her hands, gripped tightly at her slim waist, and the tic of a muscle near one dark eye revealed her tension.

He bent closer and she placed a hand on his chest. "Wait." Color suffused her and she inhaled. "We can marry in Scotland."

The buzzing started up in his head again and the big bed past her shoulder beckoned him. She wanted to marry him, and to be quick about it.

He eased in a breath and tried to think around the swelling in his trousers. She knew he wanted to go to India, and she wanted to serve both their purposes and elope to Gretna Green. And what the devil purpose of hers would be served?

"In Scotland?" he asked stupidly.

She clenched that wee hand into a fist, as if he'd just challenged her. He wrapped it in both of his and lifted it to his lips, feeling a tremor ripple through her.

"Why Scotland, Paulette?"

She exhaled. "You do not categorically object to the idea then?"

His head swam with visions of the wild north. Object? Hell, Scotland was a good idea. With the settlements already in place, eloping offered expediency and privacy, no bother with two more rounds of banns or Doctors' Commons. "I'm warming up to it. But why Scotland?"

"Lady Tepping said if we marry in Scotland, we can divorce later—"

His chest squeezed. "Divorce." He dropped her hand.

"You…you want to…to *tup* me, but you don't want to marry, not truly. You want to go to India, Thomas said."

The summer light sparkled off dust motes and blinded him. "And you'll be settled here in this big, empty, decaying house."

Managing Little Norwick, bringing it into order, would keep Paulette occupied, and close to the Hackwells who'd be sure to look in on her. And maybe that had been Shaldon's plan. The old man had sensed her restlessness from afar.

And perhaps she didn't truly want to be alone. Perhaps his own restlessness would be curbed for a while by helping her manage. He reached for her hand again and kissed it. "It's not a bad plan." Except for the idea of divorce.

A smile lit her face. "We can split the income equally. You'll have your share."

"I imagine we'll need all of it until we can bring this place around." He spotted a shelf filled with games and slim books. "And then, of course, if there are children—"

"*Children*?"

He cupped his hands on the proud bones of her shoulders. "Do you think, after last night, I'd be content to remain in my own bed when we marry?" He stroked a line down her jaw. "I don't think you'd be content with that arrangement either."

She started up with more trembling and heating, her scent filling his senses. Heart thrumming, he drew her close and kissed her.

She wrested herself away and touched a hand to straighten her bonnet.

"I would not hold you from your dream. If there is a child, you may still go, and we will decide how much money is needed."

Blast the woman. Could she not see what she wanted? What they both wanted?

They might make a bloody mess of it, but now that she'd pushed it this far, he would have her, honorably.

"Do you suppose, Paulette, I would go off and leave a child of mine?"

Her frown slid into understanding, her brows furrowing.

"What would it have meant to have your father at least in the same country?" Releasing her, he stalked to the window, shoved aside a table and turned the latch, struggling with the sash.

It was stuck, and he pounded and pushed, unable to budge it.

He heard the swish of her skirts and with his next breath took in her scent again. "There is another lock here." She slid back a bolt he hadn't noticed. "Try now."

This time the window lifted. An insect whizzed past them, and the late afternoon breeze brought the smell of mown hay. In fact, someone was farming near here. He wondered how many tenants there were.

She slipped her hand into the crook of his elbow. "I have upset you. I'm sorry, but you must tell me. Will you marry me or not? Or will you only keep your promise and see me safely to London? Whether I am Miss Heardwyn or Mrs. Gibson, I still must go there and see what is what."

He slid an arm around her waist, trying to collect himself, like some silly lass.

"I know it is not done," she said, and her voice was tiny, "I know you are wanting to do your own proposing, to choose your own wife, someone more to your liking. I just—"

He kissed her fiercely then, for long minutes, to stop her, to reassure her she was to his liking.

Voices in the hall made him break off. He straightened her bonnet and smiled at her dazed look. "Yes, I will marry you," he said, panting. "Yes, we will go to Scotland, and then to London." He lifted her onto the table and held her gaze. "But there's to be no talk of divorce."

"All right."

"And the marriage will be consummated."

She nodded, and this time *she* kissed *him*.

The next morning at dawn, Hackwell met up with him in the front hall.

"Take this." He slipped a purse to Bink, and when Bink tried to give it back, he held up his hands. "Take it. You may have need of it, and either way, you may consider it a wedding gift." He clapped a hand on Bink's shoulder. "Remember, avoid the roads around Manchester."

Fears of an uprising had been the topic at every aristocratic table, and Hackwell's frown reflected his own worry. If the government was called back, he would want to be there, and if he went, Lady Hackwell would insist on accompanying him with all of the children, which would probably be safer than staying in a great country house alone.

And of course, there was the matter of Agruen's valet, still sequestered in a shed.

He gripped Hackwell's hand. "Thank you. Call on Little Norwick's caretaker if you need help. Otherwise, the staff will hold the household together. Grey can help with correspondence. We'll be back, five days at the most." And then they needed to leave for London, but how was he to explain that to Hackwell?

He would fix that battle plan later.

Hackwell led him out and stopped on the front step. A sly grin creased his face. "Don't cut short your wedding night, man."

The Hackwell coach waited, the horses restless in their traces. Johnny stood holding two mounts, and Ewan was tying a case to the coach roof, chatting with Kincaid, seated next to the coachman.

"Some honeymoon, with this lot along." In addition to Paulette's maid, Mabel, and Shaldon's three men, Paulette had insisted they bring Jenny.

Hackwell clapped him on the back. "Five more minutes alone in the Little Norwick nursery, and you'd have had the honeymoon done, and been on your way to filling one of those nursery cots."

Bink couldn't help smiling. Paulette's enthusiasm had matched his own, and they were fortunate the throat-clearing interruption had been Hackwell's. Once they'd returned to Greencastle, they'd endured a tense dinner with the assembled guests, including an unapologetic Agruen, before making known their plans to Hackwell and his lady, and then in the hustle of secret preparations, he'd not seen her again until the morning's hurried breakfast.

The coach door opened and the lady in question poked her head out. "Shall we leave soon?"

She was cross, tired, lacking sleep. He forced back a laugh and shook Hackwell's hand again. "I have my orders."

Hackwell waved to her. "He's coming right along."

He leaned in close and whispered. "Get used to it. And I'd heartily suggest you put the two maids on the roof for a bit and ride inside."

Bink laughed and went to mount his horse.

Mr. Gibson changed horses so often and so quickly they were almost flying along the Great Northern Road.

"I'm about jostled to death," Mabel muttered.

"It could be worse," Jenny whispered.

The poor girl peered out through two blackened eyes, and her voice had not yet had a chance to recover.

"We could be riding on Mr. Cummings's dog cart." Paulette rearranged herself on the cushioned seat for the hundredth time. "This carriage is actually rather well-sprung."

"Well, that would be Mr. Gibson's doing," Mabel said. "And the poor man, spending an entire day on horseback."

Paulette looked out the window. She'd thought—hoped—he might come inside for part of the journey. Nothing would happen, but she felt a need to see him, to know this was real.

"Thank you for taking me," Jenny said.

Mabel patted the girl's hand. "She'll replace our Mrs. Everly, won't she, Polly."

Mabel was trying to coax a smile. Jenny obliged, looking half-hearted.

"If she tries to replace Mrs. Everly, we're putting her to work in the dairy."

Mabel leaned forward. "Is there a dairy at Little Norwick?"

"I don't know. I suppose there could be."

"Fresh cream and good home-made cheeses. Imagine that, Jenny."

"Who is Mrs. Everly?" Jenny asked.

"Why, she was Miss Paulette's companion. When Paulette's mother died, Mrs. Everly took over teaching Paulette how to be a lady."

Neither woman had taught her anything about being a woman. Paulette had asked about what went on in a bridal chamber, but both her mama, and then later, Mrs. Everly had mumbled and stalled until they thought Paulette's curiosity had passed.

It hadn't passed. She'd consulted with Mabel, who'd offered no answers either, perhaps because she didn't know herself, though how could that be at her age?

The coach rattled on, and when Mabel began to snore, Paulette crossed to the rear-facing seat. "You are much younger than me, I think, Jenny."

"I'm sixteen, miss."

"I imagine...you might know more, in some ways, than I do. Having lived in London."

"Not much that is pleasant, miss."

Oh. She fumbled around in her mind for words. She did not wish to stir unpleasant memories.

"What is it you wish to know, miss?"

Mabel snorted loudly and went back to sleep.

Paulette lowered her voice. "The wedding night. No one will tell me exactly what goes on. Though I have an idea."

Jenny's gaze was solemn. Paulette clasped her hand. "I do not mean to stir bad memories. Forgive me."

"That man didn't enter me in the laundry, though it were close."

"Oh, thank God."

"It weren't God. It were Mr. Gibson." Jenny squeezed her hand hard. "With a kind man, it is pleasant, leastwise that's what the girls say."

Jenny shared the whispered details of her education, her early years crouched in the corner of a room warmed by many bodies, some of them engaged in carnal acts. "I did see his...his shaft, miss. It did seem very big, but they say it does fit, and some say they even do enjoy it if the man knows his way about a woman's body, and if they like him."

Heat blasted through her, remembering the kiss that had been more than just one kiss.

"And pardon me saying, but I think Mr. Gibson does care for you."

Her body thrummed with excitement, or need, or both.

Across from them, Mabel stirred and yawned. "I wonder if there is any of that loaf left. I'm ever so hungry."

Paulette felt the emptiness of her stomach, but no hunger, and she had barely touched food all day. They'd been traveling since dawn, sustained by the cold meats and cheeses packed by Greencastle's cook. She had no idea what the men had eaten. Even their few privy stops had been quick.

She wondered if Mr. Gibson was too excited to eat also.

A smattering of cottages passed in their side view.

"Where are we now, Polly?"

She pressed her nose to the window's wavy glass. The twilight was thickening. "I don't know. I hope we've reached Scotch Corner." Mr. Gibson had explained the route at breakfast. At Scotch Corner, they would turn off the Great Northern

Road and use the summer route, from Barnard Castle, following the River Tees through Alston and Brampton and Carlisle. They were all just names on a map to her, except for their destination, Gretna Green.

If they made good time, he'd promised to stop for a meal at Scotch Corner before they pushed on, like they were in one of Wellington's campaigns, running toward battle.

Her stomach was so rattled, she wouldn't be able to eat, but at least she would see him and talk to him.

The thought sent a shiver through her.

Minutes later, they'd stopped in front of an inn. The coach swayed as the men on top climbed down, but the usual quick bustle of horses being changed was absent.

"Praise be to God," Mabel exclaimed. "We're stopping for dinner."

Moments later, Johnny reached a hand to help Paulette down. She looked around, unable to spot Mr. Gibson. While Mr. Kincaid spoke with an ostler, Ewan unstrapped their travel bags and handed them down to an inn servant.

They were spending the night. Relief and the need to stretch out in a proper bed...

Her breath caught. Perhaps she wouldn't be all alone in her bed. Perhaps Mr. Gibson would want to be with her tonight. The thought sent all of her nerves dancing and heat rushing through her center.

And worry crept in. A stopover hadn't been part of the plan. What if he'd changed his mind?

"Where—" She bit back the question—*Where is Mr. Gibson?* She was always looking for him, always a step behind. She needed to let him ask after her.

Anyway, she didn't need to ask where he'd expect her to be. This inn surely had a private dining room. She lifted her chin and marched across the yard.

The meal was a good one, and Bink plowed through it. After a full day on horseback with sparse food he was glad to have one appetite satisfied.

"Fetch two brandies," he told the serving wench. "Will you not eat, love?" he asked Paulette. She hadn't touched a bite.

She turned a scowl on the maid's back and when the door closed, scooted her chair closer.

His pulse thrummed. If he crooked one of his fingers could he move her into his lap? In another twenty-four hours, she'd be his to do as he pleased with, and by God, he wanted her right now.

Her hand touched the back of his collar, a tremble traveling from the point of contact up her arm and all the way down to his cock. Either she'd had more experience in that tiny village than anyone knew, or she was one of those women with a natural sensuality.

Didn't matter. He was taking her, and the sooner the better. The thought tightened his trousers and made him ache.

She stood and leaned over the table to reach the flagon, her breasts straining against her gown. His to bed.

And his to protect, and from what—besides the usual louts—he still hadn't been able to discover. He'd questioned Kincaid, to no avail.

He tugged at his neck cloth. He should have stayed at Greencastle and posted banns, and to hell with Scottish divorces. He'd meant what he said about that marriage loophole. What was his,

would be his. His own lust to take her honorably—
and quickly—had made him agree to this hair-
brained scheme.

On the road, they'd passed groups of men from
the north, traveling afoot to join the worker's rally
scheduled to take place in Manchester.

In his best burr, with his pistol tucked into his
belt, he'd defused the tension, and tension there
was aplenty. The loss of a livelihood and hunger
drove men and women to do fearsome things.
Hadn't the French demonstrated that?

The next day's route should be less traveled,
but if a fight came their way, either through
travellers or Paulette's mysterious threat, he
needed a rest, as did the other men.

Paulette spoke, but he barely heard her words.

"What did you say, love?"

She frowned at her plate, her fork making
circles in the untouched peas. From the line of her
jaw, she was brewing a head of steam.

The serving wench reappeared with a bottle
and two glasses, and Paulette's frown turned into
a glare.

What the devil was wrong now?

Drat the lass, and damn him for a fool. It would
have been easier to keep her safe at Greencastle.

Except, Agruen was there. And Bink hadn't
kept the place safe for wee Jenny.

He swiped a hand through his hair. He should
have ignored Paulette's pleas and ferried her
directly from her cottage back to Cransdall where
the spymaster's army of loyal lackeys could keep
her safe until the wedding. Except, if they hadn't
seen Little Norwick, there'd have been no
wedding.

The thought brought him back to his senses.
She was marrying him for the property, not for

some great passion. Best to keep that in mind, take his pleasure, and make the best of it.

While the girl cleared the table, he passed a glass to Paulette and they drank in a less than companionable silence.

Devil take it. His sore arse and his aching body begged for sleep, while his nerves wound up tight, the way they had before battle, and his shaft...his shaft was a damned distraction.

He escorted her up the stairs. Outside her door, he handed her the candle, took her free hand and saw the storm brewing in her eyes. "Tomorrow is another hard day. We both need to rest."

She lifted her chin and he saw that her lips trembled and his heart started up a brisk tattoo to match.

"If I kiss you, I'm not sure I'll have the strength to stop. And if I don't, I'm not sure I'll have the strength tomorrow to keep going."

"Good night then." She opened the door, and slipped in.

The snick of the door brought him up. Too quick that had been. He shook his head. *Ah, Bink, you dog, you'd hoped to be seduced.*

Chapter Thirteen

Paulette set her light on the bedside table. Her travel bag rested on a bench, her writing case perched on top. Mabel had laid out her nightrail on the wide bed. She'd had a chance to freshen up before dinner and had seen that big bed, her body quickening with the possibility she might share it.

Mabel and Jenny's chamber was just down the hall. One of them would sleep on the narrow bed there, the other on the floor on a pallet.

Unless they switched rooms.

She paced to the window and looked out into the dark dale beyond. This room was quieter, and Jenny, after her brutal bruising, needed the quiet and the comfort of a bed, even a shared one.

She draped the nightclothes over her arm. Perhaps Mr. Gibson's chamber would have a wide bed, and he would be alone in it, wouldn't he?

Heat rose in her, her jaw tightening painfully. The buxom serving wench had cast him an eye, several eyes actually, and her bodice had dipped lower with every platter delivered.

Not that he'd noticed. He hadn't noticed Paulette tonight either, almost as though he was losing interest.

Like Papa had lost interest. He'd ignored her and Mama, as had her guardian, Lord Shaldon.

In those letters to Shaldon, she'd asked first to visit him. She could feel him out about the treasure, but there was more she wanted.

She wanted a purpose. She wanted a life.

When his man put her off, she'd dared to put the offer in writing—her services to the crown. If Mama could do it, so could she.

Instead, Shaldon had given her this husband. She couldn't let the man lose interest before the wedding night. He'd promised to take her to London, and the way he'd kissed her in the corridor outside her chamber...Warmth unfurled in her. Now that her path was set, she *would* see it through, at least through the wedding night.

A knock announced the flirting maidservant with a bucket of steaming water for her and a stack of bedding tucked under one arm. "Some hot water, miss. And I've got the pallet for your girl right here."

Paulette took the bucket and set it near the cold hearth. "We won't need the pallet. We are switching rooms."

The girl's mouth dropped. "This chamber's much nicer, miss. Ye'll have the noise of the courtyard there."

"Never you mind." She ushered the girl out and down the hall to Mabel and Jenny's chamber. "If anyone asks, I'll be in this bedchamber." In fact, it would place her further from the room where she planned to spend the night, but if anyone should suspect, the maid's testimony would preserve her reputation.

A safeguard if after bedding her, he should decide to change his mind about marriage.

While the house settled, Bink stripped off his coats and his neck cloth and sat down to write Hackwell a report on the roads. He would send it south with the morning mail.

The public rooms quietened, and here, on this dark side of the building, only the distant hoot of an owl and occasional snorting of horses in the back stalls of the stables filtered through the wide open window.

It had been a warm afternoon, and the breeze still had not swept the heat from these upper story rooms. He yanked his shirt over his head and went to the basin, splashing himself with the cool water.

Outside, a horse was being led to the stables, the shuffle of hooves muffled.

He froze, and strained to discern what had raised his hackles.

Whispers in the hall slithered over him and he threw aside his towel. Paulette was abed, and someone was creeping along the corridor, close to her door. As he reached for his pistol, his own door latch creaked.

The scent of flowers wafted in on a draft that sputtered the flame of his candle and eased his breathing.

"Mr. Gibson?"

The husky, whispered voice sent him to half-mast and his chest tightened with a different kind of wariness.

He set the pistol aside, grabbed for his shirt and groped his arms into it, catching them in the tangled sleeves.

A set of small hands worked the linen up his arms and down his body and pulled the hem into place, covering the evidence of his arousal—before she noticed it, he prayed.

He looked down into two dark, intense eyes, and then noted the robe with its slack belt, the fringing of lace at her creamy neck, and her hair flowing in waves past her shoulder. He fisted a hank of hair and tried to catch his breath.

You shouldn't be here. She had nothing on but a robe he could rip off her shoulders, and a nightrail he could lift in a wink. And he could be in her in seconds, pounding out this need like the madman he was right now.

He leaned and touched his forehead to hers. "Go back to your room, lass."

"I, I..." She cleared her throat. "I want...you..."

His pulse raged, his cock throbbed and he couldn't form words.

She exhaled a hint of a minty tooth powder. "I want you to... to talk to me." She took a step back but gripped fistfuls of linen. "If you would, please. May I stay with you tonight? It is only a few hours. And we'll be wed tomorrow."

He squeezed his eyes shut on the vision of her in his bed, under him, tried to think of something, anything else—horse droppings, foul privies, the stench of a tannery.

When he opened his eyes, she was frowning, and he saw it there—fear. The girl was frightened.

Shame trickled through him. She feared he couldn't protect her unless she was in his very bedchamber.

Her teeth slipped over her lower lip and began to gnaw, and it hit him—what a fool he was. It wasn't her physical safety that rattled her.

Not fear for her safety then, but what?

Shame turned to fierce warmth, setting his body afire. Pulse pounding, he slid a finger under her smooth chin and tipped it up. "Why?"

"Will we go to Scotland tomorrow? Will you go through with this wedding?"

"Have I given you reason to doubt me?"

She lifted an eyebrow. "You barely spoke to me all day."

His chest eased even as his trousers tightened more, all of his thoughts in a jumble. She wanted to be sure of him, she wanted his bed, and not just for money, not for security and safety. This was the price of a warm woman as bedmate—talking, and lots of it.

But as her gaze and those hands slid over his chest, his dick reminded him there was a way to silence her.

No. If they opened this particular tinderbox, the fire would rage until dawn, and she would not be able to sit for a week. They'd never make Gretna the next day.

"I have a plan," he said.

She lifted that determined chin and his finger followed it up. "So do I."

He held back a chuckle. "You plan to seduce me tonight. To make sure of me."

That flustered her and left her gulping for air.

He drew her closer and stroked a length of soft hair. "It is a good plan. One I'd like to partake of, believe me."

"But?"

"But I'm not sure you'd be able to ride all day in a coach tomorrow after I've ridden you all night." *And it would be all night.*

Her eyes went wide. "Does it hurt that much?"

Ah, she was definitely a virgin. He felt an odd sense of relief, glad to be her first, and terrified. Like breeding a cart horse on a pony, he didn't know how he'd not hurt her, but he must find a way.

"I don't know in fact. But I'll make sure whatever pain you feel is secondary to the pleasure."

She sighed and settled against him, and he realized his hand had started to move over her back.

"You will kiss me again?"

The heat of her sigh seared through his shirt, branding his heart.

"Aye."

"On the lips?"

Desire rippled through him. "Oh, yes."

She quivered. "And the neck?"

He planted a kiss there and smiled when she jumped. "Definitely the neck then."

She looked up, eyes wide, mouth parted. Ready to be ravished.

His pulse pounded in his ear. He had only a few minutes of control left.

She pressed her palm to his chest and swirled it. "Will you take off your shirt when you make love to me?"

"Would you like me to?"

She nodded. "I saw your chest when I entered. You're hairy."

He threw back his head and laughed. "Yes then, I'll show you my hairy chest."

"Then I'll show you my not-hairy one."

A vision of those breasts swamped him and he groaned. She tightened her embrace.

"We must get you to bed." Not that he would be able to sleep with her naked breasts bouncing around in his dreams.

She frowned and opened her mouth, but a rap on the door made him release her. He stepped in front of Paulette and asked "Who's there?"

The door opened. The wench who'd served them stood there, a candle held high, and the neckline of her frock dipping low to the pink tips of her tits. She cocked her head and smiled.

"What—"

"You might want some company, I heard."

"Devil take it. You heard wrong. Get out."

Paulette stepped from behind him and the wench's eyes narrowed.

"You invited her to your chamber?"

The crack in Paulette's voice sparked panic in him. Not wed yet, and she already doubted him.

The inn servant smiled. "Well, I misunderstood."

"Did she?" Fire burned in Paulette's eyes, and an answering heat rose in him.

The maid started to pull the door closed.

"Wait," Bink grabbed the door. "Who sent you here?"

She lifted a shoulder. Her eyes slid to Paulette and widened. "The man. He asked for the lady's chamber and said I should come to you."

He pushed her aside and rushed out. An oil lamp cast a hazy sheen on the empty corridor. Everyone was abed. Even the taproom was quiet.

At Paulette's door, he felt a hand grip his arm.

Paulette shook her head. "I switched with Mabel and Jenny," she whispered.

He eased open the door anyway. The room was dark and quiet, but he made out the forms of both maids, and heard a faint snore.

"This way." Paulette took his hand. They crossed the corridor and went down to a door at the end.

It was ajar, and light twinkled within.

Alarm rattled through him, and his hand went to his waist.

Hell and damnation, he'd left the bloody pistol in his room. He reached down and pulled the knife from his boot, silently cursing.

"Ask who is there," he breathed into her ear.

She nodded. "Mabel, is that you?"

"Yes, miss." The whispered voice could have been the rasp of a sleepy woman, but Paulette shook her head.

Bink slammed the door open hitting the wall with a *bang*. The dark figure within froze and for one startled moment so did Bink.

Agruen's valet, Spellen, stood framed in the candlelight, dressed all in black and clutching a handful of Paulette's clothing.

Chapter Fourteen

Spellen's gaze spun to the door where the inn maid crowded up next to Paulette.

"You bitch," he growled.

Bink lunged, swinging his knife, slicing a gash in the man's coat, as Spellen lurched backward, blocking another swipe, and spinning away with a kick that knocked the knife from Bink's hand.

The man reached under his coat, and Bink dove, knocking a pistol away. The gun hit the thin rug and clattered across bare floorboards but didn't go off.

Spellen parried another lunge, and Bink ducked an answering blow. From the corner of his eye he saw Paulette inching around, close to where the pistol had fallen. Spellen saw her too.

Bink roared and grabbed for the man, who dodged backward and vaulted the bed, launching a pitcher, making Bink duck again. Footsteps pounded in the corridor behind him and when he looked, Spellen had frozen in front of the window.

"I have him, Gibson," Paulette croaked.

He didn't dare turn around.

"The way she's shaking, she's as likely to shoot you," Spellen said. "Put down the gun now, there's a good girl."

He could hear the rasping of Paulette's breath.

Bink steadied his breath. "Keep your aim straight, Paulette. Why aren't you locked up, Spellen?"

"I was released. Did nothing wrong. The girl wanted it."

"Liar," Paulette cried. "Why are you here?"

He leered at the point beyond Bink's shoulder where Paulette was standing. "*She* invited me."

"I most certainly did not." Paulette pushed up next to Bink. He reached for her hands wrapped around the gun and steadied them.

"Stay back, love. I'll take this."

"No." She tugged the pistol. "Spellen, put your hands up and get down on your knees."

The jackal's smile was a dare.

Could she shoot him? He doubted it—the way her hands shook it would be pure accidental. And if he made a move for the man, she might shoot the both of them.

Taking a man's life was a burden, a soldier's burden. His burden. He wouldn't let her be saddled with that.

He glanced at her strained face and took her gun hand in both of his.

In the moment he turned away, Spellen lurched toward the open window.

The gun clattered again. Bink grabbed for Spellen and planted a blow. Spellen punched back, landing a fist on his jaw, sending Bink reeling. The villain plunged for the door again, but Bink caught him and swung him back. Spellen kicked, dodged back, and dived out of the window. Bink grabbed his legs, but another kick to the jaw stunned him, and before he could grab him again, the man toppled out.

Rubbing his jaw, he hoisted himself and looked out. Spellen lay in the shadows below, while a stable hand hurried into the yard.

"Thief," Bink shouted, "Get him."

Spellen raised his crumpled self and took off in a limping trot. Another figure shot out of the barn and gave chase into the darkness.

Paulette appeared next to him, Mabel behind her, and Johnny behind him.

"You," he told Johnny. "Stay here."

He gripped Paulette's shoulders. "Are you all right?"

"Yes," she said shakily.

He pulled her close. "I'm going after him. Stay here. Say nothing." He squeezed her, picked up the blade and the pistol, and was off.

The hastily dressed innkeeper met him at the foot of the stairs, a cudgel in hand.

"Where is he?" he asked.

"Took off. There's a man giving chase." Bink stopped him. "Your maid was in on it. Find her."

Ewan met him in the yard, lantern in hand, and they traced the broken path down the dale, moving with as much speed as possible.

"Over here."

Kincaid stood, staring down a steep incline at a dark shadow stretched at the bottom. It could have been anything—a stag, a wild boar, a stout log.

"Give me that light." Bink took the lantern and side-stepped down.

Kincaid followed.

At the bottom, Bink toed the body. The head lay askew, like a man craning his neck to look down the bosom of a woman behind him.

"Broken neck." In the darkness, Kincaid's eyes glowed blackly.

A chill rippled Bink's hair. Black eyes, dark hair and a fathomless manner, that was Kincaid. Not an enemy, though, his gut told him, not to him, and not to Paulette. And Bakeley hadn't ordered

Kincaid along to be rid of him. Bakeley hadn't sent him at all. The old Earl had ordered it before his death. Kincaid was another protector for Paulette.

What the devil was Paulette mixed up in?

He should have protected her. He hadn't protected her. "That fall would kill a man," he said. "Would that I'd snapped his neck back in the inn room."

Kincaid grunted. "Was the lass in the room?"

"Yes."

"It's as well she doesn't see this." Kincaid bent and flipped back the man's coat. "And I see here that you slowed him down a bit."

Blood soaked the side of the dead man's shirt. He'd cut him after all.

While Kincaid ruffled through the man's pockets, Bink pumped his fists, getting the feeling back. Yes, it was good Paulette hadn't seen this.

He found his voice and called Ewan down, and when he reached the gully, the boy's eyes were like saucers.

"It's all right, lad," Bink said. "He's only dead. Go back. Tell the innkeeper. And—we don't know who this man is, Ewan, understand?" It was possible Ewan had been one of Spellen's guards and recognized the man. "We'll need to be on our way very soon."

Ewan nodded.

"He came in on a big roan," Kincaid said. "See if anyone knows where he hired it."

The boy left and Kincaid went back to the dead man's pockets.

"We should have Ewan check his kit."

"Already done." Kincaid patted the legs. "Didn't see him up close when he rode in, but I had a bad feeling." He stood and brushed his hands together. "Nothing here but a few coins."

"And in the kit?"

"Nothing unusual."

Bink rubbed a hand down his jaw. "How long for the coroner?"

"In these parts? We can be to Gretna and back by then. The girl will be safer once she's yours."

Bink laughed, ruefully. "Mrs. Gibson?"

"Aye. And she'll be an Everly, also."

He held the light higher. "And who are you, Kincaid?"

"A friend. To the old lord, and to Paulette. And to you. I'd suggest we leave statements for the coroner to review. They can call us for the inquest if need be. But I think they'll rule this an accidental death of a thief."

"What do you know of Agruen?"

"Not much." Rocks clattered above them as lights approached. Kincaid lowered his voice. "But I know something of Josiah Dickson." He lifted his chin and shouted, "We're down here."

Huddled with Mabel and Jenny, there'd been no sleep the night before, and as a consequence, Paulette had finally succumbed in the coach to a fitful, dream-filled, swaying slumber, one that, she later discovered, had lasted through three changes of teams.

When she awoke, her head was on Mr. Gibson's shoulder and her maids were nowhere around, and the carriage was still moving.

Mr. Gibson awoke almost immediately and checked his surroundings. His arm around Paulette—which she hadn't noticed until now—tightened and he pulled her into a kiss that quickly became heated. Her hat fell away and he tossed it to the floor on top of her lap desk.

When his hand moved to her breast, a sharp stab of pleasure made her gasp.

He released her and studied her face. "I did not mean to hurt you."

She rubbed her palm along his bristly jaw. "It was pleasure, not pain. Do you always awake so enthusiastically?"

He smiled, and then laughed. "No. But I hope to every morning from here out."

"Why are you here?"

He huffed out another laugh. "Kincaid and Johnny insisted. And I fell asleep in the saddle."

"No."

"Yes."

A worry niggled at her. Mr. Kincaid was a question mark. She'd not spoken more than one word with him.

"Do not worry. It's open country, and if anyone is pursuing us, he'll be spotted in time for Ewan to wake me. Though here I am, already awake."

She frowned and he tweaked her nose.

"You mustn't worry."

"I'm thinking. About last night, if I hadn't gone to your room—"

"No, Paulette." His arms engulfed her.

"But you thought the same thing. Is that why we left before dawn? You were worried about Agruen?"

"That's part of it. Spellen was Agruen's man, and we don't yet know why he wasn't still locked up. I sent an express to Hackwell."

After Bink returned with news of Spellen's death, she'd shared Jenny and Mabel's room, Johnny guarding their door, and thought about Agruen's words to her in the library at Greencastle. Spellen was searching the bags, which meant the rings weren't enough. He needed something else to solve the puzzle. "What was the other part?"

"We wanted to leave before the coroner could arrive to detain us. We left our statements."

"What did you say?"

He squeezed her hand and sighed. "You should probably know. I said I met you in the corridor leaving your maids' room and escorted you to your chamber, where you found the intruder. That we fought and he jumped out the window. That I saw him running away."

"And then he fell and broke his neck."

He looked down at their hands locked together and finally lifted his eyes to hers. "I did not kill him, Paulette."

She let out a tense breath. "Jenny won't say much, but I know she's terrified. She thinks he went looking for her."

"Because it was her room."

"Yes." A chill went through her.

"And what do you think?"

"I...I told the innkeeper's girl," she frowned. "I told her, if anyone asked for me, to tell them I'd changed rooms."

Mr. Gibson's jaw hardened and moved and she went on.

"Where did she go? Was she working with him?"

"He paid her I think, to keep me out of the way. Which wouldn't have worked, Paulette. I've no interest in any woman but you."

A warm ripple uncurled in her and all she could manage was a strangled "Oh."

Could that be so?

By Mrs. Everly's laws, men were creatures who'd take any woman who came along, and such doings at inns were a common occurrence.

Could Mrs. Everly have been wrong? She'd been wrong about other things. Paulette shook off the thought until later.

"He was searching, wasn't he? He'd upended their bag. What could he be looking for? Agruen already has my mother's ring."

"That wasn't your clothing, then?"

She shook her head, and his fingers smoothed hair away from her eyes, his touch gentle and warm. It was close in the carriage, the windows shut tight and the shades drawn, and she felt beads of moisture coating her face.

"Perhaps he was looking for the letter of your mother's you found."

She turned away in her seat. The man noticed everything. The man forgot nothing. It had been a mistake to mention the letter. And yet...

"I doubt it." She lifted the lap desk from the floor, undid the clasp and reached under the playing cards and the few sheets of paper. "Here. You may read it yourself."

"I will. But later. Put it away."

"Will you hold the letter for me? Will you keep it safe?"

"Yes. Certainly." He stowed the paper into an inside pocket and kissed her again, this time more gently. "Is there aught else I should know about this puzzle Agruen mentioned?"

His eyes held hers, searching, and a sick feeling slid through her. They were marrying and he should know.

Except, her mother had scoffed at Jock's talk of a treasure. It might not be real. She wouldn't know until she knew.

"It must have something to do with whatever the solicitor is holding."

His mouth firmed and he glanced away. Satisfied with the answer or not, she couldn't tell.

The coach slowed and a knock on the roof warned them. Mr. Gibson opened the shades, while Paulette retrieved her bonnet. They were entering a hamlet.

"We're almost to Brampton."

"We've made good time."

"Yes." His face was grim. He was a man fit for action, wanting to be outside, looking for danger. "And I intend to do even better. Try to rest, love." He chucked her chin, his eyes glowing. "You will have no rest tonight."

Her heart clanged wildly as the coach stopped. Mr. Gibson was out of the door before she could form the words to respond.

First they would marry, then they would settle into an inn.

Paulette smoothed her skirt. The desire for speed and efficiency, she could understand, yet it seemed a backward way of doing things. For one, she would like to rearrange her disheveled hair and straighten the wrinkles from this traveling gown. Or change into her spare one.

She had, however, agreed early on to the plan, before she understood what thirty hours in a coach would do to one's appearance. She hoped there would be a bath before the wedding night.

Her fingers curled as a ribbon of anticipation unfurled in her. After his rest, Mr. Gibson had returned to his vigilance, spurring on everyone— ostlers, post boys, grooms—to hasten. Privy stops were hurried, refreshments rapid.

He could not control the roads though, which, having succumbed to recent rains, slowed them in places to a precarious walk. Thus, when they entered the village of Gretna Green, the summer sun was low on the western horizon.

Nerves buzzing, she removed her bonnet. "My hair is a fright, isn't it?"

"You look lovely, miss," Jenny said.

Mabel crossed and sat next to her. "Turn then and let me re-pin it."

The blacksmith's shop and a grand inn came into view, but they passed by without even slowing.

"Where is he taking us?"

"Be still, Polly. Mr. Kincaid knows just the place, Johnny said."

Mr. Kincaid again. He had been the one to chase Spellen down the hill. Yet he hadn't himself fallen.

He'd been Lord Shaldon's servant until the very end, fit and able. And he'd not been valeting Mr. Gibson, that was a fact.

Drat, she should have been asking questions instead of kissing.

"There." Mabel pinched Paulette's cheeks. "You will do very well as a bride."

The coach turned down a quiet lane and stopped in a graveled courtyard. This must be an inn, a smaller one, set back from the heart of the town.

They sat for interminable minutes, and finally, Paulette opened a window and shivered. They were far to the north, and though the sun was still high, a chill breeze was coming all the way from the Irish Sea.

Mr. Kincaid appeared at the door, his face swathed in its usual gravity. He extended his hand. "Miss, Mr. Gibson is inside making arrangements. If you please, I will escort you."

She climbed out of the carriage, and he draped her in a long piece of woolen plaid.

"A tartan," she cried.

"The wind off the firth brings a chill," he said.

She studied the moss green cloth with its intersecting black and red lines.

"'Tis the Kincaid plaid. You would honor me by wearing this."

The gentle tone compelled scrutiny. Kincaid was brown-haired and brown-eyed, and almost everything else about him was middling—his height only a bit above average compared to Mr. Gibson, his physique sturdy, his age somewhere about forty. He could pass through a crowd and never be noticed, as she'd not really taken time to notice him. Yet now, he seemed almost *familiar*.

A hint of humor touched the corner of his mouth and he offered his arm. "May I have the honor?"

She drew the plaid tighter around her. An unaccountable emotion gripped her throat and she couldn't find words. Ducking her head, she took his arm.

"He's a good man, Gibson is." He whispered close to her ear. "He will protect you."

Paulette nodded again, and then his words registered. "From what?"

The pause told her he had misspoken. She did not think this man did that often. He hesitated, like he was choosing his words carefully.

"You must ask him to explain."

Anger tightened his voice, directed at whom, she did not know. Mr. Gibson perhaps. Not at herself, certainly, because as they entered the inn, Mr. Kincaid turned to her with a kind look.

One lone maid—this one older, respectably dressed—worked the bar in the taproom. Two men put down their tankards and stood when they saw her, and started in their direction. Kincaid nodded to them.

"Do you know them?" she whispered.

"Aye. Good men, they are. We are dead on our feet. They will be keeping watch for a bit."

Watch for what? And then she remembered: Agruen. Perhaps he had another evil servant to send after her.

There was no time to ask questions, as Kincaid led her through a door into a private eating room. Her eyes fixed on Mr. Gibson. Color rose under the stubble of his cheeks, and his lips curved up.

His beard had roughened over the course of the day, and she itched to strip off her gloves and *feel* him, and that thought made her face as warm as his must be.

Chapter Fifteen

A barrel of a man with his sleeves rolled up—the innkeeper surely—was smiling at her. "Ach. Here is the lass," he said.

She heard rustling and saw Mabel and Jenny and Johnny crowd in behind her.

"Who gives this woman?" the innkeeper asked.

"I do."

The words had come from Kincaid. She had no time to be startled though, because he was handing her off to Mr. Gibson, and the look in her groom's eyes all but melted her.

The rest was a whirlwind of breathless promises, hearty good wishes, and brimming toasts that included their servants and those of the inn. But no other inn guests, as there seemed to *be* none.

She had no time to ask questions though. This time it was Mabel and Jenny who whisked her away to a chamber where a huge bed held center stage and a hot bath had been drawn.

Mabel took the tartan cloth from her, and Jenny started on her lacings.

"Do stop a-trembling, Polly." Mabel folded the cloth. "'Tisn't cold in this chamber. A body would think you were nervous." She laughed and traced a finger on the intersecting colors. "This plaid is lovely."

"Mr. Kincaid's gift. His family tartan."

"Is it then? It's very Scots, don't you think?"

"It is." She pulled the bodice down and stepped out of the gown. "Help me out of these stays. I so need a bath. Where is your chamber? You must have them bring you hot water—"

"Never you mind, miss." Jenny unrolled Paulette's stockings. "Now off with the chemise and into the water. I'll take your things to be brushed and Mabel will do the rest."

"Go with her, Mabel."

"I'm not scared, miss. Mr. Kincaid promised we'll all be safe here."

The door closed on her and Paulette sank into the water, letting it ease her trembles.

Mabel unpinned her hair, pulled it over the side, and began to brush it. "Rest a minute while I untangle this."

Paulette closed her eyes, but no restfulness came. "Hurry."

"We'll wash you up thoroughly, including your hair."

"It will be wet when—"

"It smells a bit, Polly. I've brought the rosewater. And we'll add a log to the fire in the grate if need be."

There was indeed a low fire burning. No wonder the room felt so cozy.

When she'd been thoroughly washed, Mabel held up a lacy white gown. "Lady Hackwell sent this nightrail along. Said she's never worn it."

Paulette fingered the sheer silky fabric. "It's very dear."

Mabel grinned, her face reddening. "She said his lordship orders them by the dozen."

Oh. Her face must be flaming also. She slipped the nightrail over her head and swept a hand over the lace. It was scandalous.

"Here is the robe." Mabel helped her into the matching white silk and unwrapped her hair. "Now, over to the fire to dry off. Jenny and I will bring up the dinner, and then we'll send *himself* up."

She nodded and let herself be led to a chair.

"Polly."

Mabel's eyes glistened with tears, and her own eyes began to water.

"No, no, you must not," Mabel cried. "Doan't mind me, girl. I wanted to say, I've watched over you since you were tiny, like you were my own little girl, and I've worried whether you'd find a man good enough for you. And I think you have. And I think your mother will be pleased, looking down from heaven, and even Jock if he managed to talk his way past St. Peter, and I don't know about your father because I only met him the once." She sniffed loudly. "There now. I've no need to wish you happiness. I know you'll have found it. Dry your hair now."

At Mabel's signal, Bink downed his last shot of whisky, accepted the back-slapping good wishes of the men, and found his way to the stairs. A warm whisky buzz filled his head and helped keep him at half-staff.

Kincaid would send Johnny and Ewan off to bed and would retire in a bit, he'd promised. His absolute confidence in the inn and the men he'd hired reassured Bink. His knowledge of the district was one of the reasons they'd chosen Gretna over Coldstream.

When he rapped on the door, quick footfalls sounded and the latch turned.

Warm, rose-scented air greeted him, but no woman.

She was hiding behind the door, poor lass. Probably nervous, wearing what, he could not imagine and didn't care since he intended to take it off her, the quicker the better.

His shaft swelled and he forced in a breath. *Slow your bloody self down, Gibson.*

"I hear there is food here." When he crossed the threshold, she stepped up.

And he froze.

A white dressing gown rippled from her shoulders to the floor, sheer silk covering lace that outlined the mounds of her breasts. Under the thin fabric he could see shadowy nipples already taut.

Eating could wait. With tightly coiled muscles, he eased the door shut and turned the key in the lock, his eyes filled with her.

She folded her arms over her breasts, then stretched them out again, curling and uncurling her fingers. His hands prickled and itched, needing to touch her.

Tension rippled from her, reminding him the girl had a case of the virgin nerves.

She scooped two hunks of hair and flipped them over her breasts, sending waves of heady perfume his way. He followed the two lines of dark silk down her shoulders to where the coiled ends reached her tiny cinched waist, and further, over curved hips, down to the bare toes peeking out from the puddled silk of her robe.

Desire swamped him. He wanted her, and he could have her. She was his, his to have and to hold, and forever. He could rip off the white lacy gown and devour every inch of her, right down to those tiny feet. He could hold her naked atop him, the veil of her hair draping them, tickling his chest.

He held out his hand, and when she gave him hers, the madness lifted and the famished need became more bearable.

"Are you hungry?" he asked.

She frowned and shook her head. "You may eat, but please kiss me first."

He fixed his eyes on hers to help maintain his control. "Are you sure you would not like to eat first?"

Her bottom lip trembled. "Now you are avoiding looking at the rest of me. Do I shock you?"

He lifted her hand, kissed it, and her face puckered again. "Oh, aye. You look shockingly beautiful."

"Ah," she breathed. "Well, if you first wish to eat—"

His kiss stopped her, chaste, and short. Holding only her hand, he took a step back.

Her lips trembled. "You're teasing."

"Am I, lass? Well, then..." He pulled the tie of her robe, undoing the bow. She inhaled sharply, sending her breasts higher, unwinding that wild need in him again. He pushed her hair aside, and traced a shaking finger down her neck, over the top of one creamy mound.

Her hand open and flew to his cheek landing softly. "Your jaw feels a bit swollen from Spellen's fist. And you haven't yet shaved."

And surely he stunk of sweat and horses. He *was* a selfish brute.

He lifted her hand from his face and kissed it. "Nor washed. I'd best go take care of that."

He tried to drop her hand, but she stepped up against him and enfolded him in her arms.

"No."

Bink felt her grip tighten and the madness rose again. God's bones, how he wanted her. He clamped his eyes shut and gripped fistfuls of silky damp hair.

"I'll have you just as you are." Her breathless murmur warmed his chest as it had done in the room at the inn.

He tilted her chin and kissed her again, working the robe from her shoulders, slanting his lips to plunge himself deeper. While her hands found his neck, he grabbed handfuls of sweet arse, squeezing like he'd wanted to do the day they'd first met.

With one hearty leap she was up in his arms, her skirts up, her legs wrapped around him.

Sweet Jesus, he could not be this blessed.

He kicked the pooled silk of the robe aside and staggered to the bed, settling there while she pushed off his coats, her breasts straining the thin lace of the gown.

She yanked at his shirt. "Lift your arms."

Bink laughed and complied, and her sigh almost undid him. "You have so many freckles." Her palms skimmed his chest, a look of wonder in her eyes. "And the hair here is soft. Not at all like your beard."

Let's see how soft is your chest.

He should shave. A bloody gentleman wouldn't burn his bride with his beard on their wedding night.

But he was no bloody gentleman. He was a bastard and a beast and a raging cock.

Hands shaking as he fought for control, he fumbled the gown's straps over her shoulders, tugging until it fell to her waist, her mouth dropping with it, hands flying up as shields.

He lifted them away and savored the view, his vision fogging and tunneling. The creamy smooth skin here was lighter. Never exposed. Uncharted territory no other man had explored.

She was his.

A surge of power, a desire to claim, roared through him. He bent his head and licked at her nipple, swirling his tongue on the rosy pink bead.

Her sharp inhale sent her closer, deeper. When he suckled, she bucked, her soft core rubbing against his shaft.

Bink froze and unlatched from the teat, trying to stay the urge to spill. Her answering tension he could do nothing about at the moment.

"Did I...did I do something wrong?" she whispered.

He held her close and tried to think of something—the account books, the autumn harvest, the repairs to the roof. Anything.

"Mr. Gibson." Her voice had gone timid.

His Paulette feared him, feared this. Shame slowed his lust, and he gripped her hunched shoulders. "You're a dream, Paulette. So beautiful, so right, I must slow a bit, or I'll rush like a ravening barbarian and you won't feel the pleasure I promised."

"Oh," she said on a long breath, unclenching her hands.

"And you may only call me Mr. Gibson when you're angry—no, *very* angry—with me."

She dragged a thumb over his hairy cheek.

She can't stop touching me. His cock twitched against the fall of his breeches, raging to get down to business.

"What shall I call you then?"

"What do you want to call me?"

"Your real name is Edward, Bakeley said."

"Bink is really my name also. It's my middle name, true, but the one everyone knows me by."

The corner of her mouth lifted and he so wanted to kiss it.

What she called him, he didn't care, as long as he could have her in his bed every blessed night, just this willing.

That was probably a dream all right. He'd be Mr. Gibson to her sooner or later. And he didn't give a damn, as long as he had her in his bed tonight.

"You don't look like an Edward. And, you're such a big man. Too big to be a Bink."

Let me show you just how big I am.

"I suppose I don't need to decide now. May we proceed? Have you rested enough?"

He ran a finger down her cheek, her neck, her chest, and circled each breast. "Now who is teasing?"

Her laugh sent a warm thrill through him.

"Let me take off my boots, love."

"Let me." Paulette clambered off of him and moved to pull up the top of her gown from where it rested on lush hips. From the top of her head to the crease of her hip and the soft swell of her belly, he could see everything.

"Leave it," he said. "Please."

She colored deeply, but complied, breasts bouncing as she struggled to pull off his boots and unroll his stockings.

When she'd finished she studied the lump in his breeches, her parted lips sending sparks flaming through him, making the lump frantic.

"Shall we take off your trousers?" she asked.

Or your gown first? He took her hand and drew her next to him on the bed. "Do you know what to expect?"

"You are... engorged?"

"Because of you. Because of my desire for you."

"I hear a man can become that way with any woman."

He held his breath and fought down the memories. Battle lust had turned men into beasts at Badajoz. Not him. He had a man's body and a man's needs, and a man's ability to stand down when it wasn't right.

Was this right?

A cool hand touched his cheek.

"I'll be true to you, Paulette."

He stood and stripped off his breeches and his smalls. Her look of shock made his shaft throb against him.

Bink knelt before her. "Don't be afraid."

"I'm not."

The sweet pink of her cheeks had drained.

His bride feared him, and why shouldn't she?

She inhaled deeply, sending her breasts higher. Bink leaned in and kissed a breast, his hands working the hem of her nightrail up, up each shapely leg, over her knees with gentle squeezes.

When he looked up, her color had returned, her eyes gleamed, wide and dark.

He set his lips to her leg, kissing his way higher.

"Wha-at are you doing?"

"Shhh." He pushed the silk up and saw the first dark coils. His fingers slid under the gown and swirled.

"Oh." She sucked in tight breaths. "B-bink."

Bink or Edward, he'd answer to either if only he could have her like this, every night.

"Will you lay back, my love?"

She made it as far as her elbows and lay watching, her interest sending ripples of pleasure through him. He dipped his head and inhaled.

Even here, her scent was cloaked with the fragrance of roses.

Kissing his way up each inner thigh, he stopped just before reaching her sweet-scented muff, found the soft button at her center and blew on it, watching her wriggle.

"Shall I kiss you right here?"

Real distress played on her face.

"Will you let me, love?" He set his lips close and exhaled.

"Yes." She wrestled herself higher. "Yes. If you must."

Bink chuckled. Oh yes, he must.

He slid a hand under her hips and lifted her. She was already wet with the flavor of woman, and he made her more so.

He put a finger inside her. *Gently*.

God, she was so tight. Her hips bucked, she writhed, and finally fell back, gripping fistfuls of counterpane and moaning.

He took a long breath and went back to her, inching a hand up to her breasts, swirling his fingers over her nipples.

Aye, please hurry, Paulette.

The moans increased. Her fingers swept through his hair, clenched his scalp, pressed him to her in a writhing, mad, instinctive dance of need.

And then came a soft keening.

Yes.

She choked, held his head close, and cried out, pulsing against him.

He was up in a flash, done with the selflessness, stretching her limp body on the bed, parting her legs and raising himself over her.

"W-wait." She wiggled the nightrail higher, whipped it over her head and lay back, spreading her whole bounty, every shadowed curve, every smooth mound, every enticing curl, every wriggling, needing, wanton bit of woman.

Desire lit through him like the spark on a bomb fuse.

He fought for breath, for control. *You're a savage, Bink. You're a mad dog not fit for decent society.*

He *could* be gentle, *must* be gentle. She was so tight.

She bent her knees and braced her feet, and reached for him.

Now, his cock demanded.

He poised himself at her entrance.

"Please," she said.

He eased himself in. It was so tight, so tight. Bink closed his eyes, paused and went deeper.

His shaft hit her maidenhead and he halted.

She planted her small feet on his arse and squeezed, and the shock sent him plunging, burying himself deep in her softness.

Beneath him, she'd gone still as death, and when he looked, her face had wrinkled into a fierce grimace.

Remorse swirled around the frantic need to explode, the confusing, disturbing guilt of a necessary hurt.

"I'm so sorry, love." He kissed her hair. "So sorry. So sorry. It won't pain you again."

She turned her face to his and took his mouth, wrapping her arms around his neck. "Kiss me," she murmured.

He did, pouring all of the passion that should be happening below into the kiss, waiting for what he knew not.

And finally, her legs unwound from him, her hips rolled. He braced on his elbows, and lifted her to him, and one, two, three thrusts, and he exploded, all the pleasure of this sweet universe of Paulette throbbing through him.

Paulette clung to him as he rolled to his back and she found herself straddling him. She rested her head on his chest and heard his great heart pounding.

Pleasure still hummed in her, leaving her lightheaded and still throbbing below where the pain of his splitting her had soon enough passed. She felt itchy and needy for more.

And he was still, somehow, inside her, though not as he had been.

She pressed the tips of her fingers against his arm, where warm skin covered muscles like hardened oak. His shaft must be like that. "It will not hurt again, they say."

His hand stroked her back. "No. Not if we take time to prepare you."

She lifted her head and framed his face with her hands, raking the nails of her thumbs through the bristles. "I like the way this feels."

His eyes gleamed golden in the candlelight. "So do I."

"Is that how it is done? Preparing a woman?"

His eyes went to slits and his lips curved up. She felt a movement inside her and wondered if she should get off him.

"It's one way."

"What are the others?"

"There's the kissing. You like that."

"Yes."

"It gets your juices flowing."

Juices? She sat up and his eyes jerked wide, his mouth dropped.

And he moved again inside her. He was *growing* again.

He pulled another pillow under his head and began touching her breasts. Pleasure unfurled in her anew, pleasure and a feeling of power. He liked her breasts.

She leaned closer to hold him.

"No." He nudged her back, stroking her skin. "I want to look. I want to watch."

Hot warmth coursed through her.

"Don't be bashful. Never with me." He lifted his head and put his lips to her breast and the pleasure shot straight to her loins.

Instinct made her hips move. Somehow he had filled her again, and she ached, *ached* to feel that explosion of bliss once more. Desire built in her, flooded her, and she sensed she could feel *it* again even without his wicked mouth on her.

He lifted her, dropped her, showing her what he wanted. She wanted it too. She rode him, watched him while he watched her, until the ache overtook her, the pressure unbearable, and ecstasy, waves of it, exploded within her, and he clamped her tight and moaned out his own release, pulsing within her in rumbling vibrations.

She collapsed on his chest. The short hair there tickled her nose, and she turned her head to his neck.

His breathing eased and became regular, the pulse in his neck smoothing out, his scent filling her nose. She stuck her tongue out, tasted saltiness, and chuckled.

This was the reason a woman took a husband. Marriage was good for something after all.

"Is it always like that?" she asked.

"Hmm?"

"Is it always like that?"

He opened one eye. "Now how would I know?"

Chapter Sixteen

Paulette propped herself up on one arm. "You've had other women."

The battle on Bink's face made her want to laugh.

She put a finger over his mouth. He didn't have to lie. It wasn't that sort of marriage. "You don't have to tell me. I'd rather you said nothing than lie to me."

"I'm not quite the man of the world."

"But you're not a virgin."

"No. But I haven't been with a woman in a very long time."

"Why not? Every inn maid you meet wants to bed you."

"They just like to flirt, most of them. They see how safe I am."

If he believed that, he was lying to himself. She let it pass.

"So why no lover? No mistress? Even stewards have mistresses, or affairs. Maybe especially stewards. All the lonely widows in the county."

He rolled her to the side and cuddled her, his fingers stroking through her hair. His eyes looked heavy. "Must we have this talk now?"

"You're sleepy." No doubt he was that after two days in the saddle.

"Yes."

"But I would like to know. Else thinking about it will keep me awake."

His sigh rumbled up from some deep unhappy place. "I'm careful. Always. I'm a bastard."

His frown deepened, freezing his jaw and locking it in place, and all of her senses alerted, waiting. He was deciding whether to tell her something more interesting.

"And you should know there are bad things in the world. Diseases that can pass from a man to a woman or a woman to a man. Not a pretty sight, what it does to a body. One thoughtless tumble can leave a man stricken for life, and his wife, if he has one, and any lovers, and even his children."

She raised up on an elbow. "The pox?"

"Yes, and other ailments. And London is crawling with all of them. When I returned there with the Major—Lord Hackwell—it was as bad there as it had been on the Peninsula." He swiped a hand over his brow. "No, it was worse. There is no war in England, and yet women spread their legs for their next meal while great lords gamble away fortunes."

He turned a fierce look on her and her courage wavered.

Anger burned in him. Too much anger for a man running away to India, which surely could not be any better of a place for disease and such.

"I've married a radical," she whispered.

"No." He pushed her hair back, his eyes even more aflame.

She'd seen his temper with Agruen, had she not? That night in Hackwell's library, Bink's anger had flown into his fists and been just as quickly dispersed. Once Hackwell appeared, he'd shown no signs of ire.

Tonight he held this flare-up with a control that might slip any moment.

But his hand on her cheek was gentle.

"I saw first-hand the results of a bloody revolution, remember?" His tight jaw worked. "Never. Never that here. I favor changes, with order. With sense."

"So why go to India?"

"I thought I couldn't do any good here."

The flame in his eyes smoldered higher. Her breath caught.

Thought, he'd said. He'd changed his mind about leaving, and a thrill jolted through her. He was staying. They would be doing this every night.

"Now I have you." Those big fingers moved over her face again.

"And now you can do good?"

"I can protect you." His eyes drifted closed.

She remembered the conversation with Kincaid, which seemed like a lifetime ago. "What are you protecting me from?"

He opened his eyes and studied her.

She was the daughter of spies. She might not be very good at the task herself, but she could see a lie coming.

She tapped a finger on his great chest, so firm with its muscle and bone, so distracting. "Kincaid said the same thing. That you would protect me. And I asked him from what. And he said I must ask you."

A loud rumbling rolled out of him.

"If we are to have trust between us—"

He clamped a hand on her shoulder. "I don't know, Paulette. I don't know what danger. Or from who. I only know what Shaldon said, that you would be in danger."

Shaldon said? *When* did Shaldon say? And *why* had no one told her?

She sat up, reached for the discarded nightrail, and covered herself. "Which Shaldon, the old or the new?"

"The old. I don't believe Bakeley knows about this. He wasn't present when I talked to the old man, and I didn't discuss it with him."

That sent her mind into a dizzying calculation. She was in danger. Yet Mr. Gibson had been planning to return her to Cransdall, even though Bakeley knew nothing of the threats to her.

Hot anger flared in her. "You don't know what. You don't know who. What *do* you know?"

A frown burned the line deeper between his eyebrows. "We will discuss this in the morning."

"Oh no, you don't." She found the hem of the nightgown and pulled it over her head. "Oh no, we will not. I will not be fobbed off until morning."

"Paulette."

She batted his hand away, leaped off the bed, and retrieved her discarded dressing gown.

"Paulette." Exasperation laced his slurred voice.

No doubt he was exhausted. She didn't care. "I must know. Or I must puzzle this out. I'm not a child."

He threw his legs over the side of the bed and stood.

Gloriously nude. Her gaze flew to his groin, and she forced it away and then turned her whole body.

Drat the man. There'd been the start of a grin on his face. He was trying to distract her.

Hands stroked her shoulders.

"I shall...scream. I shall cause a scene. A fight on our wedding night. The other guests will be shocked."

"There are no other guests."

No other guests. The empty courtyard, the two men in the taproom who were guards, Kincaid had said.

When she turned, she kept her focus at shoulder-level where a small scar she'd not noticed before traced over his muscles. "Explain, please. Why are there no other guests?"

"Kincaid arranged it."

"But..." *The cost*. She'd pinched pennies her whole life. The cost would be enormous. The journey itself was a fortune with the changing of teams, and...

No. The cost of this journey was not her concern. Mr. Gibson, Lord Hackwell, Lord Shaldon, Mr. Kincaid. One of them could pay for this.

"No other guests. Two men to keep watch because I am in danger. Spellen knew that was my room. He was searching my room. He was going to harm me. But why did he attack Jenny?"

"Because he was a beast.

She felt woozy. "As is Agruen." She squeezed her eyes shut. "Agruen had wanted to meet me in the kitchens." She shivered, and strong arms steadied her. Would Agruen have set Spellen on her?

She couldn't think about that now.

"Agruen is surely part of it," he said.

"The man who stole a useless ring and called my rusticating mother a whore."

A growl escaped him and he pulled her into him, his arms moving around her.

Jock had said there was a treasure, and Agruen must know about it. He must be after it, he, and perhaps, others. Did Shaldon know of her father's treasure? And if he did, why did he not bother to see her and speak of it? And had he told her husband?

Guilt pricked her. Should she tell him?

"Come. I'll pour you a brandy," he said.

"And you'll tell me about this threat."

Another unmanly sigh. "And I'll tell you as much as I know."

So much for paradise. Bink handed his bride a brandy and went to wash. He had no dressing gown, but his shirt would render some respectability.

When he glanced back at his bride, she looked away quickly.

He swallowed a grin. The lass liked his arse. His shirt might do, but nakedness had its advantages. He draped the shirt over the back of a chair, wrapped her tartan low on his hips, and joined her, in all his almost nudeness. Anything to distract her from the hot-headed miff she was brewing.

He poured a glass for himself and lifted the cover of the food tray. "Do you mind if I eat?"

"No, of course not." Her tone was wooden, polite. "Are you not cold?"

"I did not bring a dressing gown. Is my nakedness disturbing?"

She colored.

Old wounds flared, making him bristle.

"I suppose a gentleman would dress for dinner, even on his wedding night."

She dismissed him with an aristocratic wave and averted eyes.

He was definitely no gentleman. He was coarse and crude. A beast and a burden, and best she knew it. "I'm not either. I can dress if my lady insists."

Deeper color washed over her. "You are not either what?"

"I'm not cold, and I'm not a gentleman."

She jerked her belt tight, wishing it was around his neck he'd warrant. The contrast of the tiny waist and the flare of her hips went a long way to taking the edge off his own ire. He focused on the transparent silk, the flashing eyes, and the unleashed passion, and settled in for his first wifely tongue-lashing.

"The tartan you're wadding up was a wedding gift to me from Kincaid, though God knows why he would give it to me. And you lie, Bink Gibson. You *are* a gentleman, as much a gentleman as Bakeley or your Lord Hackwell. It's the other you play whenever you want to. It's what you've been playing for years." Her hand flapped out again. "But it is fine with me, if you do not choose to be the gentleman you are tonight, or ever. Because you should know, sir, I am no 'my lady.' What do you think I am? I am the daughter of two spies—one died on the Continent, and the other was buried alive in the country." She bit her lip and blinked furiously. "Who am I? Shaldon, the great bloody villain, died without telling me anything. You must tell me whatever he told you."

His hands itched to hold her, but she was not out of heat yet. He helped himself to bread and meat and cheese instead. "You *are* a lady, Paulette. And you are *my* lady."

"No. I am your wife. I am not a lady. Ladies are sniveling, weak creatures wholly dependent on men, and I choose not to be one of those. I will take what money I can gather and go to London and meet this solicitor, Tellingford, and find my trustee and get the rest of my money."

She paused for a breath, and looked toward the window, and the skin on his neck rippled.

What else was she plotting to do? And what was she not telling him. For sure, there was some of that in this fuss.

She swung a level gaze his way. "I will take care of myself, and you may run away to India if that is what you wish to do."

He chewed carefully and swallowed. He would not be going to India, ever. The dream of rajahs and riches faded blissfully away, with not one tiny whiff of a pang. "A solicitor in London is in charge of the trust—"

"Which is now coming to me, since I have married."

Actually, technically, it was coming to her husband, in the usual way. He did not need to raise that conflagration, since he was the husband in question.

Bakeley had pulled him aside on Sunday just before his departure, and he'd been in such a hurry to get to her, he'd barely heard.

Now, the words flooded back into his memory.

He would get to this solicitor first. Before she could lay hands on any documents explaining the usual trust arrangement or hear the news directly, a new game would be in play. The money would be signed over to her full control.

"Bakeley said this solicitor was the executor of your mother and father's estates, and arranged the terms of Shaldon's guardianship over you. He is holding property to be given to you upon Shaldon's death."

His spine tingled. Whatever that solicitor held might be the thing putting her in danger.

"And someone else wants it."

Her brow furrowed, her gaze flitted, hither and yon, while she chewed on those snippets of information. There'd be no rest until he talked to the solicitor.

He filled a plate and handed it to her. "Eat something."

She bit into the bread and covered her mouth while she chewed. "As I said, my father was a spy. He died on the Continent, was all Mama would say."

He'd seen more than a few spies passing through the Peninsula. Paulette's father could have been one of them.

"When did he die?"

"I don't know exactly. I was little more than a child when my mother received word eight years ago, but I believe it took some time for the news to reach us."

They'd learned of the death in 1811 then. In the years before and after that, he'd been in the thick of the Peninsular battles. Death had visited the area then, freely and often.

Bink rested his fork on the plate. The Portuguese priest had passed through around then. And before him, Josiah Dickson, he who would be Agruen.

That dark memory filled his vision again. A woman as small as Paulette, so beaten she'd not been able to speak. Bink had stumbled into the fight in a Portuguese hovel while on patrol.

He rubbed at a pain in his temple. Dickson was bloodied, the other man too. *That man did it*, Dickson had said.

Dickson, who'd been at the Major's table the night before.

Bink beat on the other man until Beauverde showed up and pulled him away.

And months later, in the humble hut of a defenseless mother and her girls, this one in Spain, Bink found out the truth about Agruen.

A soft touch on his arm brought his gaze to the present, into eyes dark as that Spanish woman's, but so very alive with intelligence and concern. "It's Agruen then. Something to do with him." Her voice was low and fierce.

Somehow, she'd gone inside his head and taken a look around. The flood of intimacy brought him back to the problem at hand.

He'd protect her. He'd keep her safe. The monster would not have another chance at her. "It would be my guess also." He clamped a hand over hers. "I will go, Paulette."

She straightened. "What?"

"I won't let him harm you. I will go. As your husband, I can conduct this business."

She pulled her hand back and folded her arms. The storm returned, flashed in her, like lightening on a dark Channel night, winds ready to topple any boat within range. "And I will be where?"

Safe. You'll be safe. He bit his lip. "Greencastle."

Her hands flew up again, a flock of mad doves. "It's not safe there. *It's not safe.* Look what happened to Jenny."

His chest tightened. Jenny had been wandering in the kitchen at night, and Paulette had done her own wandering. Lady Hackwell would never allow him to lock Paulette in her room. Her maid offered no restraint. The thought of her roaming that estate, the thought of her tied down with Agruen over her...

He rubbed his jaw. Worse, if there could be a worse, Agruen would harm all in his way, including Lady Hackwell.

"Cransdall then." The spymaster's retainers were all fully checked out and endorsed, many trained, retired operatives. It was safe as the Bank of England. And he would share all with Bakeley.

"No."

"Paulette, Agruen is a brute."

Her gaze sharpened. She saw too much. He did not want her to ask about that time in Spain. He did not want to have to talk about it. He wanted to shove it back into its tomb and seal the stone.

"Yes," she said. "He's ruthless, and possibly has more men like Spellen. You'll be in danger, also."

He let out a breath. "I can take care of myself."

She huffed. "And what of me? Who'll protect me while you're gone?"

"Bakeley. Kincaid."

"Leaving you unguarded, unprotected." She shook her head. "No."

"That's how it must be. I'll hire runners, but when it comes down to it, I can look after myself."

She bit her lip. Stood. Sighed. Picked up the brandy bottle and reached for his glass, letting her robe flop open.

His shaft stirred and he swallowed a chuckle. She was trying a new tactic.

He rested a hand on her round bottom and some of the brandy spilled over the side of the glass.

She turned her attention on him, her eyes veiled by long lashes that shimmered.

Tears. Real or summoned, he wished he knew. All spies were liars, and whether she'd inherited her parents' skills, he couldn't tell, not yet.

"I will not leave you unprotected," she said. "I will not let you go into danger without me." Her husky voice turned the ripple running through him into high waves. His hand moved over the soft curves.

Desire, hot and urgent, rose and swamped him, wiping out fatigue, and thirst, and hunger for anything but her. "Will you not?" He slipped the slick silk out of its knot, dragged the tips of his fingers down her leg and lifted the hem of the gown, all the while inching her nearer.

Her knuckles went white round the head of the bottle. He was, perhaps, in danger of a coshing.

"You'll protect me? Make sure I'm unharmed?" he whispered.

"You must promise, Bink. You must promise to take me."

Aye, he would take her. "Love, will you release the brandy bottle?"

Her eyes widened. Her gaze flitted to the bottle, and he saw the moment she recognized the weapon in her hand. He shouldn't have brought it to her attention.

Perhaps now coshing would come as naturally to her as kissing and coupling.

He chuckled. A man could not complain about two out of three.

"You *must* promise, Bink."

"I'll promise. I'll promise to talk about it more." He sent his hand up under the thin silk, and watched her eyes darken and glaze.

"I'll hold you to that promise and—*oh*." The bottle plopped, tipped, and a river of sweet-scented amber coursed over the table.

Bink pulled her out of its path, onto his lap. Brandy laced the top of her foot. He tipped her back, brought her foot up and licked it clean, down to the tips of each toe.

She gasped and wriggled.

When he released her foot, he lifted her into a straddle, and pushed her thin silks high, drawing her closer until her breasts huddled against him, muddling his brain, rendering all of his senses to only that softness, that seal of her skin against his.

"We're not finished." Her breath came in tiny, barely audible puffs. "With this discussion."

And then her kiss took away all his ability to think.

Chapter Seventeen

As a husband, Bink Gibson was proving to be a puzzle, one she was struggling to solve. He played many characters—bluff yeoman, shrewd steward, fierce warrior, skilled lover.

No. That last wasn't a character. That was truly him. He'd been crafty enough turning her own plan to seduce a promise out of him into a ravishment.

Heat rose in her face, and she shifted on her seat, her foot hitting one of the two hampers of food Bink had insisted on. They'd not stopped except to change horses and replenish those hampers.

Thankfully, the two maids slept, giving Paulette time to think. The pace of this grueling trip made them collapse, almost immediately, but *she* could not sleep, not after her wedding night, not after what she'd discovered.

And what was that, Paulette?

Warmth curled in her heart, warmth that felt like joy.

Or could it be love? She pushed it down. She had no sense of how such feelings could last, and perhaps she had no right. They'd married for money, hadn't they?

Besides, Gibson was being obstinate, and she didn't entirely trust him. He'd promised they'd talk about going to London, but after one more round of lovemaking, she'd awakened alone in her bed and found Mabel and Jenny mopping up brandy and packing her bag for a hasty departure.

Word had come, in the person of two hard-riding Greencastle grooms. Spellen had gone missing, Agruen was bound for London, and cavalry was advancing on Manchester. Her husband had shared the news during their hurried breakfast, and promised they'd talk about London later, after he'd brought her safely to Greencastle.

Perhaps he thought when they reached Hackwell's estate, he would talk, and she would listen. Perhaps he thought he would lock her up with Lord and Lady Hackwell, or transport her to Cransdall.

He could *try*.

She leaned against the squab, wriggled her aching bottom, and let her eyes drift shut. They'd not stopped the night, nor would they, and each change she managed to stay awake for taught her something new. She'd learned much on this trip about traveling, about inns, about the coaching system. Her funds would hold her until London.

Outside, a low conversation rumbled, audible, but not understandable. Their numbers had swollen to include the two new Hackwell grooms, ex-soldiers Mabel had learned, and Kincaid's two Scotsmen. And Bink had tied her knife's sheath to her arm. *If need be, go for something soft*, he'd said. The belly, the kidneys, the eye.

The eye. The thought made her insides squirm, and she scolded herself. Jock had told her the same thing, years ago, when he'd tutored her. And she must not be squeamish. Her mama hadn't been, Jock had said. If it came to it, she would defend herself and her maids.

She must stay awake. She must at least try. The ache of her bones, the prospect of a fight, the plots to be made about escaping to London, all kept her on edge. A day, a night, and another day—if her husband could stay awake seated atop a horse, so could she in this plush coach.

A smattering of bedraggled walkers, men and a surprising number of women, had stepped to the side for them, eying the coach, the riders, the servants up top, and especially, the butt of the pistol at Kincaid's waist, and the shotgun in the hired Scotsman's grip.

Bink had kept his pair of Mantons more carefully concealed. When he'd stopped to question the first group for news, fear had shut them up tight. They'd not been at St. Peter's Field, they said, and he knew they were lying, looking over their shoulders with wary eyes. Something had happened, and maybe these were the rabbits who'd run at the first sight of the uniformed foxes.

Fools, they were, the lords, and the soldiers serving them. People were starving. The war had wreaked havoc abroad, and the peace was doing so here.

At the last coaching inn, he'd hurried the women through their privy stop, picked up two new hampers of food, and heard from the innkeeper the rumor of a great bloody riot, a trampling to death of men, and women too. A bloody power play that set him fuming, and worrying more.

He was dead in his saddle, and tried to hide it, else he'd shame himself in front of Kincaid, who sat erect, alert, determination written upon his face.

And just what that bit with the tartan had been about, Bink would like to know. Kincaid didn't seem a man to go weak about a girl's wedding—a spy wouldn't be sentimental, but he'd offer lies aplenty. Kincaid hadn't convinced Bink he was a Scot neither, no matter how he curled his words.

Ah, but if he were, that might explain the plaid. Weren't the Scots, like the Irish, a hard-nosed bunch who, with enough whisky flowing, would drop to a sniffle at the sound of a ballad?

The two Scotsmen they'd acquired held their part well. Greencastle was mere hours away. They'd rest there, consult with Hackwell or his lady if either still remained, and assess the security of the estate, which was still his to manage. Since leaving Gretna, they'd traveled with all haste. No inn stops of any length.

They'd left the high dales and come into a stretch of tall beech hedges, the farmland beyond thick with corn. The harvest would be soon, if these fools didn't burn down the country.

He was glad he'd shared the express from Hackwell with Paulette. When he'd told her of the danger on the roads, his bride hadn't been cowed. The courage that flashed in her eyes, well, if Mabel hadn't been in the antechamber, if the team hadn't already been hitched, he'd have taken her again.

He sighed. He was a beast after all, bothering her all night and then throwing her into a bouncing coach for days. Surely the girl was sore. Though when he thought of it, she'd not complained about the pain from his great manly shaft in her.

He'd fixed her knife's sheath to her forearm and tucked a spare knife into the seat next to her. He would have given her a pistol if she'd known how to load it. That ignorance, he'd remedy later.

The daughter of spies, she'd said. Well, he couldn't teach her the spy's knack of lying, but he wouldn't deny her the basics of a soldier's knowledge.

As soon as he felt assured she would not use the pistol on him.

His loins stirred. A night of making love had not sufficed for either of them, but he must give his brash bride the rest and the chance to mend she did not know she needed. And he must get her to safety.

And then, he must dodge her next spy's tactic, whatever it might be.

Her obsession about London was not likely to abate, but his gut told him there was more to the story than what she was sharing.

The woman was a bother, but as long as she bothered him in bed he could accept almost anything.

Perhaps he *could* take her to London. He'd promised, and they had enough outriders to keep her safe. But there was still the danger that Shaldon spoke of to contend with—about what, he still didn't know, but he had a feeling Paulette did.

Hackwell House was no safer than Greencastle, though. Agruen would look for her there.

An inn or a hotel maybe. Or Annabelle Harris's house in Soho.

Ah, now that was an idea.

The house stood, almost vacant now, with only old Mr. Lewis and his new wife as caretakers. No one would know about that house, and Mr. Lewis had proven himself a man who could keep secrets.

No one would know to look for Paulette there, but they could follow her home from one of the outings she was certain to make. And the neighborhood was on the edge of a seedy area.

He would have to muse more on this. Short of locking her up at Greencastle or Cransdall, he didn't have a solution.

A crackle of gravel, a shuffle of leaves, and the low murmur of voices came to him over the creaking of the coach's wheels, stirring his senses.

Around the next bend, a crowd of walkers appeared, tramping along in the middle of the already cramped road, sticks in hand, heads to the ground, like bloody hounds of the shire. The post boys saw them too and between him and the men up top, had the devil of the time halting the team before running them over.

Another wave of apprehension sparked through him. His hand went to his pistols while he scanned the crowd. All men. He spotted no women in this group, not even dirty, disheveled ones dressed like men.

Kincaid shot him a glance, and all of his nerves prickled. It was easy enough to mix trouble in with a group like this.

Bink brought his horse up the steep bank and leaned close to the coach window. Paulette peered through the lowered glass.

"What is it?" she asked.

"Be on your guard. And stay inside." He spurred and moved up with the fidgety team. Kincaid shadowed him, and Johnny and the others surrounded the coach. They were all armed, even Ewan.

He counted bodies, a dozen, perhaps fifteen, and all of them marked with fatigue, the dust of the road, and anger. There were no shivering rabbits here. Whatever the army had done, they hadn't cowed this group. They'd only stirred more ire.

This crowd could easily flank them and endanger Paulette. And if one of them should be Agruen's hired man...

He raised a hand and fixed a deep frown. "Good day. Coming from that madness in Manchester, are ye?" He scanned the group. They jostled and exchanged glances and grumbles.

Who doesn't fit in?

A spokesman emerged, a thin man, a bit better off, from the looks of his coat. "What's it to you?" Weariness lined his face, but his voice was vibrant. And wrathful.

"We're wanting news, man," Kincaid said in a thick burr. "My new son-in-law and I, we've just come from Gretna. What the hell happened at St. Peter's Field? What have those fool mill owners done?"

A smile creased the man's face. Not yet a friendly one, which worried him more.

"A wedding? Caught up with the villain, did you?" He scratched at his scruff. "Want us to take care of him for you?"

Bink moved his horse a step closer. "Here now. I had his blessing and the wedding was honorable, traveling as I did to marry with her kin being present."

"Aye. And I'm seeing to my girl's safe delivery to her new home. Will you tell us what happened? Will the bloody British soldiers be trampling us down afore I can bring her to safety?"

There.

Bink wheeled his horse to the verge where two men were sidling closer. He sent them his sergeant's glare. "Are ye all mates? All together?"

The two men glared back. He fingered a pistol at his waist, strained to define the difference between them and the others, and could not. It was only instinct discerning. "These two here. Were they with you at the gathering?"

"'Twere thousands there," one man grumbled.

"We saw women before," Kincaid said. "There are no women with you."

The spokesman drew himself up to his full height. "There were many, it's true, but we wouldn't allow our women to such as this. And we're honest laborers, not highwaymen. Leave off."

Tension crackled. The two suspicious ones merged back with the larger group. Kincaid's man with a shotgun had turned their way, and Bink backed out of the Scotsman's range.

"See if they're hungry, Da." The voice, feminine, loud, and convincingly burred, reached all the way to the crowd of men.

Blast her. The coach door opened a crack.

Ewan swung from the roof like a carnival trickster and both of his feet hit the door. "I'll see to them, mistress," he said.

The boy was fast, like his kin, who'd reined up behind Bink.

Ah well, Johnny was Shaldon's man, as was the young Ewan.

Inside the coach, Paulette muttered a curse as the door shut firmly, and leaned down to shift one of the hampers of food wedged up against her lap desk, all of it crowding her feet.

"Thieves?" Jenny asked.

"Weavers, most likely, come from the demonstration." Mabel gripped Paulette's hand. "Leave it to the boy."

"Mistress." The ginger-haired man at her window was Johnny and he kept his voice low.

"There may be goats in this sheep herd. Keep low, mistress."

Fear pricked every nerve. Hand shaking, she fingered her knife and pulled her bonnet lower.

Mabel stumbled over the hampers and sat next to her.

"Mind the knife in the seat," Paulette whispered.

Mabel shifted and brought out the sheathed knife. "I don't know how to use this."

"I do," Jenny said.

Paulette nodded, and Mabel handed it over.

She leaned her ear to the open window. Mr. Gibson was asking questions, gathering information about the rally and the riot that had followed, about the army's attack, the workers' grievances. In the long stretches of listening, she could not make out the responses.

He was acutely interested, though, that much she could tell, and so could the men on the road. His interest and sincerity would disarm them, she hoped.

"As my wife suggested," he boomed loudly, "we have food to share if you'll have it."

Men's voices rumbled and the door opened. Ewan tipped his hat and pulled out one of the hampers.

"Take them both." Paulette nudged the other one over.

This was why he'd purchased them and kept them filled—not to push forward without ceasing, but to buy them some peace on the road.

She watched from the window as he directed Ewan. Buying peace wasn't his only reason—Bink Gibson had real compassion for those men and women, running from their own British troops.

He had a strong protective instinct, and not just for the woman he'd taken to wife.

With an estate and an income, he'd never leave for India. He'd always be underfoot, slamming the coach doors closed if he thought there was danger.

And she'd not yet told him of her father's treasure.

The carriage began to move and as they rolled down the road, she saw men grouped on the embankment, delving into the food baskets. At a flat stretch, they picked up speed. From a fast walk, to a trot, to almost a gallop.

Goats in the herd. How many? If they were afoot they couldn't catch up with them, could they?

She frowned out of the window. What would Agruen's men do?

They wouldn't really travel afoot. They'd pretend, they'd walk a short way with the group. They'd have horses tucked nearby.

"I'll give you this back, miss." Jenny held out the knife to her.

She shook her head. "Best keep it handy, Jenny. We've given away all our food. We may still have need of it."

When they came to a rough patch of road the coach slowed. She stuck her head out the window and called "Mr. Gibson."

His head went up, and he let the coach roll until he was next to her.

"Are you angry with me then?" he asked, looking grim.

"I'm being polite in front of the servants. I wish to speak with you."

She craned her neck to look up at him. His gaze was cast down the road ahead, not backward, as it should be.

"Is it possible we will be followed?"

"Yes. But we've dealt with it."

"How?"

"Kincaid's two Scotsmen are straying behind us. Do not worry."

She let out a breath. Perhaps it was well they had four extra men. Perhaps her husband could get her to London safely without requiring the poke of her knife into someone's eye. As exciting as the prospect might be, she didn't want to have to try it.

"Now tuck yourself back inside, love. There's a fast stretch ahead and we'll make a quick change very soon." He stepped up his pace and moved out of her range of vision.

She plopped against the squab. *Tuck herself back inside?* Like she was a thick bit of Stroud cloth folded up and stored in the coach for cold nights?

The spike of irritation turned into a sick feeling that grew and lodged near her heart. The pleasure they'd shared, the wonder of being held by him, the comfort of being protected, it all came at a price. One she wasn't sure she was willing to pay. She wouldn't last twenty years being confined to the country without even a Jock to break up the boredom. She wouldn't last another twenty minutes.

What would Mama have done?

Mama had most assuredly let herself be tucked away in the country, but she'd had a child to look after.

And she'd gone off a few times on business, even before they'd received news of Papa's death. Only a few, and in retrospect, for only a few days, though to the young child Paulette, it had seemed like forever each time. Mama'd had that small bit of freedom, to come and go.

Mama wouldn't have lasted being tucked away with no hope of escape. And neither would Paulette.

Bink glanced at the level of the sun and felt hopeful. At this pace they would reach Greencastle before full darkness settled. Bringing Paulette to safety was all he could think about.

Well, almost all. His bride had been stonily polite at the last two stops. She was tired. He was dead in his saddle himself, and quite willing to match tempers with anyone, even Paulette, in lieu of taking on the unseen threats stalking their group.

Perhaps he'd especially like to take on Paulette. An uproar was brewing with her. As soon as they got through their dinner at Greencastle and the bedroom door closed, she'd be demanding he take her to London. And his answer would mean he'd sleep in his own chamber.

Damn it, better that than endanger her for some foolish whimsy. Her father had been a spy for Shaldon. Perhaps her mother had spied at one time, but she'd made the sensible choice to stay in the country taking care of her child instead of running all over Europe with her.

The appearance of two men on the road yanked him completely into the present. In the distance, two gentlemen sat astride two horses.

He signaled his riders and scanned the terrain on both sides. The hedgerows here could conceal an ambush.

One of the riders raised his arm and both spurred their mounts forward.

"Hold up," Bink shouted, and rode forward to meet them, another set of hooves on his heels.

Chapter Eighteen

As he neared the two riders, the quality of the horses reassured him more. He'd seen Agruen's cattle at Greencastle. The man had squandered whatever money he'd won through death or marriage, and the best he could afford had been no match for these mounts.

Closer still and his hackles rose once again. One of the riders was Bakeley, and the grin on his face spread from ear to ear. "Greetings, brother, I hear congratulations are in order."

Bink nodded. "Bakeley."

"So glum." He peered around Bink to glance at the coach. "Was the wedding night that bad?"

Behind him a throat cleared. Johnny backed his horse away, stone-faced, just as he ought to be.

The man with Bakeley had hung back, but Bakeley motioned him to go join the others near the coach.

When he was out of earshot, Bakeley turned to him and said "Well?"

The brush drew his scrutiny again, his nerves prickling. This road didn't lead to or from Cransdall, and why the devil Bakeley was here, he couldn't imagine.

"I'll not be waxing poetic about the wedding night to you. It's none of your damn concern. What the hell are you doing here?"

"Ah, ha." Bakeley clapped him on the shoulder.

Bink's horse shied, not appreciating the closeness of the other mount.

"As to that, brother, Hackwell and I devised a plan to keep your lady safe."

Irritation spiked through him. Paulette was *his* wife, *his* to protect.

A breeze picked up and the brush nearby rustled, sending his horse side-stepping again. Bakeley frowned at the trees and reached under his coat.

A hare ran from the cover, bounding across the lane.

Struggling to settle his mount, Bakeley laughed, and Bink released a pent-up breath.

There was real danger to Paulette, and taking offense at the offer of help was pig-headed and unfair. With Hackwell there'd always been more camaraderie than command, and Bakeley was his brother.

Brothers helped each other.

So, best listen, Bink, and don't be too proud to turn down help.

Bakeley looked up at the sky, "Rain's coming in. Shaldon had a manor house not three miles off this stretch. It's a small, secret safe house. Found it among our father's papers after you left."

Bink's tension eased. In truth, he was glad he'd not been born under all those piles of Shaldon papers.

"Paulette can stay there, well-guarded," Bakeley said. "Hackwell's sent his family off to stay with the Cathmores in Sussex. Now, I've a coach down the road. You've visited your last coaching inn for the day. We'll transfer the lady, her servants and her bags and send the hired horses on their way."

"What news of Agruen?" Bink asked.

"He headed for London and did not arrive, as far as we know. His man Spellen is also missing."

His nerves prickled. How was it possible Bakeley didn't know about Spellen?

"He's not missing. He went over a ledge in the dales. Broke his damn neck." And Hackwell would know that if the express had arrived.

Bakeley's lips turned up and he laughed. "Look at us, brother. Caught up in our father's games. Did the valet put up much of a fight?"

Bink told him about finding Spellen searching Paulette's room.

"I only chased him as far as the window he jumped out of. Kincaid took over the rest."

Bakeley's eyes gleamed. "Kincaid. Have you discovered his secrets?"

"What secrets would those be?"

"If I knew, I wouldn't ask you. But, ah, you're being cagey. You know something of him."

"He's a Scotsman, he says."

"If that's his real name. Shaldon would not discuss him. Said you and I would have to find out on our own."

"You and I?"

Bakeley laughed ruefully. "Him and his damn secrets. Now it's our turn to play at this game, I only wish I knew what the hell it is, and what Agruen was after with Paulette."

As did Bink.

"In any case, we'd best move on before we lose the light. She'll be safe in this cottage while we head down to London to meet the solicitor."

She might be safe, but whoever was left to guard her would be in for trouble.

Bink signaled to the coach to move on, the question of who would keep watch on Paulette weighing heavily. In her own way, she was a winsome thing, pretty, and passionate. If it was Bakeley or Kincaid, or himself, she'd be in good hands. He wasn't sure, under the circumstances, he'd trust any other man.

"Why have we stopped?" Paulette asked Ewan as he helped her down the steps of the coach.

Her husband came over and relieved Ewan of her arm. "Get the bags," he said gruffly.

Around the bend in the road she spotted a plain black coach stopped further down, pulled to the side in a flat stretch, leaving enough room for another coach to pass.

The evening was warm, yet she felt chilled to her very bones, stiff from the days of bumping and sitting, and so tired it was like wading through a dream.

And her prickle of nerves told her the dream was likely to turn to a nightmare.

She allowed herself to be led down the road to where the new coach sat. "What is this, Bink?"

He grimaced and clamped his lips shut.

A gentleman on horseback paced closer and her heart dropped. The corner of her eye ticked, the trembling threatening to spread through her every nerve. She stiffened her jaw and tightened her fists. "You are not. Sending me. To Cransdall. I won't go."

"Good evening, Paulette." Bakeley swept off his hat and gave a little bow from the saddle. "My congratulations on your marriage. We are officially brother and sister now."

"Give us a minute, Bakeley." Her husband's hand had moved to her shoulder in a gesture that was much like an irritating petting.

Bakeley shrugged and took his mount away.

"Shaldon has a manor near here. Hackwell is worried enough he's sent Annabelle off to stay with Lady Cathmore."

Her breath eased a fraction.

"We are all going there in this new coach, and letting the postilions take the other one on. If someone is following us, they won't be able to trace you through the coaching inn."

That made sense. "So much secrecy. Is there news?"

"I don't know any more than you."

She searched his eyes for a lie. "Does your brother know anything?"

"He says not. We'll question him more tonight."

She exhaled. They were going to this manor together. He was not leaving her, at least not tonight. "And then?"

A grimace puckered his brow. "And then we'll talk."

His attention flew to the baggage being loaded and her heart plummeted, and she *knew*—this manor was to be her prison. Gibson was locking her up and leaving for London without her.

Well, they would see about that.

Jenny and Mabel approached, carrying her lap desk and a satchel. He led her around to the other side of the coach and reached for the door.

She snatched at his arm. "Mr. Gibson—"

The line in his forehead deepened. "So I'm to be Mr. Gibson."

Blood raced and clanged in her head, clouding her vision. Her jaw ached from clenching it.

"There's no one close by to hear, Paulette." His voice rasped.

She gritted her own teeth. No one would hear, and that was supposed to placate her? "Edward."

She yanked open the door. "Bink." She stomped a foot on the stair. "Gibson."

Swallowing, she glanced back at him. "Mr. Gibson." She took in an angry breath. "Mr. Bloody Gibson. May you rot."

"Wait." He tugged at her elbow, and when she looked, he was frowning.

Not frowning. His face had crumpled. The line was there, between his eyes, and both eyes shone.

The kiss, hard, passionate, caught her all unawares and knocked her off balance. She clutched at his shoulder, though there was no need. He'd swept her in close, so close she could feel his heart beating.

The coach shimmied and he pulled back from the kiss, pressing her head to his chest and knocking her bonnet askew.

"You may call me whatever you wish, Paulette, as long as you continue to kiss me like that."

Her hands fisted, and she swallowed a sob, fighting for breath.

"I'll only be able to keep kissing you if you take me with you to London."

He set her away from him and stood looking at her.

Damn him. He *was* leaving her.

"Into the coach with you," he said. "Bakeley says we'll be there within the hour and he'll have hot baths and dinner waiting."

She pressed her lips closed on a curse. She'd have her hot bath and her meal, and then she was leaving.

He all but lifted her in and she settled upon the seat. Jenny and Mabel climbed in from the other side.

"That was quite a kiss." Mabel bent over to wedge the lap desk on the seat, effectively hiding the smirk Paulette had glimpsed. "Ah look, there's a basket of food here. We won't starve before reaching wherever we're going. Where might that be, Polly? Do you know?"

Did she? She'd paid attention to the route from Gretna, and she knew this road would eventually lead to London. She could figure this out.

"A manor nearby. One of Shaldon's properties."

Mabel offered her a hunk of cheese but she waved it away, and Jenny took it gratefully.

Jenny had known much of hunger, Paulette thought. She'd taken her assault in stride, also. And she could handle a knife, she'd said.

Mabel would be of no help in her escape from this manor. Mabel would tell Johnny, and Johnny would tell Mr. Gibson.

However, Jenny, she might be able to confide in.

What would Mama have done?

As the hired coach pulled around them and the rattle of the horses died away, Paulette remembered the stories Jock had told her about her mother's escapes from one predicament or another. Her mother had been, like Paulette, a small woman. She'd easily passed for a boy.

She set her hand on the lowered window and counted the turnings. She would need to find her way back to this road that led down to London.

The house was no cottage but a three-story manor, tucked back in a grove of trees behind a sweeping overgrown lawn.

A squat, older serving woman with a bland demeanor delivered Paulette to her room, where she waited impatiently for the promised hot water. When it finally arrived, an hour had passed.

She swished in and out of her bath, rushed Jenny through helping her dress, and was twisting her hair onto the back of her head when a knock came.

"Mr. Gibson will be taking me down. Hurry with the pins, Jenny."

Mabel opened the door. The same maid carried a covered tray. "Here's your dinner, madam," she said.

"My dinner? You're not serving dinner downstairs?"

The woman colored deeply. "I was told to deliver it here."

Mabel rushed to take the wobbling tray. "This will be fine. And doesn't this smell lovely?" She settled the tray on a table, and the woman turned to go.

"Wait," Paulette said. "Are you or are you not serving the gentlemen dinner downstairs?"

The maid's lips moved wordlessly and when sound finally issued she said "Well, yes, his lordship did request I do that, but he said you would be eating here."

She felt her jaw hardening. "I see. You may go."

The door closed, and Paulette stood.

"I'm not quite done, miss," Jenny said.

A lock of hair still tickled her neck. She grabbed the pins from Jenny's hand and stabbed them in. "There. Both of you eat. I'm dining downstairs."

In the corridor, she looked around. There was still enough light trickling in through the windows to see her way from this third floor garret to the stairs.

The smallish bedchamber was the sort where a poor relation or a governess would be housed, and the narrow bed would be cozy for honeymooning lovers, but neither her husband nor his bag had arrived.

There was no key in the lock. Not yet.

Hone your instincts, Jock had taught her.

But her mother, when she'd begged her for answers about her past as a spy, had called her too fanciful, and when pushed, had firmly denied her life as a spy.

If only Papa had come home, or Jock had not died. She would have learned more. She wouldn't be so alone.

It was possible she was being too suspicious. Perhaps Bakeley and Gibson would not conspire to lock her away.

She shook her head and swallowed hard. No, excluding her from the discussion at dinner was a sure sign. She couldn't trust Bakeley. She couldn't trust her husband.

Well, let them try to lock her away. Jock had taught her about locks.

She gripped the banister and moved quietly down the carpeted stairs to the second floor. No creaks on the stairs—the house was well-kept for people who needed to sneak in and out. Several doors lined each side of the corridor, which ended in a sharp right turn into the building's one wing.

Paulette moved down the hall, counting doors, and turned into the second corridor. More doors lined the walls, bedchambers most likely. At the end was a servant's staircase leading both up and down. The smell of savory meat and pudding rose up these stairs and made her mouth water.

Satisfying her hunger was the least of her problems. She needed to know what they'd planned for her.

Which room would be Gibson's? She placed her hand on the farthest door latch, and apprehension tingled through her. Who would Bakeley house in this place? Spies on holiday? And if she opened the door and found one sleeping, what would she do? She'd left her weapons in her bedchamber. *I'm looking for my husband,* she could say.

She remembered Agruen's grip on her arm.

Chin up, Paulette. You can scream loud enough to bring at least someone from the kitchen.

This room was unoccupied. Her curiosity piqued, she checked each room, all of them unlocked. No servants interrupted her. The small staff was undoubtedly serving the dinner downstairs. Four rooms held men's things. Bakeley, Bakeley's companion, whoever he was, Kincaid, and she finally found the room with Gibson's traveling kit. She slipped in and looked around.

It was very odd. Husbands and wives were usually settled next to each other, in adjoining chambers if possible. The bed bore a man's outline. He'd rested, then washed—the water had cooled in the basin. He'd shaved also. The razor sat gleaming on a piece of white toweling. He'd taken more care for this dinner with Bakeley than he had on their wedding night, not that she'd minded.

Had he changed for this dinner? She opened the small case.

He'd packed away his soiled shirt, so there'd be no need to stay while his laundry dried. The razor could be packed in moments. He was leaving, and soon. And, his pistols must be with him.

She stepped back into the corridor and collided with Jenny, who had Paulette's soiled gown draped over her arm.

"Oh, Miss."

Paulette pulled her into her husband's room. "They've put Mr. Gibson in this room."

Jenny frowned. She knew enough about the arranging of guests to know this wasn't usual.

"They're planning, I think, that I should stay here."

"'Twill be safer, won't it, miss?"

"Perhaps. But I don't want to stay here. Will you help me?"

"Of course."

"You must not tell Mabel. Will you promise?"

The girl's hesitation sent anxiety coursing through her. Perhaps it was a mistake to trust Jenny.

"No matter what happens, Jenny, you will have a home with me. I promise you."

The girl nodded.

"I saw two handsome lads working here, not much bigger than me either of them."

Jenny nodded again. Boys that handsome, of course she'd seen them.

"I need trousers, a shirt, and coats. My own boots will do, I think."

The girl's eyes widened. "I dressed as a boy once." She frowned. "The usual boy for the sneak had took sick and they needed—well, I almost got caught. If something happens to you—"

"Nothing will happen. I'll follow close to them. I'll need that second knife back from you." And a pistol. She needed a pistol. Gibson had two, but if she took one of them, he would notice. "They're plotting to lock me up and keep me locked up until they've secured the money my father left me."

The maid's face fell. "Mr. Gibson would do that?"

Guilt stabbed at Paulette. All the servants admired Bink. "His intention may be only to keep me safe. But I don't trust his brother, Lord Bakeley. I mean, Lord Shaldon. And I don't know the other man, but I thought he looked—"

"Shifty." Jenny's lips firmed.

The girl saw much. "Yes. I won't use the knife unless I need to."

Jenny nodded. "I didn't see a key up there. I was locked in once, miss." She frowned again. "Not for long. There'd be those going upon the dub...er, that is...I know a bit about picking locks."

"Really?" Her heart lifted. She'd had the lessons from Jock, and some practice, but it would be good to have the help of a professional.

"Oh, miss." She would swear Jenny blushed. "I would never steal—"

"Of course not. Anyway, I know a bit about it too."

"You need picks."

She patted her head. "I have my hairpins."

"A real set would be better. One of the gentlemen might have one."

Kincaid. If anyone had a set of picks it would be him.

She'd seen his black bag resting on a chair in the next room.

Chapter Nineteen

Bink quaffed a large glass of ale while Bakeley droned on. His brother had convened this meeting at the table spread with hot dishes. Old battlefield habits died hard, and Bink ate. It was wise to eat when one could during a break in the fighting. He'd barely tasted the beef and the pudding, so much on edge was he from fatigue, worry, and nagging apprehension.

Kincaid had joined them, as well as Bakeley's man, who called himself George Stewart, a man with the refined narrow face of a popinjay poet, and the silent dark eyes of a hawk.

He was, Bink decided, another of the old lord's operators.

"They'll be calling on Parliament to gather," Bink said. "You'll be wanting to take your place in the Lords."

Bakeley winced. Stewart chewed blandly. Kincaid shot Bakeley a hard look and went back to his plate.

Bakeley's flinch was the sparest of shudders, a mere whisper of movement, and strange. The absence of grief at Shaldon's passing hadn't surprised Bink, eager as Bakeley must have been to get the old man off his back and take on the full role of his Lordship. That would include donning his cloak and coronet for the Lords.

Bakeley adopted a nonchalant look and waved a hand. "Plenty of time for that."

"Not if this bunch starts a rebellion. It will be all hands to battle if that happens."

"It won't."

"I'm not so sure. We encountered a bunch on the road and had a chance to chat. They want blood back. When the choice is between starving and lopping some lord's head—"

Kincaid cleared his throat loudly.

Bink stood and went to the window. Day was sliding into night, a sliver of a moon making its way higher.

"How many men do you have outside?"

Bakeley lolled back in his chair. "Do not worry, brother."

"There are two with the house," Kincaid said. "As well as the coachman and groom who escorted us here, plus our six."

Bink lifted an eyebrow.

"The Scotsmen have returned," Kincaid said.

"And?"

"Those two did break away from the group, but they didn't follow us."

Bink turned back to the window and reexamined his memory of the group on the road. The two men had been dressed just as roughly. They'd grumbled with the others when he'd asked about the demonstration. He could not put his finger on what had made them stand out.

He'd rather have heard they'd been disposed of. "Where did they go?"

Kincaid's jaw moved. "They followed them west and then they lost them."

His hands curled into fists. "*Lost* them?"

The older man grimaced. "They were good, or else lucky."

"And then what, your men doubled back and found us how?"

"I put a man on the road," Stewart said.

"In any case," Bakeley said, "there's no telling if they were Agruen's men. They might have been weavers for all we know. Bink, your men are resting, as should you. We leave at first light for London. Paulette will be safe here."

"And who will see to her safety here?"

"I will." Stewart said, no emotion detectable in his narrow, cold face.

Like bloody hell, you will.

"Well, *you* can't," Bakeley said. "You're needed at the solicitor's office."

"What solicitor's office is that?" The door had opened noiselessly and Paulette stood, her head cocked.

A burst of shame burned Bink's face. Damn Bakeley, and damn himself for being maneuvered into speaking of this with the men before he'd had a chance to talk to her.

He walked up and took her arm. "Have you eaten, love?"

She lifted her chin and let her lips turn up a fraction. "His lordship sent a tray to my room. But I found I wanted more company than my servants." She shook off his arm. "What have we here? Ah yes. A very nice repast. And no extra plate." She sat down in the empty chair and pulled a bowl over. "And no footmen. To preserve your private conversation, no doubt." She reached for a bread plate and piled food on it. "Now what solicitor's office are we visiting?"

Paulette's insides were shaking, but she sawed at the food with utensils that must have been her husband's, as the other gentlemen occupied the other seats at table.

They'd not yet reached their brandy course, but no matter. If they thought they were sending her away, they were mistaken. They would have to physically remove her.

She'd shocked Gibson. Good.

He'd be more shocked before this was over. They'd both married for money, but she was no Smithfield bargain cow to be penned in the barn.

She ignored him and turned her attention to the others. Kincaid frowned. Bakeley looked tongue-tied. His handsome friend's eyes glinted, sending a shiver through her.

She inclined her head to him. "No one has taken the trouble to introduce us, sir, but I surmise you are a friend to Lord Shaldon. I am Paulette Heardwyn."

Her husband's throat-clearing sounded like he had a fish bone stuck. She felt his heat at her shoulder.

"Oh, pardon me. I'm Gibson now. Paulette Heardwyn Gibson."

The man's face didn't move. Bakeley's mouth parted a bit.

Hot anger rose in her. She reached for the glass on the table and took a drink, trying to wash it down.

It was a very good ale and it steadied her. "Who are you, sir? Will no one here have the courtesy to introduce me to this gentleman who is privy to the plans for my inheritance?"

Bakeley sat up straighter. "Paulette—"

"George Stewart is the name he uses," her husband said, in the low rumble that signaled trouble. His anger felt reassuring. She was sure it wasn't directed at her.

And if it was, blast it, she didn't care. "I see." She took another drink. A big hand oozed comfort into her shoulder. She wanted to lean into it.

Instead she froze. No need to encourage him. It was only a trick anyway, trying to woo her compliance. "What are the plans then?"

"You know it's not safe for you in London," Bakeley said.

"But it's safe here?"

"Yes. This is one of my father's safe houses for his people."

"And you will all go to London and leave me here with my two maids."

"No. Of course not. We'll leave the four grooms and Stewart here—"

"No." Bink squeezed her shoulder. "Paulette does not know your man here. And neither do I."

Hope touched her heart.

Bakeley frowned. "You'll be comfortable here. It will be only a matter of days for us to take care of business. Bink will settle with the solicitor. We'll smoke out Agruen and see what he's after, and Bink will be back to reclaim you. In the meantime, you may enjoy yourself. You'll be well guarded. You can walk in the garden. You can even ride within the surrounding woods, providing you take men with you."

"My lord," Kincaid interrupted this pleasant vision.

She'd forgotten his presence. His eyes were not unkind.

"I believe, my lord, it is you who must stay with Mrs. Gibson."

Pink rose in Bakeley's cheeks.

Her breath caught. His father's *valet* held sway over him. Even Stewart had more authority here.

He might be as much under the thumb of these others as she was.

"We'll discuss this later." Bakeley glanced at Paulette and she heard his unfinished words— *after Paulette goes to her chamber*.

Her chair creaked under the weight of Gibson's hand. "Tell us what you know, Bakeley," he said. "What do you know that Paulette and I don't?"

While the silence stretched, she leaned in and refilled her glass, willing her hand not to shake. She took a sip and pushed it away. The ale was too strong. She needed her wits about her. She rose, found the bell pull, yanked on it, and went back to her seat.

A maid appeared. "Bring a pot of tea," Paulette said.

The woman looked at Bakeley, who nodded, and turned.

Heat rose in her and she clenched the edge of the table.

"Just a moment," she called. "Did you know I'm to be the mistress here for the next undetermined amount of time? You'll take instructions from me, you will."

The woman's face paled, but she bobbed a curtsy, said, "yes, madam," and left.

Paulette's head began to pound. None of this was the maid's fault.

"So you'll cooperate," Bakeley said. "You'll stay and not give Bink here any trouble?"

"Bakeley." Bink's voice rumbled dangerously in her ear. "Paulette is my wife, and neither of us are children to be spoken to or about thusly."

Bakeley drummed his fingers on the table, frowning.

"Let us start with a discussion of that trip to the solicitor," Paulette asked. "Do you have plans for my inheritance, Bakeley?"

Bakeley's mouth firmed. "You think I would steal the orphan's mite? Of course not. We are trying to trap a traitor."

"And if I were to not, as you say, *cooperate*, stay here like a good girl, would you deny Mr. Gibson and me the settlement your father promised if we married?"

Bakeley rose and walked to the fireplace. Walked back again. Behind her, Gibson radiated tension. She glanced over her shoulder. He was as hard and as fixed as a statue, jaw clenched, brow furrowed, lips firmed.

"Of course not," Bakeley said.

Confusion swamped her, sweeping away all her moorings, leaving her hollow and alone.

A warm weight touched her shoulder.

No, she was not alone, at least not yet, not until she left for London. And then, in spite of his words now, Bakeley might very well withhold the settlement.

The truth from Lord Shaldon? You might as well hope to get wine from a milk cow.

Bakeley was Shaldon now.

"It does not matter," she whispered. She'd take whatever mite her father had left in trust and use it to find the treasure. Or if she couldn't, if there was no treasure, perhaps she might, if he would still have her, follow her husband to India.

Bink turned glittering eyes on her, eyes sparkling like sunlit amber. Then he offered her his hand.

What would he do? Did he mean to take her to the room and lock her up? Or would he actually speak to her? Or...

No, she must not let the kissing start. She must not. She had to think clearly. She had to rest. She had to escape.

He practically carried her up the stairs, stopping at his room, where he tucked away his razor and snatched up his bag before strong-arming her out the door.

"What are you doing?" she asked. "Where are we going?"

He stopped in the dim corridor and looked both ways. Someone had lit a lamp near the stairs.

"Which room is yours?"

His voice, husky and ragged, sent chills through her. He was upset about what she'd said. He thought she'd married him for the money. Which she had. And he'd known that. So why was he angry now? And what would he do?

She'd seen what he'd done to Agruen and Cummings. Fear traced a path down her spine.

"Why?" she asked.

He must have felt the trembling she'd been fighting because his grip on her arm eased. "We're going to have that conversation you've been wanting."

Such an inconvenient time for her vocal cords to freeze.

His face moved closer, his eyes glowing golden in the light. "We're going to conspire together," he said, and dropped a kiss on her nose.

"Oh." She expelled the word on a puff of air. They would conspire.

Her eyes slid to the stairs leading up to the third floor. She had already conspired earlier with Jenny, who had promised to send Mabel to bed and go and find clothing. If she appeared now with a suit of boy's clothing, the timing was inopportune.

"They put you a floor up from me?"

His voice was rumbling again. "Yes. Like a story our man Jock told me about a girl named Rapunzel, confined to a tower."

His lips firmed. "We'll see about that. Lead the way."

She hurried up the stairs, his hand still attached to her elbow, the connection melting away her anxiety.

It was always like that with him—comforting, exciting. Still, she would need to get rid of him.

Or she could put him to sleep. After so many days in the saddle, whatever bit of rest he'd enjoyed hadn't been enough.

At the door of her room, his hand found the small of her back. A shot of pure animal awareness coursed through her, sending her breath into short little gasps.

She closed her eyes, caught her breath, and shook herself.

She didn't have time to make love. She needed to plan her escape and gather her things. Jenny would come soon with whatever clothing and information she'd found. The time for her to leave was now, tonight.

The bedchamber was empty—Mabel had gone to bed after all, thank heavens. A small lamp burned low on the table where her mother's ornate hair brush and comb were arranged. She would bring only the comb. Nor would she need any of her clothes.

The door closed behind them, and he pulled her into a kiss that melted away all thoughts of packing. His bag plopped on the floor, while his lips, so firm and determined, sent shivers through her.

She opened for him, her tongue twining with his, while his arm locked around her and he brought her so close there was no space between them anywhere. Pleasure drummed through her, sending warmth spiraling. His hard shaft poked at her through her skirts.

Perhaps one very quick tumble and then he would fall sound asleep. Perhaps after so many days on the road it would take only one go around.

His fingers raked through her coiffure, sending a cascade of pins and combs, and she clutched at his strong neck, returning the favor by running her fingers through his hair.

Kisses trailed along her cheek, down her jaw, over her neck, melting her insides. And then he paused, and she heard the scratch at the door.

"Enter."

The door opened. His gruffness would scare many servants away, but not Jenny.

She took in the scene, bobbed a curtsey, and hefted Paulette's bundled dress. "I've brushed off your gown, miss. Shall I come back later?"

"No," Bink said, and "Yes" Paulette said, both at the same time.

He groaned, and before Paulette could stop him, grabbed the bundle from Jenny, slammed the door, and tossed the dress on a chair where it fell to the floor and unrolled, spilling out dark trousers, coats and a shirt.

She spun him around, praying he hadn't seen the garments, and pulled him back into that passionate kiss. He took the kiss deep, worked her skirts up, and found the opening in her drawers.

She choked at the feel of his fingers.

"Unfasten me," he groaned, pushing her back against the closed door.

She reached for his coat, and a low rumble told her he'd meant his fall.

Her fingers were clumsy; her mind filled with the need to dissemble, her body filled with his fingers working into her, her heart filled with such a wish to trust and be trusted, she thought she might burst.

She pushed down the top of his trousers and wrapped a hand around his stout shaft. Gasping, his eyes fluttered closed, his free arm braced the door frame, his big chest collapsed against her, and they were one union of grunting, panting, and moaning.

Then he was shoving at her skirts and lifting her. She guided him through the slit in her drawers, and moaned when he filled her.

So wet from him, she was. He had that power, to wring her dry, to fill her again, a power that built with each drive into her until she shattered and he bellowed his own release.

They stood, joined, braced against the door, for longer minutes than they'd needed to achieve that climax, until she felt his muscles tremble from the weight of holding her. She unlocked her ankles and slid down.

And remembered the trousers and shirts spread across the floor.

"Oh, my. That was..." She straightened her gown and forced her hand to her heart when it wanted to wander back under her skirts. She did not want to stop. She did not want to put her attention back to leaving. Perhaps he didn't want to leave either. Perhaps they should both stay here for several more days. "You must be exhausted. Do you want to sleep here?"

He tipped her chin up and kissed her nose again, his handsome face wrinkling into a curious examination. His was a strong face, the face of a man one could rely on.

Unless that was the last strong face one saw before being locked in a manor house.

But what had he said earlier about conspiring? She sorted through her sluggish brain to try to remember what had happened before he'd so thoroughly muddled her.

"Let's get you out of this dress." When his fingers flew to the lacings in the back of her gown, warmth rippled anew. They would make love again. Yes, she wanted that. It had not taken long. There would be plenty of time to carry out her plan.

She slipped the dress off, stepped out of it, and he helped her out of her stays and her chemise and drawers until all that remained were her stockings.

She stepped close, touched her breasts to his waistcoat and her lips to his neck.

"Ah, lass," he said. "You're hungry for more."

She stilled. Was he criticizing?

"As am I. Ravenous. For you." He stroked her cheek and looked at her.

She suddenly felt her nakedness. "You are too tired. Let me get my chemise."

"No. I mean, tired I am, but my willingness is not in question. What's in question is time."

"I see." He wanted to sleep. He was leaving within hours.

"And we haven't done our conspiring yet."

"Oh."

"Yes, oh." He set her back and everywhere his gaze touched her, she burned. When his eyes finally settled on her face, they glowed with a dark humor. "We need to talk, yes, and we need to see if those trousers and coats will fit you."

Chapter Twenty

His bride's face all but thundered, a momentary flash of lightning streaking across her dark pupils, quickly and poorly obscured by a look of aplomb that didn't hide her lack of innocence.

What she would say was bound to entertain. If they survived this, they could have years of fun together, him and his Paulette.

When we survive this. He would not let any harm come to her.

She rattled her top teeth against the bottom, worrying over her words. "What did you have in mind, Bink?"

Now he was to be Bink, ah, but she was trying to distract him, clever girl. He trailed a finger down her chest, over the swell of one sweet breast, across the puckered nipple and down again. "How did you think to hide these?"

A tremor went through her and he wrapped her closer. She was not cold, his Paulette, just wonderfully responsive.

"They're not so big."

"Only a woman would say that. But here's what will happen with the first man you see. A glance at this pert nose." He touched her there. "And then right to the chest for more evidence. You'll have to pull your hat low, bind these." He palmed her breast. "And make sure your coat is buttoned."

She broke free, ran to the clothes on the floor and snatched up the gnarly shirt.

"And we shall work on your walk also."

The shirt settled over her head and she strode back to him, swinging her arms.

He laughed. "Better." Leaning close he sniffed. The shirt had been laundered recently. Thank the heavens he wouldn't have to smell another man's sweat on her.

He set a hand on her shoulder and she covered it with hers. "Now we talk," she said.

"You were going to leave."

Her chin jutted out. "*You* were going to leave. You were going to lock me up and leave me."

"Is that what you think? You thought I would leave you here, alone, unprotected, with one of Shaldon's jackanape, lying, cut-throats, and go chasing after some supposed sum of money left you by your father?"

Her eyes widened. "You don't think there's money?"

"Oh yes, I imagine there's some. Not enough to cause so much excitement. I think there's something else. Something Spellen would search your room for. Have you thought more about what it might be?"

She bit her lip and looked away, holding back.

She still didn't trust him.

"There's nothing. Agruen took my ring years ago, and if he's still searching it's obvious that was worthless to him. There's nothing else of her. Well, except for the knife and the letter."

And there was nothing in that letter.

He knew. He'd read it after she'd given it to him to hold, and he'd gone through the rest of her things before they'd left Gretna.

Her bags contained nothing but clothing and a few personal items. No false linings, no secret compartments.

The same was true of the small wooden lap desk where an unsigned silly rhyme in her father's stiff hand had been stowed between some blank sheets of paper, a pencil, playing cards, a tiny sewing kit, and a cheap travel guide.

"Finish dressing and let's see if you need any alterations. Does Mabel know your plans?"

"No."

"Best leave it at that."

He watched her struggle with the trousers, long locks of hair dangling and getting caught.

The hair was an issue also. There was just so damn much of its loveliness.

She tucked in the shirt and fastened the trousers.

"They'll do." He patted his coat. "I'll keep hold of your mother's letter. Is there anything else here you can't bear to part with?"

Her eyes lit on the blasted lap desk he'd helped her to rescue from the tree and from Cummings. She'd hauled it all over England and Scotland since then.

"I'm sending one of Hackwell's men back to him. We'll pack that along to Greencastle for safekeeping."

"It's a small thing. I can stow it into a saddle bag."

"Traveling by horse, are we? Fine. We'll strap it on somehow and have a game of piquet when we stop for our dinner."

Her grin made his heart swell. No doubt it was foolish to take her, but he knew he couldn't leave her here.

She pressed against him in a tight hug. "Thank you, husband."

She wasn't strong enough to push the breath from him, yet it took him moments to be able to speak.

"I can't work out what the devil is truly going on, Paulette. I don't think Bakeley knows either, but Shaldon did, and Kincaid...well, he might or might not. Bloody damn spies with their games and their lies—they don't even share the truth with each other. I don't know why any of this would involve you. All I know is, I don't want to lose you."

She gripped him tighter, all womanly sinews and soft strength, her breasts swelling against him, reminding him they would need to be bound, and he must get at least an hour of sleep. And load his pistols. Ah. He'd not had a chance to train her.

"I do wish I'd had time to show you how to manage a pistol."

"But I know already."

He set her back. "How?" Jealousy sparked in him, and then he remembered—if her mother was truly a spy, perhaps she'd learned it from her and not from another man.

"Jock taught me."

"Jock."

"Yes. He was an old man, a friend of my father and mother, who came to live with us. He was a spy, too. He taught me many things, and told me stories about her."

"He taught you how to load a pistol?"

"Yes. And to shoot. He taught me how to swim if I fell overboard, like he had. And a bit about knives." She grinned. "And lock picking." She took up her jackets. "Shall I finish dressing?"

"Try on the coats."

The waistcoat was tight at her breasts, but it buttoned. The jacket was big, thank the Lord.

"Now, have you scissors in your sewing kit?" he asked.

She cocked her head, nodded, and went to get them.

Bink made a show of swinging his lamp as he strode through the dark corridors and the shadowy stable yard, and Paulette scooted around in the gloomy perimeter with the bags he'd had her carry.

It was proof they would travel light, as they must. If she was to play a gentry groom, she'd have to heft his kit and her own, at least when they were around others.

And he would not be sure they weren't around others until he'd cleared this manor by many miles.

Bakeley's coachman came into his circle of light and greeted him.

"Any report?" Bink asked.

"Nay." The big man matched the quiet of Bink's question.

"What of the grounds?"

"I've a boy near the gate."

"And the others?"

"Getting sleep, sir." He sounded weary, as if he envied the others. That was to Bink's advantage. "Found cots for them in the servants' quarters. His Lordship wants them rested afore you leave." He glanced at the sky. "A couple more hours, I reckon."

Bink looked up also, hiding a great look of glee. The grooms and guards were in the house, not stretched on a blanket in the stable loft. Not having to saddle the horses quietly was a boon. He had a timepiece to gauge the hours, and knew every second would count if he and Paulette were to have a head start. Galloping cross-country in the dark was out of the question.

Trickery wasn't. He took a long breath. What he had in mind, wouldn't take long.

"There's a fire in the hearth, and bread on the board. Go have a hot cup and something to eat and a rest. I'll watch out here."

Bink helped Paulette up into the saddle and handed her his reins. "One more thing," he whispered.

"Shouldn't we leave soon?" she hissed.

He'd reminded her there were times a soldier nodded agreement, even in the dark. There were times when a soldier didn't talk. It had been a difficult lesson for her. The sooner he had her away from here, the better.

He'd opened the stalls and the horses had already started to mill. He'd stopped short of leaving the stable door open—it went against his grain to endanger the animals. Yet if Bakeley's men had to run through the fields to catch an errant horse, they'd be slower still. He didn't think he would hang for it.

He patted her leg and shushed her. "I'll be right back."

A branch crackled nearby and he froze. His hand went to the pistol at his waist.

Johnny stepped out of the brush, and Bink's breathing eased a fraction.

"Sir." The darkness almost swallowed the greeting, but Bink could see the man touch his cap.

Though Johnny had agreed to come work at Little Norwick, though he'd made his claim upon

Paulette's jolly maid, Johnny had been Bakeley's groom, which meant he'd been Shaldon's, and Shaldon's men might not truly shift loyalty so easily.

On the other hand, all spies were liars and some could be bought, and the affections of Paulette's maid might just be the price. He mustn't give up.

"Well, Johnny?"

"Horses is all out of their stalls." He still spoke in a hush. "Hmm. Don't know how it happened but I'll see to them. Should take a good while. Won't bother the others."

He could hear Paulette's excited breath, too loud, behind him. "See to it then. Quietly. And thank you."

Johnny saluted. "Overheard there's a third man at watch in the line of trees just off the meadow they didn't want you to know. I can keep secrets too. You and this boy here take care."

"Mabel." Paulette's voice came softly.

"Don't worry yourself, lad. She's a tough bird, as is that young one."

Johnny disappeared into the darkness.

"Can we trust *him*," she breathed.

"Aye. I believe so."

"Will they hurt him?"

Hurt Johnny? "No."

He took the reins and led them off down the edge of a hedgerow to the back of the property. Paulette was an inexperienced rider, and the horses untried. He would walk this part of the journey until the shadows started to lift and they'd reached a road.

It required concentration but still wasn't enough to distract from her question. *Will they hurt him?*

His brother wouldn't, he was quite sure. But he wasn't sure his brother was the man in charge.

Paulette's mount stumbled and he heard her stifled gasp. Johnny had Ewan, Mabel was stubborn, and Jenny resourceful. He must trust them to fate and put his attention on his own lady and the way ahead.

Paulette stretched her legs and rested her back against the gnarled bark of a huge oak tree. The branches above offered some protection from a drizzly rain that colored the afternoon grey and kept her miserably damp. A thorough soaking might have been preferable.

Bink handed her a flask. "Have a swig. How's the backside?"

It ached like the devil, now the numbness had waned, but she refused to whine.

"The polite term is *derriere*. And it is excellent." She lifted the flask to her lips.

"Indeed it is."

Choking, she looked up into his grin.

"Perhaps I should massage it for you anyway."

Heat curled through her, and an answering smile threatened. "You cannot be rubbing your servant boy's bottom in the bushes off a public byway." She handed him the flask and gripped his arm to haul herself up. "Should we not be going?"

He looped an arm around her waist and nuzzled her. "There's no one about."

The journey had gone well so far. She'd proved herself a good enough horsewoman, or else his choice of horse had been inspired. In any case, she doubted her backside was much sorer than his must be.

If Bakeley's men were in pursuit, they surely were miles behind.

The rattle of wheels loosed Bink's arm. He nudged her back further into the brush where the horses rested.

A cart went by, a dark woman clad all in black driving a spry little horse—quite different than the farmers and drovers they'd met more than once. In the box, a man lolled, only the back of his hat visible.

Her skin prickled, her nerves jigging like the barroom full of boys in their cups at the inn where they'd stopped for food late the last night.

She couldn't say why. They were not far from London, in a country area of gabled cottages and produce farms. The woman was traveling towards the way they'd just come, so she wouldn't be Bakeley's.

And surely Agruen would not have a woman in his employ.

Agruen hated women.

She reached for Bink's hand, smoothing her thumb across the calloused knuckle. He should be wearing his gloves.

His big fingers wrapped around hers. "I'll get you there safely."

The weight of worry had grown worse, Agruen's men, and now Bakeley's, would be following them.

Bink always seemed to sense what she was feeling, and always managed to lift the trouble, to keep it hoisted so it didn't crush her. He'd done that from the start, first with Agruen, then with Cummings, and now—now who was she running from, truly?

She shook off her nerves and leaned into him. In fact, her husband's knack for knowing her had begun earlier, with Bakeley's announcement of their inducement to marriage. And the thought of how that situation had changed made her smile.

"Up with you then." He helped her into the saddle, and she bent and dropped a quick kiss under his hat brim, hitting his ear.

He flattened his palm along her thigh, a great slab of warmth moving higher. Steam should be rising from her damp trousers, as it was in her eyes. She sniffed.

His hand stopped. "What's this?"

She let out a slow breath, taming the quiver inside her.

She'd found love. She loved Bink. Bink, the tough bastard, Bink, the kind gentleman. Both men. She loved them both.

She cleared her throat. "A great drop plopped on me from the branch up there." She pointed at the offending limb. "Hit me square in the eye."

His long look turned her incipient tears into vapor. On a drier day, on a more secluded road, in a proper dress that could be discreetly lifted—and didn't she now see the advantages of dresses for ladies?—he would have had her against the trunk of that oak tree.

The thought brought back her smile. "We should get to this house of Lady Hackwell's. Does it have a bedroom?"

He mounted his horse. "As her steward, I've had occasion to inspect the place. And yes, it does."

Bink led them out onto the road, now empty as far as he could see. It was fitting the master should lead the way, and he'd kept an ear tuned to the horse clopping at his rear flank.

She'd done well, his Paulette. Though whether she would be truly his upon receipt of whatever secret had been hidden for her—and by her—remained to be seen.

And anyway, they were not out of danger yet. That ancient cart had more than niggled at him. The man lolling in the back could be any laborer, but there was something familiar about him. The woman driving he'd seen in profile. She looked to be a Rom, but the dress was wrong, too well-made for the rest of the setup. Perhaps she was a Spaniard, or a Frog. And he'd seen a woman like her at one of the inn stops the day before.

He shook his head. The dress, the posture, the demeanor of that woman had been different. And in the decades since the Terror, there were more than a few dark-haired women tripping through the English countryside.

He glanced back to where Paulette sat tall and straight. Ah, that was it. The woman on the cart, the woman at the inn, they both reminded him of his Paulette.

Paulette's coats outlined twin flattened mounds. It wasn't in her to round her shoulders, but he would remind her to slump. They would arrive in London in the busy evening traffic. With luck, no one would take much notice of a rube and his boy.

Chapter Twenty-One

A scant mile back on the path trod by the big red-haired man and his retainer, the dark haired woman stopped her cart in the narrowest section of road. She handed a mallet to the man in the back.

The cart bed shimmied and pitched as they both climbed down, the mare rolling her eyes in a foolish fashion.

"*Cálmate, querida cora—*" She caught herself and stroked the horse's nose.

She had slipped from the English. She did not usually do that. Seeing the girl with the besotted man she'd taken as a lover was making her heart ache just a bit. How foolish they both were, like this lovely horse, not knowing that she, Mrs. Nichols, was here to help them.

She went to work on the tack, ignoring the man's stare, while keeping an eye on his movements. He was one of two ruffians she'd hired for a great deal of money.

She clucked her tongue at the horse as she worked, and led her away from the traces. The cart dipped on the shafts.

"Now," she said.

He grinned, smashing at the spokes, destroying one wheel and pushing the cart on its side, blocking the road completely. Shaldon's noble son would stop for this cart. He would wonder if the girl had been on it.

The brute picked up the mallet and approached. She slid a hand into a pocket and he stopped, a sly grin revealing yellowed, gapped teeth. "Is there aught else, Mrs. Nichols?"

As a *nom de guerre*, Mrs. Nichols was working out well. A dropping of the eyelids, a turn down of the lips, a ducking of the head, and no one questioned a soldier's foreign widow, especially not one so clearly struggling to, as the English said, *keep up appearances*. There *had* been those sideways looks, filled with speculation. After all, she was today a Frenchwoman, and not so far past the breeding age.

However, she'd seen right away, with all the laborers traipsing about, she'd stick out following the girl's path from Scotland.

She whipped her hand out, a coin flying at him. The mallet fell softly, and he snatched up the bit of silver. "That's the rest of your payment."

Mouth curling, his gaze on her narrowed. The smaller of the two men, he'd come along for this last bit of work.

After he'd used that mallet on his comrade.

Another coin flew. "And this for that extra bit of trouble."

He rubbed both coins together. "An' how 'bout an extra bit of summat else?"

These English men were no different than the Spanish, no different than the French, no different than the Portuguese, the Austrians, the Italians, the Belgians.

Men were men, and it was blissful they could not see past the shape of her bosom.

"Here we are, all alone," he growled.

She brought out the pistol, making him smirk.

"Here now. Don't want to use that. They'll hear the blast in the next county and come running."

"Oh." She let her voice and hand quiver. "You are most certainly right."

He stepped closer, and she edged back, the brush at the side of the road catching her skirts. Her boot slipped in a muddy patch and she went down on one knee, the pistol hitting the soft dirt a yard from her.

His cackle cracked the silence, his eyes flitting between her and the gun.

"There now," he said. "Knew we'd come to an agreement." He nudged the gun aside with his foot and began fumbling with his fall. "Lift up your skirts and let's have a go."

She edged further down the embankment, closer to the overgrown hedge of a farmer's field. "I've already paid you."

"Well, you're a little bit more, aren't you, a little thing like you. And then there's the rest of them coins in your—"

He choked, eyes widening, and grabbed for his throat where the dagger had stuck. He jerked at it, sending an arc of blood over the damp ground, and fell forward, releasing the blade.

She watched until the twitching stopped.

Oh yes, she was at a prime age to take charge of those who crossed her path. Or who crossed her.

She frowned, bent for the weapons, and retrieved her coins. Except for those very few, who would see through the game she played? There were two such in *this* group of the girl's pursuers. In the other group—bah, Agruen was a snake in his own adder pit. His retainers had no loyalty. One only had to find the key and the right way to twist it. Money usually, or sometimes a swiving. She had little of the first and would not give away the latter, but she would think of something.

She considered moving the man into the brush and decided against it. Let them find him splattered along the road. His presence would be yet one more distraction.

She dragged the saddle that had fallen from the cart bed. The mare eyed her and ducked her head twice.

"Ah, this is what you like, clever girl." She stroked the long nose. "If I could I would take you home with me."

The horse pranced and shook, accepting the saddle, and allowing herself to be led into a thicket, where Mrs. Nichols stripped out of her gown, tied on a neck cloth and mounted.

Paulette strode confidently next to Bink, balancing their gear at both sides, goggling like the rustic she was pretending to be.

She'd never seen so many people in one place at one time. Bink had insisted it would be like this until well into the wee hours, and then had told her to shut up, quite rudely, because they'd been passing some men on the street, and it was his way of making her duck her head.

Along the way he'd explained the geography—Hampstead, and Mayfair, the East End, and the City, just as though he was talking to an ignorant servant boy.

The City was where they would go tomorrow to visit Mr. Tellingford, the solicitor who held her trust. Her trustees were no longer part of her mission. She was married now, and the trust was ended. Their marriage had been recorded at Gretna, and Bink had the proof stored away in a pocket. That much she knew.

She caught the eye of a well-dressed young lady no older than herself and quickly dropped her eyes and her shoulders.

He'd explained she must slump and act servile. That was why he'd saddled her with carrying the small satchels that weren't truly heavy yet were making her arms ache.

"How much further, master?" She pitched her voice lower. They'd walked for miles, it seemed, since checking their horses in at a stable.

"Shush, boy."

They turned a corner. Bink stopped abruptly and entered a store. It was a gentleman's store, thank the Lord. Had it been one of the ladies' shops they'd passed, she would have been taxed beyond all ability to not ooh and ah.

The shop clerk approached and asked if he could help them.

"My Lord's arrival from the country is imminent, and he wants his manservants in new livery."

She'd heard Bink adopt this clipped aristocratic accent before, but never with so long a nose, as if he was his Lordship himself. He'd wiped the haughty look right off the clerk's face, and explained the hideous coating of road dust they both bore, all in one sentence. For all his dislike of spies, perhaps he'd done some spying himself. She must ask him.

"I've hired a tailor for the coats and the trousers, but the other garments—"

"Certainly, we can help you. And this will be for Lord..."

Bink studied a display of linens. "How quickly can you deliver?"

Perspiration dotted the man's brow. "We have the largest stock in London and tailors at the ready. I could fit out your boy here tonight. Er, how many servants are we speaking about?"

"Four footmen, two houseboys, six grooms, and the butler of course."

"You are not the butler?"

The gaze he leveled the man would wither the bark off a tree. "I am his Lordship's steward."

The man took a step back and bowed. "Of course, of course. Er, which lord is it?"

"You will know that when I return, tomorrow or the next day." Bink handed him a coin. "For your trouble. Now show us your back exit."

The man blinked twice.

Bink handed him another coin. "I shall give you the sale when I return. I shall ask for you."

What passed just then, Paulette wasn't sure, but the man's face went blank and he beckoned them to follow him.

The alley outside was fetid and smelly and darkly shadowed.

Apprehension ate at her gut, just as Jock had described in the stories he'd told, and her tired muscles started to rebel.

Bink took the packages from her and nudged her close to the wall. There was no one around, but later, she imagined this alley would be quite dangerous.

"There are watchers," he said in a whisper no louder than a breath.

Watchers. On the street. So they must be close, yet they could not go there. Unless...

"The back way?"

She felt his head shake, and with it, she felt his worry.

"An inn?"

Another shake of the head. Of course. They'd talked about that. Agruen would check every inn and public lodging. He'd have spies there, looking for them.

"Do you trust me, love?" he whispered.

"Of course." The words were out before she could think, and that made her want to laugh.

"I've just the place." He squeezed her hand. "I'll explain on the way."

Bink's gaze swept the alley as they progressed through it. There was no one about, not hidden under a beggar's pile, or behind a crate. No sign of life whatsoever. Later, when full dark fell, there would be plenty of action, there on that rack of boxes, or there, in that recessed doorway.

He pushed back the fear threatening to swamp him. He must channel it into his muscles, like he'd done before battle. This wasn't so different. The boy watching the street might not have been Agruen's, yet he'd lit a warning flare in that sixth sense Bink had honed so well in Zebediah Gibson's home, in school, and later on the Peninsula.

He led her around, through a series of mews and across into a street, reckoning they'd reached Bloomsbury. Paulette accepted the small bag with her box stoically and kept pace with him. It would be a long walk, though as a country woman, she'd probably walked farther than this every day going back and forth to the village.

He spotted no lurkers about in the street, but kept the pace brisk, checking at corners for more watchers. To her credit, she kept silent. He could see the wheels of her mind turning like the inner workings of a clock, wondering what he'd spotted, what she'd missed, what she should look for.

She trusted him. She'd said that without hesitation, in a way that made his blood soar. And he doubted she was thinking about where they would stay. It would be yet another new experience for her if Betty took them in.

And he would have a great deal of explaining to do.

Paulette's feet ached and her stockings bunched in the heels of her boots. She did not want to complain though.

"This is Mayfair," Bink said, still speaking quietly though the walkers had thinned.

She glanced at the large townhouses. At this hour, Bink said, people were dressing for sumptuous dinners, the ladies in fine gowns, the men in their brocaded waistcoats, like the ones they'd seen in the shop windows. Hunger uncurled in her stomach, and the dogged fatigue lifted with a surge of anticipation.

"We're going to the Hackwells'?"

"No. We'll seek help from another of her ladyship's acquaintances."

"Her friend from the children's home? Lady...ah, what was her name?"

His silence lasted past a row of carriages, the horses being held by liveried men, their presence distracting her. She checked each in turn in what she hoped passed for rustic awe, surreptitiously looking for evidence of Agruen. Danger seemed nowhere, and everywhere, her ignorance was so grave. Jock hadn't prepared her for this.

They'd reached a square edged with great houses before he again spoke. "Friends of Annabelle Harris might find succor at places high or low. Where we're going happens to be one of the low ones."

The houses were far too grand to be low, but she kept her own counsel and followed him. They came at last to a lane where the houses were, indeed, smaller, closer, yet still genteel. He passed it, turned into yet another back alley, and went on to a plain wooden gate.

She'd tried to store their itinerary in her head, but she was hopelessly lost. She must learn her way around London's byways, if she was to spend time here with any sort of freedom.

Bink put his ear to the gate, and she copied him. The alley was deserted, quiet, and a good deal cleaner than the ones they had passed through earlier, and there was no noise within.

He opened the gate and they slipped inside.

Paulette looked around. This patch of flagstones and flowers was the first London residence she'd seen on the inside.

Lovely, it was. Someone with an eye for color and balance had put forth an effort here. There, where roses made a heroic late summer burst, and there, where a patch of daisies budded tightly next to a showy phlox. Even her quiet mother would have exclaimed over this.

An outbuilding hugged the walls that hemmed everything in, this small bit of nature in a raucous city. Her mother would have loved the flowers, but she would have hated the smallness of it.

She struggled for a breath and tried to quell a dawning realization. She *was* a country woman, used to fields and byways, glens and brooks, stretches of ash hedges and thick stands of elm.

Confinement to this space would leave her permanently breathless.

A strong arm wrapped her and rolled her in to a broad chest. Bink stroked over her queue of hair cinched by a thin ribbon, where he'd lopped a full twelve inches with the scissors he'd reached for without searching—because he'd known they were in her case, because he'd poked through it himself earlier, when she wasn't looking. Of course he had.

She'd chosen to defer the talk about that until later.

She lifted her chin and searched his face. He was as anxious as herself. That she should know him so well, that he'd help carry her troubles...

She dropped her gaze to his wide chest and blinked hard, her courage swelling.

"This house," he still spoke in his gruff whisper, "used to be home to Lady Hackwell's sister. The woman who lives here now was a friend to the sister and, in a manner of speaking, a friend to Lady Hackwell." He dropped his bag and gripped both of her shoulders. "I have only ever visited the establishment on Lord Hackwell's business. I have never been here... otherwise."

Blood drummed in her ears. The lady must be another high-in-the-instep matron, another who would be turning cartwheels when she learned Bink was the son of an earl, and not just any earl but the anciently titled, incredibly wily, powerfully influential, Earl of Shaldon.

"Who's there?" The voice was gruff, and when the man came out of the shadowy gangway, knife in hand, Bink whipped her around, gripping her tighter.

She peered around him and saw a tall, thin man, with a horribly scarred visage.

"Sergeant Gibson?"

Bink's hold eased. "Rowland," he growled.

In three strides the man was upon them, saluting, face grim, his eyes fixed on Bink.

She stepped out, and he dragged his gaze to her. He looked. Blinked. His eyes widened and his mouth dropped.

"Who's about tonight?" Bink asked.

The man's mouth flapped again but no sound came out.

"I haven't mollied on you, Rowland. This is my wife and we're in danger. Do you remember Josiah Dickson?"

Rowland's face twisted into a gargoyle's glare. "Aye."

"So who's about tonight?"

"No one, nor will there be anyone. Mrs. Townsend sent all of the ladies down to Hastings to take the sea air for a few days."

All of the ladies.

Paulette's brain worked through the meaning. Lady Hackwell ran a home for children, so perhaps this was a home for women who were in distress or ill. And wounded ex-soldiers.

She was not sure that would be so safe. Lady Hackwell's philanthropic concerns could be found by Agruen and Bakeley, and as easily watched.

"Here now," Rowland wiped the knife off on his gloves, tucked it into a sheath, and picked up a bunch of cut roses.

She realized it had been a pruning knife, though no less deadly in this man's hands. How else had he survived the terrible wound that marred what had once been a handsome face? "Your lady's fair exhausted. Give me your bags, and we'll go and see Mrs. Townsend.

Chapter Twenty-Two

Now they were in the safety of a private establishment, Bink felt at liberty to tuck Paulette close.

He'd forgotten Rowland had found a place here. Betty's clients were gentlemen, and not so above the common that more than one porter was required. Rowland's face alone, burned by a cannon burst, usually put drunks on the right path, with no need for fists.

In the kitchen, a cook stirred a large pot, while a maid worked at a table—two more to worry about. Though both lived in, were not likely to remember him, and were, in an establishment like this, bribable.

Rowland deposited them in the tidy parlor Bink had visited before. It was stuffy, the sunset and August heat filling the room with otherwise invisible dust motes. He watched Paulette circling, examining the tasteful chairs and settees.

"Is this one of her ladyship's shelters?" She turned questioning eyes on him, innocent eyes.

The words stuck in his throat, and by the time he dislodged them it was too late. The door opened and Betty swept in.

Paulette's gaze went to the woman at the door. Tall and handsome, she was plainly dressed and coiffed, but rouge painted her lips and cheeks, and her bodice was cut so shockingly low it revealed all but her nipples.

"Sergeant Gibson." A smile lit her face and she curtsied, as if he were the only man in the universe.

Jealousy sparked in her and threatened to burst through her fists. The woman was flirting with Bink, her husband. He, in return, was bowing, his hat clutched in his hand, the unruly hair at the back of his neck damp from the stifling heat. Paulette squared her shoulders and clomped over next to him.

She was treated to the same warm smile and curtsy, which settled her ire but inspired a new problem. To curtsy or bow, she wasn't sure, and the momentary confusion put her more out of place.

"Mrs. Townsend, may I introduce my wife, Paulette."

Mrs. Townsend took her hand and poured all of her formidable charm over it, scattering the jealousy. The lady oozed compassion. She must be a highly skilled nurse for the residents here. Her dress was odd, but she'd heard it said town ladies were given to scandalous décolletage.

Bink had stayed away from the house, only visiting on Lord Hackwell's business, for propriety's sake. The one man here was too scarred to be a threat to the shelter's residents, but a man like her husband, well, rumors would start.

"So lovely you are, even playing a boy, gentlemen would be smitten. And I can see there is a story here, one you may not wish to share, and that is all right. The ladies are gone and we are all having a little holiday here also, just me, Rowland, the cook and Trish. I'm afraid it will be bread, soup and cold meat tonight, some sweet punch with our dinner that we can fortify with a good brandy, if you wish, or perhaps you would prefer ale, Sergeant Gibson? Meanwhile, I have a wholly unoccupied room. One of the girls left last week to be married, imagine? Come along and you can refresh yourselves before dinner. I'll have water sent up."

Mrs. Townsend was already out the door, and Bink's hand was on Paulette's elbow, so she went.

"I don't have a proper dress for dinner, ma'am."

Mrs. Townsend smiled. "We are all at our leisure here. But if you are more comfortable in a dress, I believe I can assist you."

They went up a flight of stairs and down a long corridor.

How many ladies actually lived here, Paulette wondered. There were multiple doors. The rooms must be as small as a nun's cell.

Mrs. Townsend opened the door and swept into a room. Red curtains drenched the window and wide bed. The chair was upholstered in red, the carpeting red. The mantelpiece had been painted a dark burgundy.

There was so much red the room was on fire.

When she looked up, Mrs. Townsend was staring at her. Bink wouldn't meet her eyes.

"You didn't explain, Sergeant Gibson?"

Fear spiked through her, as hot as the flames of this room. Her hands started to numb. She took a step back.

He grabbed her hand. "No, Paulette. You'll not be confined here, and you've no reason to fear Betty Townsend. We'll only stay the one night, visit the solicitor, and then go on to Hackwell House or somewhere else safe. What Betty means is...what I didn't tell you is, this is a...a..."

"A brothel." Mrs. Townsend's voice was kind and held no shame. "I do not deny it. And I do not lock young women up against their will. Trish will be up in a moment." She nodded and closed the door on her way out.

Paulette plopped on the chair. A brothel. Her husband had brought her to a brothel to keep her safe. The feeling returned to her hands and she rubbed at her eyes. His words raced through her mind. He had been here twice, and only on Lord Hackwell's business.

Her eyes started to tear and a laugh bubbled up in her, and soon she was both laughing and crying. Strong arms came around her, lifted her out of the chair and cradled her.

"Paulette, Paulette, do not cry love."

She felt his lips on her forehead, and eyes, and hands. "Oh, Bink, Sergeant Gibson." More laughter, peals of it, uncontrollable like her tears. "A whorehouse. You brought your wife to a whorehouse."

"You are laughing and crying."

"Yes." She snorted.

He tightened his embrace. "It was the best I could think of. I'd hoped to sneak up the back stairs to an attic room, but it's even better no one was here. The servants are used to keeping secrets, and Rowland is a good man in a fight."

"Did you bring a clean neck cloth?"

His grin lit up his face. He unwound the loosely tied cloth and handed it to her.

She blew her nose and took a deep sniff of the cloth. It was damp, and the smell of his sweat made her yearn for him. She turned her lips to the thick cords of his now bare neck.

His back stiffened, and though her bottom bumped his hard arousal, she sensed his wariness.

She was starting to know him. The maid would arrive soon. Plus, he was exhausted. She put a hand on his fall.

"Yes," he said and tipped her back, nuzzling her neck and sending her into fresh giggles.

A knock on the door made him lift her.

"Don't stop," she said, "I'm sure they are used to it."

"Come in." He smacked a kiss on her forehead, set her on her feet, and went to the door, where he took the two steaming buckets of water from the scrawny maid.

He poured water into the basin, and the maid returned moments later with linens and a dress made of fine figured muslin.

"Thank you, Trish." He pressed a coin into the maid's hand. She mumbled a thanks and left without ever making eye contact with either of them.

Paulette stripped off her jacket. "You know her name."

"Only through Lady Hackwell. She got Trish the position here." He pulled out the hem of her shirt, yanked it over her head, and then went to work on her cloth bindings. "Let's set these girls free, shall we?"

That bud of desire melted, oozing toward her middle.

"Betty won't care about your breasts stretching your coat during dinner."

"Or that dress she sent up? I spot a chemise but no stays. And I wonder if it will be cut quite as low as the one she was wearing."

"Then we'll stuff the cloth in the bodice to cover you. I won't have another man ogling my wife."

"Perhaps I should have stuffed some stays into my writing case."

He grunted as the binding slipped away and turned her to face him. The band of gold in his eyes narrowed as he did his own ogling, and she felt that heat all the way to the spot between her legs.

"Thank goodness. They are unharmed." His eyes lifted to hers. "Why is that lap desk so important to you?"

While his eyes held hers, his finger touched her breast and circled it. She closed her eyes and let the sensation wash through her.

"We have time before dinner, I think."

"Why, love? Why the lap desk?"

She could almost not think. She was tired and hungry and so needy she felt she would burst. And it was not a secret. There were no secrets with him.

Well, almost no secrets. She hadn't told him Jock's stories of the treasure.

"Your father sent it to you," he prompted.

Her eyes shot open. He remembered everything.

"Yes. He made it for me. It arrived after the news of his death, after Jock's arrival. It was his last gift to me. I almost lost it to Cummings, and Spellen could have taken it when he searched my room. I feel like I must keep it with me close by."

His hand stilled. "Let's have a look at it."

There it was in his eyes, the determination she'd seen with Cummings and Bakeley. In this state, she'd have trouble seducing him before dinner.

And anyway, he'd reminded her of something. "You've already done that, haven't you, Mr. Gibson?"

He blinked. Smiled. Trapped her against the post of the bed, the cool wood digging into her bottom.

"You're right. I couldn't fool a spy's daughter, could I?" His wicked lips were back on her neck. "But I will have another look at it. In a bit."

Mrs. Nichols pulled the hat lower over her eyes, bent like the furtive boy she was pretending to be, and shuffled along the Soho street where the girl's man kept his safe house.

Perhaps they would circle around and return here after all. She'd scraped through every alley around and over to Berkeley Square where Hackwell House stood. The girl and her man had been too quick.

Odd that. It wasn't often she was spotted, but he surely had spotted her. The beast had grown a brain since his time on the Peninsula.

A carriage stopped and pulled her attention. There. Finally some of the others had shown up. She shuffled along, turned the corner, did a peremptory sweep and ducked around a brick townhouse.

Josiah Dickson—Lord Agruen, she reminded herself—peered out the carriage window and raised a hand.

A street sweeper strode from the opposite corner, crossed the road, and went up to the door. He banged with his fist on the knockerless door. Though he waited long minutes, no one answered.

The fools. The carriage pulled off down the street. The street sweeper turned down an alley. They would try the back way, in vain.

The house was empty now, except for a caretaker, who was too clever to answer the door. Or perhaps he'd been sent away for his safety.

The neighbors hadn't known who was home, but they were glad the children were gone. Many children had lived there, the neighbors said, lost children, until the lady of the house had married and moved on. It would have been a perfect safe house for the girl, except it would not have been so safe. Wherever the brute had taken her was safer, because *she* did not know its whereabouts, and that meant Agruen would never find it.

Tomorrow, when the man, or if she was really so stubborn, the both of them, traveled to the City to see the so-called solicitor, that was where they would be picked up. If he came alone, he would lead back to her. The solicitor was the key. There would the real danger be.

She turned on her worn boot, with its flapping sole and spotted a lone horseman, moving languidly through the afternoon traffic.

Shrewd eyes, as dark as his hair, like Paul's had been, a spy's eyes. She shuffled on, not meeting the gaze that swept back and forth over the street like the sweeper's broom.

So Kincaid was here, and all the players were in place.

When the maid set the dishes out, Bink struggled not to dive in like a soldier on a battle break. He clenched his hand upon the table and waited, shutting out old memories of similar times, when he was starving and exhausted and there was still more of the war to be fought.

Betty had set up a round table in a small conservatory that was likely her private space. Green plants lined the walls. There was even a lemon bush sending a sweet fragrance to fill the room.

Among the many hard things about being a whore, living with all the violent colors required to portray a woman's professional stature would be one of the worst. This green must soothe all that passion.

"We are grateful to you for taking us in."

Paulette had directed her comment to both Betty and Rowland, who he'd guessed had become more than just Betty's strong arm.

Friend? Lover? Perhaps partner?

It was possible the man had the financial resources for the last. Bink had found him in London, leasing his rooms.

Rowland's return home to his family in Staffordshire had been troubled, and living every day scaring the wits out of the neighborhood children, tiresome.

His mind immediately went to work calculating whether Rowland and Betty could be trusted. A month ago he would have said yes. Now he was undecided.

"You are hungry, I think, Sergeant Gibson, Mrs. Gibson." Betty passed a platter of ham around. "Dig in then."

Rowland laughed. "Like old times, is it not, Gib?"

Paulette quirked a pretty eyebrow at him. She'd given up on a coiffure and left her shortened hair to spill over her shoulders. The few bits of sun they'd encountered had lifted a freckle or two on her skin, nowhere near as many as he had, but sure enough proof that whoever her parents were, she was no purebred Spaniard. She looked young and far too innocent for these dinner companions.

A blush rose on her cheeks. Betty's lips pressed, squashing a smile.

"We never had many meals this good, as I recall," Bink said. "I shall not forget your hospitality, Mrs. Townsend."

"Call me Betty." She passed the bread around.

"Betty and I have talked, Gib, Mrs. Gibson. We stand ready to help you with your troubles."

"You may call me Paulette. And that is very kind." Her eyes shimmered and she quickly looked down.

Sentimental, was his bride. She'd never be a spy, but she would be his, if he had to tup her five times a day to convince her.

"We would not cause you trouble," Bink said.

"You may trust us," Betty said. "We hear many things. See many things. And we can be discreet. You know that I think."

Aye. He did.

Betty had proven herself by a good deed done for Lord and Lady Hackwell, a secret she'd revealed only after a soul-searching agony. And Rowland, of course, he'd been in the troop when they'd found out Josiah Dickson's villainy.

"Do you know of the Marquess of Agruen?" Paulette asked.

Betty and Rowland exchanged a look. Rowland's mouth firmed and he said "Josiah Dickson."

"He's after something I supposedly have or will receive. I can't imagine what, except that..." She bit her lip and looked at Bink.

"Paulette's father died on the Continent working for Shaldon. She was a ward of Lord Shaldon."

"Shaldon. I see." Betty rested her chin on her locked hands. "Your mother is not living?"

"She's deceased also. I didn't see my father more than a few times. I don't truly remember him." Paulette cleared her throat and took a sip of punch.

"I've heard of Agruen," Betty said. "You understand, I do not gossip. However, if he's after you to do you harm, I will share."

Rowland nodded, and Betty went on.

"He's pockets to let, they say. The money his wife brought is gone. Yes, he keeps up appearances, but he owes every shopkeeper around. They only provide custom because of the title. And, here is the puzzle, no one knows precisely why. He doesn't gamble much more than other lords. He doesn't collect art or buy the best horses. His home and his estate are said to be in disrepair. Though there is one other thing. He's not...forgive me, but you're a married lady now so I will say this, he's not allowed into any of the better establishments like this because of his...predilections. I suppose finding a house to accommodate his tastes might be more expensive."

Paulette's mouth dropped.

Rowland's gaze flitted from her to Bink.

"Worse than his heavy hand?" Bink asked.

Betty shrugged. "He left a girl unable to walk. Is that not bad enough?"

Bink's head pounded with the memories. "He might have been French, the way he treated the Spanish locals."

"'Twould have been better had he died on the Peninsula," Rowland said.

"What was he doing in Spain?" Paulette asked in a tight voice. "Was he a soldier?"

"No," Bink said. "He was attached to the Embassy or such."

She stirred her fork in the dish, and lifted her gaze to him. "A spy?"

"He'd have been carrying information, like everyone else, that's a certainty." For which side was in doubt.

Paulette nodded. "I suppose he'll have a man watching the solicitor's office and will be waiting for us there."

"Must you go there?" Betty asked. "Cannot the solicitor come to you?"

Hope registered in Paulette's eyes. He hated to dash it. "He'll no doubt be followed himself."

Paulette sat impossibly straighter, her hands fisted at each side of her plate. "We'll go there. Once we receive what we're due, we can perhaps leave by a back way."

He reached for her hand and squeezed it. The back way would be watched also.

"I'll send a message to Hackwell House on the off chance the Major is there."

On the off chance Bakeley had been lying and Hackwell was not off ferrying Annabelle out to the country, but was ensconced in his own home preparing to do battle in Parliament.

"And we can summon runners from the solicitor's office to help," he added.

"It's not a bad plan, Gib. Will you but wait for a day, I'll get some of the boys to come along."

"I don't want to wait," Paulette said. "I want this settled. I want to know what he le-eft for me that is causing so much trouble."

"Do you have something to wear," Betty asked.

Rowland winked at him and he grinned into his napkin. Leave it to women to worry about what to wear.

Paulette colored deeply and her chin set. "I can dress as a boy, or wear this. We traveled quite lightly."

"It's a lovely dress, but I think I can arrange a better disguise." Betty snapped her fingers. "And a veil. You must wear a veil. There is a hackney stand on the corner. We'll bring one round and send you both along in that."

"They'll recognize Gibson here, all right," Rowland said. "No way to hide a museum pillar with a crown of red gold."

Betty sent him a frank and assessing gaze. "Can you dissemble, Mr. Gibson?"

"He can," Paulette said.

"I have a wig left by a barrister—"

"No wigs."

"Are you sure? I promise it is most certainly free of vermin. You might be a barrister accompanying a client—"

"No wigs, Betty."

She sighed.

"The man has said no wigs." Rowland's good eye crinkled. "It must be some blackening then."

Paulette giggled and covered her mouth at his glare.

"It's foolish. I'll pull my hat down low."

"Perhaps it won't matter. Perhaps they'll know you anyway, dark haired or not. In any case, I'd wait until morning to color the hair, to preserve the sheets, you know. You may sleep on the idea, Gibson, and decide in the morning."

She rang a bell, and Trish delivered fruit and cheese and scurried out.

Betty toyed with her raspberries. "In any case, I believe Rowland and I should accompany you."

"I agree," Rowland said.

Unease turned his stomach. Not over a lack of trust, he decided, but the danger to them.

Paulette caught his eye. "We wouldn't take advantage of your kindness to endanger you," she said.

Betty went on as though she hadn't spoken. "I know a bit about the legal world. It's not unheard of for ladies in my profession to seek the assistance of a solicitor. And perhaps, a carriage bearing two veiled ladies will be more easily disregarded."

"You mean two ladies and two gentlemen," Bink said.

"Rowland is right. You'll be quite noticeable, Gibson. Rowland knows how to play the servant, don't you my dear? We can bring Paulette safely there and back."

"No." He squeezed Paulette's hand. "I've promised to keep her safe and I will do so. And I will not allow you to risk any more than what you've already done for us."

Betty tilted her head. "Well, I had to try." She sighed. "There's also the consideration the solicitor may insist on dealing only with your husband."

"What?" Paulette cried. "That is so unjust."

"The Rights of Man are only the rights of men," Betty said. "No, I suppose Gibson must go with you. One of the ladies here has a very respectable dress that will suit. She's your height, and we'll take it in where it's too large. And I have a bonnet and veil that will do nicely."

Paulette turned her hand in his and her grip tightened.

"We're grateful, Betty. And the loan of a dress would be marvelous. I shall return it, or replace it. And I should like seeing my husband with dark hair, but how shall we cover all those freckles?'

Paulette donned the chemise, stays and puce gown Betty had brought her, barely able to make out the closures, barely daring to breathe lest she wake Bink.

He'd slept a mere five hours out of the last thirty-six, yet she didn't trust that a man who'd survived violent warfare could slumber through the escape of his bride.

For escape, she would, for his sake. It was *all* for his sake. Rowland and Betty's words had weighed heavily on her. Bink was impossible to not notice. She, on the other hand, would be garbed more finely than Agruen or Bakeley would ever expect, for indeed this dress *was* elegant, and the veil would do the rest.

The solicitor would talk to her. He *must* talk to her. That was the other reason she must go alone. If Bink accompanied her, Tellingford might completely ignore her.

She slid a pistol into her pocket, sheathed a blade on her arm, and another in her boot, and shoved the set of picks she'd lifted from Kincaid's bag into her other boot.

His breathing was the steady, loud snore she was growing accustomed to.

A bit of light leaked through the muffled window and she crept to the door.

They'd discussed the best time of arrival. They'd discussed hackney fare, and she'd tucked coins into her reticule. She was leaving far too early, but without Bink, she'd no idea how long it would take a hackney to reach the City. Solicitors had clerks who worked from dawn to dusk, she hoped. Surely they'd allow her to wait for Tellingford's arrival.

She tiptoed through the house. Below stairs, all was quiet, and she gave thanks Betty's house kept late hours for even the servants. She eased into the back garden and out the garden gate. The corner they'd passed the night before had no hackneys, so she went the other way. Dawn was coming, and market men were out already, delivering goods. She made her way down the alley toward the busy street ahead.

After many wrong turnings and obscure signs, the hackney paused at an elegant building with a black-lettered sign *Tellingford, Lippscombe and Latrice.*

Her heart eased and then started up again. Her dither had turned into a panic about finding the solicitor's office. Now she was here, she must worry about who else might be waiting.

"This be it," the driver said, none too kindly. He recited a fare that was more than they'd agreed to, but then she *had* led him astray.

Perhaps she would walk back, if someone would but tell her the way.

The building housing the solicitor's office was not what Paulette would have expected, grander than the lone solicitor's office in the market town near her home. A deep portico swallowed the entry door, its shadows lending an extra gloom to the overcast morning.

The streets of Mayfair had been quieter. Here, laborers, tradesmen, clerks, even some early-rising gentlemen bustled about. Watchers, she did not see, but then she wouldn't, would she?

She gulped down the fear, paid the driver, and climbed out. A shadow moved in the portico and a dark figure loomed and terror slammed her.

In a flash, he was down the steps reaching for her.

Chapter Twenty-Three

"Breathe," Bink whispered, all but carrying Paulette up the steps and through the door, where he plopped her against the wall, flipped back the veil, and ran his hands over her arms.

The prickling in his hands was easing, the blood flowing back. Dear God, he'd wanted to throttle her, but her trembling was shaking his anger away.

He pulled her close, their chests heaving together. That was terror there. She was good and afraid, and rightly so. When Trish had pounded into his room to tell him Paulette left, all he could see was visions of a defenseless woman—his woman—walking the streets of London.

Who knew she could find the hackney stand so quickly, or be so foolish as to go there by herself, without him? Even without Agruen's or Bakeley's interference, there was the usual danger. London was no place for a woman alone.

The porter entered, and Bink set Paulette back from him.

"Mr. Tellingford's clerk will see you now, Mr. Gibson." The lean fellow eyed Paulette's heaving bosom with far too much curiosity. Bink sent him a withering look that quickly detached the gaze.

"Come along, my dear." He latched her to his side. The scolding would keep until later, to a more private setting.

"You came without me," she whispered.

Well, perhaps they *could* have a word or two now. "Only after I discovered you gone. What bloody nonsense was that?" he whispered as they moved down a corridor.

Their greeter ushered them into an office, introduced them to a clerk, and left.

"Mr. Tellingford is with another client."

"He's in?" Paulette asked. "So early? I didn't expect it."

"Would you like to take a seat?"

The man addressed his words to Bink, ignoring her. Irritating that. Worse, though was the thread of suspicion racing through him. He had a knife and a pistol, and—he patted her arm—Paulette was wearing her sheathed knife.

"Perhaps we should have expected another *client* to be here, my dear." He kept his voice steady. "And I believe we will stand."

The inner door opened, and he shoved Paulette behind him.

"Brother." Bakeley filled the doorway, his face breaking into a smile that looked like relief. Behind him Kincaid's head bobbed.

Kincaid nudged past Bakeley and advanced on them. "You didn't trust us."

There was no accusation in his tone, only a bland matter-of-factness, but the older man picked up Paulette's hand and chafed it. "You've made it this far, so you've been careful. Where did you stay the night?—no, no I won't ask." His sigh displayed an uncharacteristic fatigue. The man rarely slept, yet this was the first time he'd seemed tired. Bink imagined him scouring all the townhouses of Hackwell's acquaintances, and all the hotels and inns. "We're going to help you the rest of the way. You must trust us, Gibson. Paulette's safety is paramount to us, as is yours."

"Where's your man, Stewart?" Bink asked.

"Did including him make you lose trust?" Bakeley asked. "He's off arranging your rooms. Good God, when we saw that body upon the road—"

"Body?" Bink asked.

Kincaid sent Bakeley a glare. "Never mind that. You've arrived safely." He squeezed Paulette's hand. "It was excluding Paulette made you both lose trust, wasn't it, lass?"

Paulette's head swam with the up and down of fear and emotion. Kincaid's touch was comforting, almost paternal, very trust-inducing, except...after all she'd been through that morning she had no certainty in her own judgment.

A body? There'd been a body? She must pull her head out of the water and start swimming.

"What of my servants?" Paulette said.

The chafing turned to patting.

"They're safe. Don't worry. They have the grooms and my men to assist them. They're on their way to London."

"I don't know Stewart. I don't wish to stay in some secret rooms he's arranging."

"Then we won't," Bink said. "We'll stay at Hackwell House."

Kincaid's eyes narrowed. "'Twill only be for a short while."

"What of this body?" she asked.

Kincaid's mouth firmed before he spoke. "Upon the road. We found a laborer with his throat spiked besides a broken, abandoned cart."

"No horse?" Bink slid his gaze to her.

He was remembering also the woman they'd seen from their place in the bushes, the woman driving the cart, a man lounging in the back.

A shiver went up her back. "That woman driving…"

"What woman?" Kincaid cut in.

"We saw a cart upon the road, a woman driving it," Bink said.

Anger rose in her. "Agruen will have taken her."

Bink frowned. "Unless she was employed by him."

She shook her head. "He hates women."

Kincaid's frown had faded back to his usual inscrutability, and she studied him.

"Did you track the horse?" Bink asked.

"Into the woods," Bakeley said, "where we lost the tracks. But we found no woman, nor any trace of one."

Bink caught her eye, and glanced back at Kincaid. Like her, he thought the wily man was concealing something. But what?

Never mind. Questioning him would be useless. She pulled out of the older man's grasp and looked up at Bink. "Thank you, my love." It was time to face up to whatever her father had left for her, and wait for Agruen to show his next hand. "Is this solicitor ready for us, Bakeley?"

"I am, Mrs. Gibson." A man of middling years stood in the doorway, a tall handsome man who yanked a thread of memory in her brain so violently she felt her breath leave her. She stood very still, pushing away the urge to swoon and beating her stomach into settling. Bink's hand touched her waist again, gentle and warm and as reliable as the back of a sturdy chair.

This man, this solicitor, had visited her mother. She'd seen him touch her mother, the way Bink was touching her now.

She eased in a breath. They'd been lovers, surely.

She blinked, shutting out the picture of her beautiful, aloof mother and this man, tucking away the knowledge. "I know you."

He approached and reached for her hand. Another man wanting her hand. She gave it to him, allowed him to bow over it. "Yes. I was a friend of your mother's. You were a spirited child, and I see that hasn't changed. Mr. Gibson." Bink freed up a hand to shake. "I'm glad you've kept Paulette safe. Let us get her seated before she faints."

"I do not faint."

"She doesn't," Bink said. "But let's take a seat anyway, Paulette."

Bink had done much to help fill the empty chasm in her heart, but it hadn't closed over. Not yet, and the news the solicitor provided tugged at the frayed opening, made the wound stretch a bit wider. Outside of the details of a pension—a very small, very precarious-upon-the-whims-of-government-and-lost-upon-her-marriage pension—her trust was indeed as small as she'd learned from Bakeley.

Actually, it was even less than that. Had she not married Bink, she'd be living in the tiniest rooms, in the smallest village, in the remotest part of the kingdom. London or a grand estate would be out of the question, unless she could reconcile herself to the unsavory part of this town, or to living the life of a genteel servant.

There'd been nothing personal, not even a letter from either of her parents.

Her chest swelled with aching and pushed the pain into her throat, freezing around everything she wanted to say, obstructing her hearing. They were talking, signing, going over details, settling her back into her fathomless hole. She gripped the arms of her chair and squeezed them until she could clear her throat.

Bakeley—or Shaldon, she must think of him as Shaldon—had been present for this affair, still clinging to the old lord's sense of his rights over them. If she could speak, she would order him out. Why Bink didn't do it...

Her breath caught. Bink had rested the quill, leaning forward, ready to propel himself out of his chair.

She'd missed something—no everything. They'd finished this business.

She forced in a breath. "Wait just a moment."

Mr. Tellingford loomed over his grand desk, his face a blank. Kincaid's eyes were dark and grave, and not without compassion. He'd also stayed, another man who thought he had a say in her life.

She didn't need his compassion or his pity. She eased in a breath around the constriction in her chest. "You knew my mother, Mr. Tellingford."

"Yes of course."

"Were you her lover?"

He blinked, the only alteration to his demeanor. No color rose to his cheeks, nor did he appear to tense.

Oh. Of course. He was another one who worked for Shaldon.

Memories snaked in through the fog in her head. Jock had limped into the cottage, his head in a bloody bandage, ranting in Spanish and delivering the two letters. Mama had put Jock in the spare room, changed his dressings, and fed him. Days later, this man arrived and took Jock away. And then brought him back.

Months after that, the lap desk arrived from a merchant in Cornwall, misdirected there by the smuggler who'd rescued it and who, Jock said, feared the wrath of Paul Heardwyn's masters more than he coveted the profit of selling the finely crafted item.

Mr. Tellingford expelled an expansive sigh, designed to push all the air from the room. "My dear—"

"So that is a yes. I was but a child, but I saw things, sir. And I don't, I don't criticize. She was tossed away to rot in the country while my father ran off to the Continent or the Peninsula, or wherever. She was lonely. She didn't fit in. After living the life of a spy it must have seemed like an early d-death."

Oh drat. Her eyes were threatening to water. She took a deep breath and thought of something distracting. Money. That would do. She should be angry about how little they'd left her. The treasure Jock whispered about was probably not even real. She must ask about that.

She lifted her chin. They were all watching her, including Bink.

Who didn't know what she knew about her father's supposed treasure, because she hadn't told him.

She dropped her gaze to her hands and blinked hard.

"Paulette is right." Bink's hand engulfed hers and squeezed. "You must tell us everything you know about her parents, and you must tell us why Agruen is after her. It most certainly is not for these pieces of paper here. Her inheritance won't cover his brandy bill for the year."

"She wasn't a spy." Kincaid said.

Her head shot up, and she looked at the dark eyes, kind, perhaps even truthful. "Jock said she was."

"Jock was wrong," Tellingford said.

"He wasn't. He couldn't have been. He told me stories, very detailed ones about Mama's b-bravery spying during the terror, before I was born." She struggled to swallow the bile rising. If Mama wasn't a spy, what was she? Who was she? And why had Jock lied?

"He shouldn't have," Kincaid said.

"He was trying to comfort you." The solicitor came round the desk, swallowing up the air in front of her again.

So devious were these men. Perhaps Bink was right and they were all liars.

"There now," Tellingford said. "Your mother was a Spanish émigré's daughter from Cornwall. Not a spy. She fell in love with your father when he worked in the Home Office and had occasion to visit your mother's family."

By the time Paulette was old enough to understand, her mother had been estranged from her own people.

"Why would the Home Office visit my mother's family?"

Tellingford looked to Kincaid, who wouldn't meet the other man's eyes. Bakeley hadn't moved either, and tension radiated from her husband next to her. They all looked to Kincaid. He was the man with the answers.

Kincaid's long pause told her she was about to hear a lie.

She bit her lip, waiting, remembering. Jock had told her no stories of Cornwall, but she remembered her geography lessons. In Cornwall, there were inlets and hidden coves for the smugglers who owned that wild place.

She freed a hand and smacked her forehead. "They were smugglers." The gift had been misdirected to Cornwall, one smuggler to another, before finding its way to her. "Why could she not tell me that?" She took in a deep breath. "I want to meet them."

"Your grandparents are gone," Kincaid said.

"I see. How?"

"Your grandmother died when your mother was young. Your grandfather died when he returned to the Peninsula."

"Well, that was suitably vague." Bink's voice rumbled up deep and angry. "We're getting but lies and half-truths, Paulette."

Her stomach tensed. She'd hidden a secret from him also, hadn't she?

Kincaid's gaze drilled hard into her husband, sparking darkly. "Ye've not asked about your father, Paulette. How he died. It was in Spain, outside Talavera. He was beaten to death."

She nodded numbly. "By a big Englishman. Jock told me that." He'd watched from the bushes as her father entered the parley, before heading out with her father's messages for Paulette and her mother. Only later had he learned Paul Heardwyn had been killed.

Her husband twitched in his chair, his hand growing tight around hers.

"You're...you're hurting me," she whispered.

His face paled and he yanked his hand away. She reached for him, holding both his hands in hers, and turning back to Kincaid.

"A big Englishman," she said.

Of course. Papa had something that Agruen wanted. Agruen was a big man compared to Jock. "Was it Agruen who killed my father?"

Kincaid turned the dark gaze on her and gave a terse nod. "Agruen, aided by the fists of a British soldier."

Numbness poured into her, locking her in place, and she couldn't say why. Her legs, hands, arms twitched with a need to move, and her empty stomach turned inside-out. The room went dark, except the pinpoint eyes of Mr. Kincaid. Spies's eyes. Calculating eyes.

She choked in a breath. She'd believe it of Agruen, but who was the soldier? And Kincaid surely knew more. Perhaps he knew what she was supposed to have that Agruen wanted.

"Why? Why was he killed?"

Kincaid swiped a hand across his face and stalled, like he regretted telling her, but that couldn't be right. A calculating man like him would never err.

"There was a woman." The words came from beside her and she turned. Sweat coated Bink's unshaven face and threatened to drip. He contemplated her hands, still clutched around his and...trembling. Only the shaking was coming from him.

"A woman?"

His eyes glowed golden with their own sheen of moisture.

"What, Bink?" she whispered.

Nearby, someone cleared a throat.

He stared at her hands, but his gaze was carrying him far away, and she knew.

He'd met Agruen in the war. He'd slipped back to Spain, and he was seeing all the horror again, anew. She'd seen moments like this with Jock.

She squeezed Bink's hand, wanting to do more but sparing his pride in front of these other hard men.

Kincaid leaned in and took up the thread. "Agruen beat the woman half to death and your father fought him."

"And the soldier?"

"Stumbled into it." Bink's voice sounded strained. "Found the woman. Was told by Dickson the man had beat her."

"Yes."

The word spoken by Kincaid had a note of finality, but he went on. "Now. Agruen thinks your mother had something from your father, something about him. And that leaves you in great danger."

Her thoughts whirled. Could the treasure be a means of blackmail?

A thread of nausea twisted in her and she swallowed it down. "She had nothing. Nothing. A letter he sent her, a letter that said nothing."

"Where is it?" Tellingford asked.

Her mother hadn't shared that letter with Tellingford.

"I have it." Bink's voice was wooden.

"It might be in code. We'll need to see it." Tellingford and Kincaid held a private conversation of back and forth glances.

Her husband stirred on his chair. "I have it in safekeeping."

Her heart skipped. He'd left it at Betty's, with her desk.

Pah, the desk was nothing, an empty shell without even any secret compartments.

She swallowed hard. Paul Heardwyn left her almost nothing and no one would believe it, least of all Agruen.

But of course, there was also the ring.

"Agruen took my mother's ring."

"What?"

"I found a ring among her things. It was, according to Agruen, a part of a puzzle ring. The pieces go together, you know? It had a, a hand."

"A gimmal ring," Kincaid said.

"Yes, well, Agruen took it from me. He stole it when I visited Cransdall the summer after Waterloo."

"How do you know?"

"I was there, and it disappeared from my room. He'd been interested in it, so I had a maid snoop around, and then I confronted him, and he told me he was keeping it. And if I told anyone, he would say that I had been..." she squeezed her eyes shut. She'd been such a fool. "He would say I'd had congress with him." She shivered. "Which I didn't."

"I will kill him," Bink said, gruffly.

"The rings might hold a key," Tellingford said.

"To what?" But even as she asked, she knew—the letter must be coded. They must get the rings back to uncode the letter, to find—

"What are you not telling us?" Bink asked. "What are you seeking, and why should Paulette give it to you?"

"Sit down, Tellingford," Kincaid said. "Bakeley, go and check who's listening at that door." He settled on the corner of the desk and began his story.

Chapter Twenty-Four

Bink's head thundered so badly he strained to hear. He'd killed Paulette's father, unjustly, unwisely, on the word of a villain.

No. *No*. The man had still breathed when Beauverde pulled Bink off him. The woman had still breathed also, though neither of them could talk.

He blinked at the pain and the images and forced his attention to the key facts of Kincaid's story, the ones Paulette's survival depended upon.

Agruen had been working with France and the Spanish traitors, the *Afrancesados*. That was no surprise. Paulette's father, and the woman, had been working with Agruen and against him at the same time. There had been money, a great deal of it, and a ransom that had gone missing.

"But Agruen has no money," Paulette said.

"Yes." Kincaid looked far too much at his ease on the edge of the desk. Bink longed to knock the man down. He'd told Paulette a story that would destroy what they had, this tender green love.

And who's fault is that, Bink, you miserable brute.

He squeezed his eyes shut. Pity, he couldn't shut out his memories, or silence the voice in his head.

"Either the money was lost or was stolen from him, or we've considered that he might be paying blackmail." Kincaid was all business again.

She glared down at the rich carpet. Her panic had passed, just as the intimacy between them would. She would leave him. Kincaid, so all attentive, was perhaps grooming her to be one of their operatives. He would use her, just as he'd used her father.

The pain in his head dulled and spread, threatening to consume him.

He tried to focus. He would hire a good steward for Little Norwick. He would make sail for India by Christmas.

"I have nothing. And you know I have not been blackmailing him. I want my ring back."

"You told him that at Greencastle," Kincaid said.

"Yes."

"He wanted to see what you'd receive upon Shaldon's death," Kincaid mused.

Bink eyed the crafty Scotsman. "And how did he know to find Paulette at Greencastle?"

Kincaid almost smiled. "We'd got word to him, round about."

Hackwell. Hackwell had been in on this game far longer than Bink had known. *What the devil.*

"When he discovered you were marrying Gibson, he knew Gibson would receive whatever was held for you, and being an honorable man, turn it over to you. And we knew you'd protect Paulette and whatever was hers."

And you knew I'd fall in love with her, like the sick, sentimental fool that I am.

Paulette shook her head. "It doesn't matter, since there is nothing. How could he think a keepsake, or whatever this is supposed to be would be locked up?" She looked at him, the trust still shining in her eyes.

That look was like a sharp kick to his gut. The trust would be gone soon.

He'd talk to her later, privately. He'd tell her everything, and if she wanted him gone, he'd leave.

"Bink. I want to go back where we stayed last night. Can we do that without endangering...them?"

He thought of Betty, and Trish, and Rowland. Agruen's hired men would cut them to pieces.

She shook her head. "No, I suppose not."

"We'll go to Hackwell House. Kincaid." He fixed the man with a glare. "You'll employ us extra help."

"Shaldon House will be better, Bink," Bakeley said. "You know how Father is about security."

Paulette's mouth firmed.

"So you can lock us up there? No, brother. I know Hackwell House, and I've hand-picked the staff. Now that you lot are involved, you can help me keep my wife safe there."

Kincaid sighed and looked at Tellingford.

"I'll make the arrangements," Tellingford said. "And we'll get you a carriage."

He slipped out the door.

"When will this end?" Paulette asked.

"I don't know." But it was a lie. He knew when it would end. He fisted his hands and pumped energy into his muscles. And this time he would finish the job on the right man.

The heavy fog had lifted and naught but a mist still hung in the air when they reached the doorstep. A black carriage came to a stop in the street, and Kincaid went out to speak to the driver. Bink recognized the man who jumped down as one of Kincaid's Scots. His fellow countryman and other of Kincaid's men ranged the walkway in front of the solicitor's office, creating a clear corridor for Paulette and him.

He squeezed her hand. "Are you ready?"

She'd drawn the veil back over her face, all her emotions hidden.

A sick feeling washed through him. Veiled or not, it would be like that now, forever.

"Yes."

Kincaid motioned and they stepped out. Two paces out, a boy skirted around the carriage boot, ducked under a guard's arm and stopped in front of them.

And raised a pistol to Paulette's heart.

Bink's blood roared and he shoved her behind him. A guard jumped the boy, and Bakeley joined in.

"Bink." Paulette's cry came from behind. Tellingford had her about the waist and was dragging her back.

He was on them in seconds, wrenching the solicitor's hand, while Paulette kicked and struggled, her bonnet and veil flying off. The man released her and she rushed into Bink's arms.

Tellingford held up his hands. "I was getting her to safety."

"I won't go anywhere with you," Paulette choked out, her cheek pressed to Bink's shoulder.

Behind them, the melee came to a close.

"Let's get to where we're going," he said.

But he paused. The boy's cap had been torn off, and long hair, as dark as Paulette's except for the lacings of grey, trailed over a torn shirt. The boy was no boy. He was no girl either, but a fully grown woman of some years.

The same woman they'd seen on the road.

Paulette gasped and clung harder. "She's the one we saw. Beaten up cart, grey horse. She followed us." She released her grip and turned on the woman. "You work for Agruen. Who are you?"

The woman's lips twisted in preparation to spit, but a yank on her collar stopped her. She huffed. "I work for no Englishman."

The accent, the face, she was Spanish, or Portuguese. Not French.

And so familiar.

He moved closer. She was perhaps forty, petite and trim, much like Paulette. Too much like Paulette.

"Filomena," Kincaid whistled. "Resurrected from the dead."

"Good day to you, Kincaid. Your men have disarmed me. Tell them to let me go."

"You'll have more than one wee pistol on you, Fil. Perhaps we shall let the Gibsons go on their way, and you and I will go inside and chat."

"How lovely. Shall we have a fine English breakfast? Some elderberry jam on a point of toast?"

"Perhaps."

Now the battle had subsided, a throbbing started behind Bink's eyes.

He knew her. He'd seen her in Portugal or Spain, lurking about a camp, delivering intelligence, visiting an officer's bed—one of those, perhaps all of those.

A fog thickened around the memory but couldn't hide the sharpness of those grim eyes.

"I think not. I've come for something and then I shall leave."

She turned on Paulette. "I want the letter from your father these men have given you."

Her mouth dropped. "What?"

His Paulette was too confounded to even attempt a lie.

"The letter. Pah, do not pretend. He told me he sent a message that would be kept in trust for you. I want it."

Paulette looked back at Tellingford. He shook his head. "You've broken into my office twice, Fil. You know there's no such message."

Her lips wriggled in a frown that turned into a smile, and then a laugh. "That was me only the once. But I don't think Dickson found it either, else he would not still be looking." She turned cold eyes on Paulette. "Where is it, then, *querida corazón*?"

"There was no message," Kincaid said. "If he sent it, it didn't arrive."

Paulette's eyes widened and she looked up at Bink, her gaze tearing at his heart.

Kincaid was wrong. Heardwyn had sent not one message but two, and neither was important, was it? Neither was worth Paulette's life.

A chill slithered through him—in the library, Agruen had said he was keeping Paulette's ring to solve a puzzle, and this woman wanted a letter, a letter Kincaid didn't know about.

Kincaid and the late Lord Shaldon didn't have the key to this *puzzle* either. What the devil was everyone looking for?

He studied the dark eyes of the woman and their halos of crows' feet. Since Heardwyn's death, the French in Spain had been vanquished. She wasn't after a cypher or a state secret.

His head pounded. His lungs squeezed like a cart had rolled over on him. And her eyes burned into him, clouding his vision.

"Who are you?" he asked.

She laughed, a stark, evil, croaking, her eyes glittering. A spy's eyes, abandoning the lie. "You do not recognize me? Though you thought once to rescue me from the girl's father."

At his side Paulette froze.

"Alas, I could not dissuade you because here" she pulled at her collar "Dickson, while he raped me, squeezed me so tightly I could not speak for a month. It was Paul who pulled him off of me. And this one," she pointed at him but glared hard at Paulette, "this is the one who beat your father to death on the word of a rapist."

Paulette's eyes widened and her mouth opened but no words came. The shock on her face sent Bink spiraling.

His world crashing should make more noise than the soft breath of his bride. The darkness descending should shut out her face. He shouldn't be able to see the words settling into her heart.

He mustered some breath in the grey calm and said, "He was not dead when I left him."

But he might as well have been so. And he wouldn't explain to Paulette on a public street, with Kincaid and his men looking on.

The eyes his bride turned on him were hollow.

My love, she had called him, not one hour ago. All the incipient promise of love had drained away. A woman could not love the man she thought killed her beloved father, could she? Not even for a manor and four thousand a year.

His pulse pounded in his ear. It was useless. He was useless, a feckless beast, only good with his fists. Once they had this madness settled and he knew she was safe—

He drew in a deep breath. No. He would not make a run for India, not yet. She could be with child, even now. The child would need him. She would need him, his protection and guidance, at least for a while, and he would give it to her and rue losing her from his bed.

"Foolish girl, *she* did not tell you of me, did she?" the woman called Fil said. "I am Filomena De Silva. I was a cousin to the woman you called Mother, and—"

A shot crackled through the air, pain stinging Bink as he dived for Paulette.

Chaos erupted. With one hand he reached for her. With the other, he clawed for the gun at his waist.

More shots blasted. Smoke mingled with drizzle. The grip of his pistol was wet. He slid it under his coat and a sharp pain pushed him to his knees, and Paulette slipped from his grasp.

No—she was ripped from him. Blood-lust flooded him. He struggled up, legs wobbling like slippery eels, chaos around him, men fighting, wrestling. The horses spooked, flew off, hooves clattering, carriage stairs dragging, door flapping. A thug reared in front of him, knife in hand and he fired, sending the man crashing.

Bakeley snatched his arm.

"*Where is she*?" Bink roared.

"You're hit. Get inside."

"*Where's Paulette*?"

Kincaid popped up from the man he was checking. "See to Gibson's wound, Bakeley." He pointed at another man. "Get horses. Now." Then he gripped Bink's shoulder. "She's in that carriage. Agruen took her. *The horses*," he bellowed.

A roar swallowed him, but no noise would come. He fisted his hand around the pistol and would have pounded his brother, but Bakeley parried and wrenched the gun away. "Let me go,"

Bink shouted. "What are we waiting for? He'll torture her for naught."

The pavement rolled like the deck of a ship. He'd failed her. He'd failed to protect her.

"See here." Kincaid grabbed his shoulders and glared into his eyes. "You're gut-shot, man. Ye'll be no good in the chase, bleeding and fainting. I *will* find her and we *will* get her back."

He looked down at his waistcoat where a thickening circle stained the cloth a darker shade of brown. "Damn you," he said, gripping Kincaid's arm. "Do it, then. Find her."

"I'll follow as soon as I have him inside," Bakeley said.

"No. You're the heir of Shaldon. Stay with your brother. We'll find them."

The horses arrived and Kincaid was off.

"Them?" Bink asked.

"They have the woman also."

Paulette rubbed tiredly at the bindings on her wrists and looked around the squalid room.

A glimmer of light floated in through the dingy windows. This was a small sitting room of the sort she thought she might have been able to afford with her income. Threadbare chairs, their cushions stained an unpleasant shade of brown, adorned the fireplace.

She and the woman who claimed to be a cousin had been shoved onto battered wooden chairs at a sad matching table in the room's corner.

Her knuckles were bloody, her dress ripped, and she had lost Betty's lovely hat and lacy veil. Agruen stood watching his minion finish tying Filomena. The other woman winked at her over the wiry, smelly man's shoulder, and she felt some of her spirit return.

She had fought hard and would have bruises to match Jenny's.

"This is a pretty set of rooms, Lord Agruen," Filomena said. "You have had more financial resources than the world knows of, I see."

Paulette held her breath, and waited for the blow. Filomena was goading him into adding more lashes to those he'd already delivered. Her face was bruised, her lips cut and bleeding, yet she still played the jaunty street urchin.

"It *was* you, then, wasn't it, Fil?"

"What could you possibly mean?"

"The blackmail. The bleeding. I'll have that item now, and you can return me my money."

What item? What money?

"I have neither, though I commend the industry of the blackmailer, and pray that the money has gone to encourage Ferdinand to restore the people's constitution."

In three strides he was on her, with a knife at the older woman's throat. "You will tell me the name of the one bleeding me. I know that you know it."

"Pah. Would a respectable blackmailer pick a lordling as impoverished as you?"

He pressed the knife tighter. "We know there is nothing respectable about you, whore."

His sort of man thinks every woman is a whore.

Paulette tugged at her bindings. "Do not call her that."

He turned his eyes on her and her heart shriveled a bit. "But she is, little Paulette. She was your father's whore."

No. Her heart pushed into her throat and no sound would come out.

"Your father's, and every French general's from Rouen to Lisbon. Isn't that true, Fil?"

Her vision went fuzzy. Her lungs would not fill. She barely remembered her father, but she knew he loved her mother. She just knew it.

Filomena's voice came to her out of a cloud. "If you say I am such a whore, your Lordship, then there can be no question of a lie. You must of course be in the right about everything."

He drew the knife back and his lips turned up in a smile that pressed a shivery ice block to the space between Paulette's shoulders.

"I will have you again before I kill you. But this one," the full force of that serpentine face turned on her, "this one I will keep longer and enjoy. Twice we have been interrupted, little Paulette. Now there is no one to trouble us. A pity you are no longer a virgin. Or are you still? Was that great bull of Shaldon's unwilling to do his duty to you? Or perhaps unable?"

He reached for her cheek and she leaned away, fighting the urge to heave. Her eye ached, and she tasted the blood from a split lip.

He gripped her jaw hard and wrestled her upright studying her. "No," he mused. "You're not devious enough to bleed me, little Paulette. But you'll restore me the fortune your father stole from me. What did you get from the solicitor, eh? Was there a letter from your dear papa? You'll turn it over now."

"She said she did not receive it from the solicitor," her cousin said. "And this one has no skills at lying. Her heart erupts from her eyes."

"We shall see." He released her, sheathed his knife, and struck Filomena.

Paulette's heart stopped. The woman had seen the blow coming and ducked, sparing herself the full force. He began to hit her again and again. Her hands were tied in back, her feet bound. She must be gripping the chair, somehow, because she held on, dodged, ducked, swung out her legs, and still she did not topple.

One final blow knocked her to the floor and Agruen kicked.

"Wait," Paulette shouted. "Stop."

He kept on. "Stop," she screamed again, with all the force she could muster, praying they could hear her as far as Mayfair.

That swung his attention back to her, sending her nerves shrieking.

Thoughts tumbled, pictures. Her mother denying her answers, her mother and Mr. Tellingford, her mother dying. Finding the letter among her mother's things—and the ring. She took small, shallow breaths and fought for control.

Jock's voice whispered in her memory—*one must reach deep inside to survive the pain.* Her pain was as yet small. Her cousin's, was not. Filomena wheezed and struggled for breath, sending her own heart pounding and squeezing so that her own breaths came just as hard.

Filomena had pointed a gun at her—she was not a friend. Yet she must keep her alive, somehow. Alive, Filomena might help solve the mystery, at least until she acquired what she herself wanted.

She mustered a breath. "There *is* a letter."

Chapter Twenty-Five

The woman lifted her head, her whole body jerking with great gasps from her place on the floor, but her eyes riveted on Paulette, like twin bolts under a smith's hammer.

The fear flooding Paulette's veins all but paralyzed her. There were no allies here, only predators.

Bink, where are you? Why did you let them take me?

In the stories Jock told her, her mother always escaped. She was always strong and convincing and unafraid.

But the stories had been false. Her gentle mother could never have lived through this.

Yet *she* must live. She must survive until Bink came for her. He would come, she had no doubt. He would find her. She must find a way to help him find her.

The letter must serve as her lifeline. "There *is* a letter. The solicitor wasn't holding it. My mother had it hidden away."

She eased in another breath. Like Paulette with Bink, her mother had not shared all with her lover, Tellingford.

"I discovered the letter after her death. It was just meaningless news, a husband's prettied up report of his business, not even true, I'd imagine. I was glad she'd kept it." She let her real tears brim. "Because it was all I had of him. And then, I was angry. There must have been more, letters she'd destroyed. I had nothing. Nothing of him."

She squeezed her eyes tight and shook her head. She must play this right. She took a deep breath. "I think, well, if it is the letter you're searching for, it must be in a code. I can't imagine how or what."

"Where is the letter now?" Agruen brushed a spot of blood on his sleeve. He sounded almost bored. "We know it wasn't among the things Cummings took from you. Did you stash it back at Hackwell's country estate, hmm? Or did you have it in your reticule?"

"N-no." She shivered, hoping it would be helpful.

Another chill went through her, a real one. He knew about Cummings, which meant the vile worm was in league with the serpent. And so he'd found his way to Greencastle because she was with Bink, and that's where Bink was likely to be. And so he'd searched her room at Greencastle, or planned to. Or perhaps his valet had been planning to search there after he'd ravished Jenny.

Agruen drew closer. She lifted her chin. "My husband has it."

He touched a finger to her cheek. "How sweet. Your husband. Shall we believe her, Fil?" His attention went back to the woman on the floor, and Paulette's breath caught, dreading the next blow.

But he was done kicking for now. He snapped his fingers, and his weaseley assistant came from somewhere behind Paulette and righted her cousin's chair with her in it, gasping.

More blood trickled from a cut on Filomena's head, and she wheezed with a grimace that meant something inside her was broken. "Have Paulette write out a note to that great bull who beat Paul to death," she said.

Paulette winced and caught the baiting glint in the other woman's eye, and her blood rose.

That Bink had beat her father almost to death— if he hadn't admitted it, she wouldn't have believed it. Never would he have put a hand on an innocent man. She'd seen the misery in his eyes when he'd learned the truth of the man's identity, and even then denied killing him.

She wouldn't die without telling him it didn't matter. It truly was Agruen who had killed her father.

She bit back the accusation.

"So Fil," Agruen said, "we'll have her write a note asking for the letter and he'll just hand it over."

"If you release me, yes," Paulette said. "The letter..." What had she said? It was all she had of her father? She mustered some tears. "You may have it. I do not care. The man who wrote it abandoned my mother and me."

Filomena's eyes narrowed and she pressed her lips together, but she didn't speak.

Perhaps she still had a *tendre* for Papa.

Agruen's beady eyes took it all in, and he smiled like a Rom reading minds. Or he was enjoying the bloody display of his handiwork.

Heat rose in her. If she could but break these bonds, she would kill him.

"Oh but, Paulette, I don't want to release you. Such a tender young thing you were in the garden at Cransdall."

His leer enflamed her more. "After you stole my mother's ring."

That news sparked a flash in Filomena's eyes.

Paulette's blood raced. *I got my part of this puzzle from another whore.* Filomena De Silva was the other so-called whore.

"Let us start with the letter and we will puzzle this out. You." He snapped his fingers again at his assistant. "Bring paper and ink, and then untie her. And dear Paulette, if you try anything, your cousin here will suffer."

He knew Filomena was her cousin?

They were all spies together, hunting, beating, or blackmailing each other. But he was English, so if he was being blackmailed, that meant he must have betrayed his country, and perhaps her father had evidence of it. Perhaps there was no treasure after all, but only a blackmailer's tool. She would gladly exchange it for her life. England had done nothing for her, after all, except to steal her father's life and leave her husband with a legacy of guilt.

She looked briefly at the sharpened point of the quill. Agruen saw and smiled evilly. She shrugged and paused over the inkpot.

> *My love, I am safe for now, being held in a foul garret I'm guessing to be in the East End since I saw more sailors on the streets and I did not pass that way in the morning. Fil has been beaten savagely but still smirks and snarls. You must bring the letter and then you must kill him because he threatens to rape and kill me anyway.*

"Get on with it," Agruen growled.

She could not write that of course. "I am framing my words."

> *Dear Mr. Gibson*

No. She set her pen to the paper.

Dear ~~Mr Gibson~~ Husband,
I live. Agruen wants my father's letter to my mother.

"What instructions do you wish me to add?"

"Write 'The person delivering this missive will provide instructions.'"

The pen scratched as she wrote.

Agruen went on, "'If he does not return within one hour alone with the letter...'" her hand trembled during the pause. The script would be hard to read. "'Lord Agruen will personally deliver one of the fingers I used to hold the quill for this letter.'"

She swallowed hard and the tip of the pen broke on the evil man's name.

"Drat." She dipped the spoiled tip and scrawled

threatens more evil.
love, P

Agruen took the paper. "You do not follow orders well."

She gripped the pen tightly, her rage building within her and warring with her fear. Take her finger would he? "It will suffice." When she spoke, her voice grated like she'd swallowed sharp stones. "I should like my mother's ring back. It is of no use to you."

He smiled. Laughed. "She makes demands, Fil. She is so like you." He gripped Paulette's chin. "Do not think to use that flimsy quill. My knife will be quicker, and then I'll send Shaldon's by-blow a hand instead of merely a finger." He slammed her ear to the table, and the shock clattered through her. "Bind her again, and then come with me."

*****

Bink gripped the edge of the table he sat upon, taking each sharp stab of the surgeon's needle without whimper. If his pain could spare hers, please God let it be done.

"Hurry up, man," he said through clenched teeth. She'd been gone for more than an hour. It had taken mere minutes for the surgeon to arrive at this so-called solicitor's office, another few minutes to strip him and probe, and another hour to pull all the pieces of linen and wool from what was merely a long, wicked flesh wound.

Bakeley sat in a chair watching the surgeon's work. His guard, he was, but as soon as the leech was done Bink would be out the door. His brother was welcome to come. He did, after all, have their brother Charley to play the next Lord Shaldon.

"Sit still, brother. That wound is deep."

"I've had worse from French sabres."

His Lordship stood and started pacing.

The surgeon knotted his thread and reached for the bandage. "I suppose I could not ask you to rest for a few days until I can take these stitches out."

He was a lanky fellow of indeterminate age and matter-of-fact manner.

"No," Bink said.

The surgeon grunted. "That's how it is with your kind."

"My kind?"

"You've fallen in with Shaldon, Kincaid and Tellingford. There now." He tied off the bandage. "Where is that fresh shirt?" he shouted.

The same clerk who'd greeted them at the door that morning entered. His eyes took in the bloody pile of cloth with interest, and he handed Bink a shirt and a neck cloth.

When Bink held it up, his skin pained him sharply where the surgeon had sewn the raw pieces of flesh together.

"Biggest one I could find. It should fit," the clerk said.

He tried to poke an arm into the sleeve and winced.

"Here." Bakeley grabbed the shirt. "Let me valet you before you pass out."

"Has anyone reported in," Bink asked the clerk who stood about watching the show, an earl dressing his bastard brother. Bakeley helped him into his torn, bloody coats.

Voices sounded in the corridor. "I'll go and check," the clerk said.

The door flew open as soon as he reached it. Kincaid's eyes swept the room and landed on the surgeon who was slipping his coat on, preparing to leave. "Well?"

"A deep flesh wound. He's survived worse."

Bink jumped up from the table. "Where is she?"

Kincaid looked at the clerk. "Get out."

When the door closed, Kincaid surveyed Bink. "You'll do."

"Bloody hell, Kincaid, where is Paulette?"

"We haven't found her yet."

He gripped the older man's shoulders.

"Stop," Kincaid said. "We've traced her to Spitalfields. We're working our sources now."

"Let's go then."

"There's been a ransom demand."

His empty stomach flipped. "How much?" Bakeley would damn well front him the money. This bloody mess was all Shaldon's doing.

"Not money. A letter. You were holding it for Paulette."

He reached into his pocket.

Blood had soaked the paper in places. Kincaid eyed the letter, his eyes gleaming.

"Good. You'll leave this. I have a man penning a decoy right now."

"No. You'll not risk Paulette's life for more of your games."

Kincaid swiped a hand across his cheek in a gesture that told more about the depth of his worry than Bink could ever imagine.

"Fair enough. Conceal that somewhere. We must hurry. The scurvy boy says there's a deadline." He handed Bink a pistol. It was Bink's own, loaded and primed. "You still have a blade?"

Bink stowed the letter and the pistol. "Yes."

"Good." They started down the corridor. "The boy will take you to Agruen's man. He will demand to return alone with the letter. Tell him you must see her. He will protest. He'll want to carry the letter. If he will not give way, kill him. We'll have the boy, and we'll get the location out of him, or be damn close." He stopped at the outer door. "Agruen will try to kill you. We would like him alive."

"If he hurts Paulette in any way, he's a dead man."

"She's a brave girl. And Filomena, when it comes to the point, will fight for her."

He doubted that. The bitch had pointed a gun at Paulette.

Paulette struggled to work the bonds at her back. From the movements of the other woman's shoulders, she was doing the same.

"Can we untie each other?" Paulette whispered.

"You do not need to whisper. We are quite alone, and that door is locked." Her voice was strong. The beating had not affected her as badly as Agruen must have hoped.

Paulette eyed the door. "We can pick that. We just need to get loose."

Her cousin laughed. "Just like that? Sela taught you something more useful than how to darn stockings. Perhaps you are right." She scanned the room. "Perhaps there is something here we can use to pick locks."

Perhaps I have a set of lockpicks in my boot along with a sgian dubh.

She kept her mouth firmly closed and stood. Fil was only a few feet away. A few hops, given the way her feet were bound. "Can you stand?"

"Yes." Her cousin got awkwardly to her feet and leaned her waist on the table.

She looked small, frail.

It was an illusion. She also probably had a weapon hidden somewhere, in spite of the search by Agruen's man.

Paulette must be the first one untied.

She backed up to the woman and felt for her hands. "When we are untied, will you kill me, Filomena?"

After a moment of silence, the woman chuckled. "You are giving Agruen the letter and he already has the ring. I think it is him I must kill."

She hadn't answered the question. "Was it your ring he took also?" Paulette had worked her way to the end of the rope.

"Why would you ask that?"

"He told me he took a ring just like my mother's from another woman." The other woman's knots were loosening. "I cannot feel your hands working. I shall go and sit down directly if you do not help out."

"You do not trust me."

"Why should I? You were going to shoot me."

"Ah that, *corazón*. I ran out of powder days ago."

The tension on her wrists loosened. She wrestled free, and turned, untying the other woman's bonds.

Filomena plopped down on her chair and started working the bonds on her legs. "Keep the rope handy at your wrist."

Paulette hurried to sit. She pulled the knife from her boot and sawed at the knot.

Her cousin's eyes lit. "*Excelente*. But do you know how to use it?"

"I will use it on you if you try to hurt me."

The woman stepped one foot out of her bonds. "I shall sit right here while you search for a piece of wire—"

A door below crashed open and men's voices echoed.

"*Shhh.*" Filomena slipped the bonds around her feet and her hands. Paulette did the same, concealing her gripped knife behind her back under a rucked up fold of her skirts. When she looked up, her cousin's head had fallen in a fake swoon.

She swallowed. She must look weak. She would draw him closer. She closed her eyes and tried to conjure Jock's lessons. Stab up with the knife, watch for the ribs. Or go in the back, for the kidneys. Or, dear God, the eye.

The door opened and her heart stopped. Agruen's knife pressed into Bink's neck.

Bink quirked a lip and gave a shake of his head, sending her his strength. His strength—would she ever feel the power of those strong arms again? Real tears pricked her eyes.

She nodded and bit her lip. "What are you doing, Gibson?" she asked. "You were supposed to turn over the letter, not bring it."

Her cousin's head did not move. A sterling performance, that.

"Did you not want him to come, Paulette?"

"I don't wish you to take my finger. But now that he's here, and you have that useless letter, let us all go. I'll even let you keep my mother's useless ring."

"Ah, but it's not useless." He jerked his head and his minion came and took over guarding Bink.

His hands were pulled tight behind him as if he were already bound.

Agruen yanked a blood-stained letter out of his pocket and two rings. "If this is even the letter. So much fresh blood, by-blow. I hope it is yours."

Her pulse quickened. Bink's coat showed a rip and dark splotches. He *had* been wounded.

Bink laughed. "Else you wouldn't have taken my wife, Dickson."

The sharp crack of the minion's fist on his jaw made Paulette jump. Her skirt slipped just as Agruen came up behind her.

Her pulse pounded in her ears like a troop of men climbing a flight of wooden stairs. The narrow slats of the chair wouldn't hide the knife. She must strike now. Stab up...the kidneys—

"You are a traitor, Agruen." Filomena had lifted her head a fraction, and her words came out dark, echoing with pain, and drawing the villain's full attention. He moved closer, his back to Paulette.

"Perhaps we're done with you now, Fil."

Paulette eased in a breath, and tried to measure a target under his layers of coats.

"No. If you want to decipher that code, you need me. Paul would have put it in Spanish or Portuguese, and, as I remind myself, you do not speak either language so well. Or at all."

He looked at the letter. "As long as you don't mind dying thereafter."

His gaze swept the room and he laughed. "All of you."

His helper cleared his throat.

"Not you, you fool." Agruen pulled out a chair near Fil and perused the letter. "Ah, the blood hasn't touched the writing. How poignant." He took the rings, matched them together and studied the markings formed on the inner band. "Paper," he shouted.

His assistant shoved Bink into one of the dirty brown armchairs and went into the adjoining room. It truly *was* just the two men against their three. Bink's feet were not yet bound. They *could* overcome them. They *must*.

"What's it say?" Bink asked.

Agruen frowned. "Shut up."

Bink got up from his seat. The minion, drawn to the drama at the table, didn't notice. "It says nothing, I'll warrant. Nothing more than 'Dear wife, how fares you, and how is my Paulette'. No secret location of Fouché's letter to you that Filomena here lifted. Nor the name on the bank account where your French gold is hidden."

A bloody corner of Filomena's mouth quirked. Was Bink bluffing, and did Fil know it? Or did she really have a letter from a Frenchman?

Paulette's grip tightened around the knife. "It's true then. You worked for the French. It's why you tried to kill my cousin. It's why you had my father killed. He found out the truth."

His pencil moved busily, but she could see the white of his knuckles. He paused to frown over the inner markings of the rings.

He looked puzzled and displeased.

But of course. There would be another ring. Bink had said there sometimes was a heart. The heart was missing, and so the code would not work.

Bink sent her another tiny shake of the head and took up her thread. "But your blood money went missing."

Paulette nodded to him and Fil. "And you inherited an estate that was broke or… You killed your uncle and your cousin. And that wasn't enough, so you married that pitiful rich widow, and that wasn't enough, either. Did you kill her also?"

The blackguard smiled. "What if I did?"

Monster. Taking this man's life would serve mankind.

"How? How did you do it?" Bink asked.

"It's easily done," Fil said. "A cut in the team's rigging, a poor load on the hunting gun. A bit each day of poison in her ladyship's tea."

Agruen laughed.

"Did you?" Bink asked. "If we are all to die anyway, there's no harm in telling us. And your boy here is a criminal just like you." The look he sent the man said he was expendable also, but Agruen was too focused on the cipher to notice.

"A criminal?" Agruen laughed. "I'm a peer of the realm."

"Traitor, rapist, murderer." Bink spit the words out, and this time Agruen looked. "Soldiers died because of you. Farm men, flash house boys, East Enders like him." He nodded toward the minion.

"Wellington's valiant scum. Men who for once in their lives had a right to a fair fight."

"What if they did? What if I am? What did King George do for any of you, you fool. When I find that blackmailer, and that money, I'll go on about my business, sitting in Parliament with the rest of my brethren. And pah, I intend to enjoy a dalliance with the fair Paulette. Though I would have preferred her unspoiled by a rutting beast like you."

"You pig," Paulette said. "You vile, greedy, bottom-sucking arse of a pig. You will *never* touch me. You will *never* lay a hand on me."

Filomena smiled. "That's my girl," she said softly.

Agruen's mouth contorted. He dropped the pencil. "This is a pretty letter, but it's not the right one. You've not brought me the right one." He jerked his head at his man. "Kill him."

"Wait," Paulette shouted, even as she saw Bink whisper to the man, who scratched at his jaw and stared at his master.

"Kill him," Agruen growled.

"M'brother died in that war. In Spain it was."

"That's where he cheated men like us," Bink said. "Bastards and lords alike. Moore and his men, driven into the sea."

"You fool." Agruen pushed from the table and flew at Bink.

Bink's foot swung out, kicking the big chair at Agruen, catching the villain's blade.

Paulette threw off her bonds and Agruen's man looked at her, startled.

"Get out," Fil shouted.

The man backed toward the door.

"Get him," Agruen yelled at his man.

Bink's foot swung again and Agruen's knife clattered to the floor. He lunged for Bink, his coat flapping up.

Stab quick. Stab up.

Paulette swung and missed.

Agruen turned a shocked look on her and bellowed, charging. She swung again, even as her feet carried her back, and Agruen hit the floor, face-down, with Bink's bulk landing atop him.

The man twisted and pounded, and Filomena was there, her boot jabbing again and again at Agruen's face.

"Enough," a voice boomed.

Paulette's hands froze around the knife and hope rose in her.

Men swarmed the room, men who were on their side.

Chapter Twenty-Six

She looked at the knife she still gripped. Blood dripped down the cross of the dagger and on to her bloody hand and the room dimmed, her vision narrowing to just that bit of wet blade. Her breath...wouldn't come. Wouldn't come. The dagger slipped from her hands.

"Paulette, love." Bink was on his knees before her, arms tight behind him, a man's head bent over him, jerking at his arms.

"Hold still," the man said.

"Paulette, love," Bink said again, the sound coming from far away. "Look at me. Deep breaths. Take deep breaths."

Even swollen and shadowed, his eyes glowed golden. The pain there resonated with each beat of her own heart.

"I've killed him." It took all of her willpower to draw in her breaths. "I'm a killer."

"Paulette."

Her knees wobbled. His voice slipped further away.

"*Corazón,*" the woman said.

"Gibson." That was someone else in this fog.

"Is she all right?" Hands gripped her waist. Someone lifted her.

*****

Bink reached for her. He needed her. He needed to touch her, to talk to her.

Bakeley pushed at him. "You're bleeding again, brother."

His neck cloth was splattered red. "It's Agruen's blood. Give her to me."

"Sit down in that filthy chair, Edward." The crackly voice made his hair stand and he turned to look.

Shaldon, the old lord, his father, risen from the dead, held the center of the room against all attackers.

He should have known. *He should have known.*

He'd been maneuvered. Tricked. Leg-shackled to the bride selected by Shaldon. And Paulette, his lovely Paulette, had been used as bait to catch a traitor.

"*What the hell have you done?*" Bink shouted.

"Sit, Edward, and Bakeley will give you your wife back."

The urge to smash the older man's face was overwhelming, until he glanced at Paulette. He sat and let Bakeley settle her in his lap.

"I am not a sack of corn." Her voice strained like the fresh stitches in his side, causing him as much pain.

Still, she could speak, and wasn't protesting his hold on her.

He smoothed her hair back and examined her injuries, bruises and small scratches only, it seemed, and the remnants of the terrible fear of facing Agruen's torture.

Anger, that fierce rage, swelled in him again. If she wasn't here, on his lap, he'd kill the man with his bare hands.

And be what? *The killer she knew him to be.*

Despair hit again. Her letter had given him hope, hope that she wasn't ready to forsake him after all she'd learned, all they'd both learned. Agruen—Josiah Dickson—had, all those years ago, played on Bink's quick temper, his great bulk, and his urge to think first with his fists.

Paulette blinked, frowned and turned toward the sound of Shaldon's voice, issuing orders.

She sat up. "You." She stretched a finger and pointed at the living, breathing man who was his father.

"Hello, Paulette."

"*You* are a scoundrel. You sold my home. *Sold it*. To Cummings, and you...you...let him take it, and you weren't even truly dead. And you *tricked* me into marriage."

Bink's heart fell. He was the husband she'd been tricked into marrying. His wound ached, but the sharp pain in his heart was far worse.

He'd risked it all, had it all, lost it all.

"And you, Bakeley." She was in a right temper, her skin pinching pink, her hair dangling at her shoulders. He wanted to kiss the anger out of her, to draw some of that spirit into himself. "You knew. You knew, and you lied, to me, and to..."

She stiffened and glared at him.

"And to me also. I did not know. And about marrying you, I'm not a bit sorry," he said in a gruff whisper. "I love you."

She went pinker still and her gaze darted away.

"I'm a useless lump, but it was not right, *Father, Brother*, to use Paulette as bait."

Bakeley jumped in. "This shouldn't have gone this way. If you had but trusted me—"

"Trusted you?" Bink swore a colorful oath.

"I'm your brother."

"And he's our father. And he's deceived us."

Agruen had been shackled and helped to his feet. He wasn't dead after all.

The room filled with men, operatives of Shaldon's. Agruen's henchman was being led away, and Filomena's wounds were being tended.

"Who is she, truly?" he asked.

"A whore," Agruen said.

"There now," Shaldon said. "Fil's not a whore. She's a patriot, though not of England. Never mind, she's helped with our strategies, unwittingly I'm afraid. Dear girl, it's always a pleasure to work with you. We shall talk. Agruen, your days of running free across England are over. How your story ends will depend on how much you wish to share with us." Shaldon tilted his head and three men hauled Agruen toward the door. "Not you, Kincaid."

He hadn't noticed Kincaid. The Scotsmen too were here, as well as Tellingford and the clerks. The solicitor's office might be real, but it was also well-connected with Shaldon's operation.

Paulette could be a statue perched on his lap, she was that stiff. She would be up and away in moments, and he must let her go.

"Paulette," Shaldon said gently, "Filomena De Silva is not truly your cousin."

"No? She bears my mother's maiden name."

"That is true. But it was the woman who raised you who was your cousin. Filomena is your mother."

"Bloody hell," Bink breathed.

Paulette heard the curse explode from him and she wobbled. "How?"

Fil frowned. "Must we have an audience?"

With one nod, the room cleared, except for Kincaid, Bakeley, Shaldon and the three bloodied victims of Agruen's violence.

Fil wheezed. "Must we do this in this filthy lair?"

"Get on with it," Bink said.

Still speaking for Paulette, when she could speak for herself. Strange, but it didn't bother her.

"Paul and I met in Italy. We were lovers. Then he went off to France. I had you. I left you with friends while I worked. When he found out, he confronted me. I could not care for you and work also, and it was a precarious time everywhere. I had an uncle in Cornwall, and Paul took you to him. I did not know that his daughter, my cousin, would steal my lover, but that is what happened. Paul met Sela and," she waved a dismissive hand "married her, and with Shaldon's help, set her up in that cottage."

Had it been another one of Shaldon's arranged marriages, with her as a pawn?

"You and he just gave me away?"

Fil shrugged. "It was war. You did not go hungry. No French pigs came to your door to rape you. Your house was not blown up by cannons. Did she...did she not care for you?"

Had she?

Her mother had been a gentle woman, not given to violent tempers, but so inwardly drawn it had been hard for Paulette to really know her. Had she accepted her lot—an absent husband and a child who was not her own?

She studied the face of the woman claiming to be her mother and wondered what answer would hurt her the most.

No. Hurting her was not the answer. There'd been enough lies all around. "She kept me safe.

She showed me love. Her lies were ones of omission."

Filomena grimaced. "There are always lies. Are there not, Kincaid? Behold, Paulette, your father's half-brother."

Kincaid cast the woman a baleful look.

"Why am I not surprised?" She looked from face to face. "Tell me. What is it truly I'm supposed to have? What is this letter from my father?"

Filomena chuckled, and Kincaid glared at her again.

"There was no letter from the French," Fil said. "Only a clever counterfeit that allowed me to bleed the man for a bit. You knew that, did you not, Lord of Spies? But as for what your father sent to you, Paulette? Why, money of course. A ransom to the French. Agruen stole it from the French, Paul stole it back again, brought it to England, and decided to keep it. Is that not true, your Lordship?"

Shaldon seated himself on a wooden chair. "Agruen thought it was true, but we don't know. It could as well be that the money is scattered across Spain. It was, as Fil says, a ransom for one of our people. When it went missing, when Agruen stole it, the French wanted it replaced. If Heardwyn took it, it was because he knew a replacement had been arranged." He shrugged. "Like all spies, your father could be enterprising at times."

In other words, her father could lie and steal. "And so you, Mother, and you, Uncle, let me be the lure for a villain chasing money you don't even know exists."

"We were not working together," Fil said. "I am not without hope that the money exists. The cause of restoring the constitution of Spain can use that money."

"Aye, the crown would like the money also, but it was never about money for me," Kincaid said. "It was about stopping a traitor and uncovering his web. And I would never let you be hurt, lass."

"But she was hurt," Bink growled. "You couldn't just scoop Agruen up and torture him?"

"This is England," Shaldon said. "Not France. Paulette, Agruen's pursuit of you was inevitable. He was getting desperate, and we knew he'd go after you long before your trust was dissolved on your twenty-fifth birthday. We feared he might even appear at your cottage and try to force you to marry him."

Her breath caught. "He admitted he killed his wife."

Shaldon grimaced. "With or without our involvement, Agruen was drawn to you. So we came up with a plan. Your uncle insisted you not be unprotected. The matchmaking scheme was his, and a brilliant match it is."

Bink stiffened and her heart lifted. He hadn't been part of this plotting. He'd been as much a victim as she was. Except...

"You matched me with the man who killed my father?"

Kincaid cleared his throat. "We matched you with a man of courage and heart and loyalty, a man who would defend the defenseless, protect women and children, and put his life on the line for his fellows. And yes, we knew he had beaten Paul, but it wasn't him who killed him. That was Agruen, finishing the job a few days later."

She turned to face Bink, and the hand she touched him with came back wet. It was covered with blood, and his face was a grim, grey mask, his eyes, tiny points of light.

"Bink. *Bink*," she shouted. "He's bleeding." She jumped from his lap and tore open his coat. "*Help him.*"

Chapter Twenty-Seven

Bright sunlight poured through the bedchamber window. Bink sat on the edge of the bed letting it burn through him. If only it could burn away the pain in his heart.

He looked around the room. Paulette's things had been delivered from all the various locations where they'd been strewn.

Her trunks from Greencastle sat in the adjoining dressing room. The small bag she'd taken to Scotland was there also, her hairbrush cleaned and placed, waiting for her lovely hair. Rowland had brought her lap desk over earlier, and it sat on the writing table under the window, along with a package addressed to him.

After they'd all but carried him out of Agruen's foul den, he'd insisted on coming to Hackwell House, where he'd been cleaned and re-stitched and put to bed for a while. Hackwell, who was, in fact, in London, had sent his own valet to help him dress, and he'd made it as far as the shirt, trousers and boots before sending the man away.

He should struggle into his coats and his neck cloth, and go and converse with Hackwell and his stalwart lady who had, after all, refused to go down to Sussex.

But his heart felt like it was torn in two. Paulette wasn't here. He hadn't heard her moving about in this chamber they were meant to share.

He glanced at the package from Shaldon again. The letter enclosed might as well have been a deathbed message. It described in terse, unflowery script Shaldon's feelings for Bink's mother—and she also a spy, for the rebels in Ireland.

Bink shook his head. He'd not seen that in her, ever.

Shaldon had also told of his pride in Bink, and his plan to publicly acknowledge him as his son. He'd even enclosed the title and deed for Little Norwick.

And there was also a ring, a gold heart with a ruby center. The Spymaster's candor didn't extend to explaining where he'd found it.

Bink struggled up and lurched to the table, sliding the ring out and holding it up to the light. The marking inside would make no sense until matched with the other rings.

And this ring was properly Paulette's. He dropped it back into the wrapping. He would leave it with her when they separated.

He fumbled his way back to the bed and plopped down.

A light step in the hall made him turn, but the catch in his side stopped him. He must stop moving around, the surgeon had said, else he would pull the stitches out again.

Anyway, this would be Thomas. He'd have spotted the valet's departure and had come knocking to cadge Bink for the day's story, since Hackwell had banished him from the room while the surgeon was working. The less Thomas knew of spying the better, else he'd trade his yen for the army for something more adventurous.

And given the boy's natural disposition, perhaps more suitable.

Instead of a knock, he heard the latch turn. He rose and faced the door just as Paulette slipped in.

She was a vision, in the blue dress she'd worn the night he'd first kissed her. She was beautiful, bruises and all. And she smiled at him.

He had no words.

At his choking, her brows drew together. "You're up."

He nodded.

"Is that wise? You lost so much blood. Perhaps you should sleep more."

No more sleeping. He had things he must do. "You look lovely. Are you all right?"

"Yes. Of course. I used another chamber to bathe. Even with the laudanum they gave you, I feared you might wake."

"You've been here all along?"

"I was here until I knew you were well settled. Then I went back to the solicitor's office. I wanted to collect my letter and my rings and talk to my...to Filomena a little more."

"What have they done with her?"

"She'll be released, my uncle said, to return to Spain, where she's plotting against Ferdinand. Him I believe. But not your father." She laughed ruefully. "What a cheat he's pulled on us."

"Yes. I want to talk to you about that. Come." He reached for her hand. "Let us sit down."

There were two chairs by the window table.

"Shall I call for some tea?" she asked.

"No. Maybe later."

He escorted her, though in truth he felt as wobbly as a bow-legged baby, and it was her helping him toddle into the chair.

He watched her arrange the blue skirts and prop an elbow to lean on. Horizontal rays of late summer light illuminated the purpling on one cheek and the shadowed mottling around her eye.

She'd been his to protect and still she'd been taken. He felt every bruise of hers like it was his own.

"I...Paulette, I will regret to my dying day attacking your father. No. Don't interrupt." Her mouth had opened and he raised a hand. He must get this out. "I should have looked more closely that day. I should have engaged my brain. I should have realized Dickson might be lying. But I'm a beast. A belligerent bull. It's what Gibson—the man who raised me—used to tell me. It's a good thing in fierce battles, but..."

But not in a marriage. Not with a lovely woman who deserved better.

"If you want that Scottish divorce, I'll give you it."

Divorce?

The word poked a fresh wound right into Paulette's heart, and her first inclination was to lash back at him.

Except...the words had been so awash in pain, she leaned closer. His handsome face, as bruised and battered as her own, was turned in her direction, his soul shining out through his eyes. The strong jaw had indeed taken many punches—for her. He was the same as that day on the road to Cransdall when he'd boosted her into a tree to rescue her father's gift. Not a beast at all, but a gentleman, a man of honor.

She'd seen into the heart of him. She'd take his rich gifts over any jewels.

She reached for his hand. "I might be with child. Your child. And you might leave a woman but you'd never leave your child."

"I'd never leave you, but I'll understand if you send me away. You deserve better."

"There is no better. And I love you."

His throat bobbed with a fierce swallow. "I have something for you."

She clung to his hand and stayed him. "Hold there, Mr. Gibson. This is where you say 'I love you, too'."

A grin spread over him, like every part of him was smiling. Ah, but she knew he loved her.

"Shaldon—my father—was right. The match is brilliant. I love you, too. And if you're keeping score, I said it first."

A chuckle bubbled up. "So you did. Now what do you have for me?"

"Shaldon sent this along. The deed for our home is in here as well." He tipped a package to spill out a ring and slid it onto her middle finger where it wobbled loosely. "He went to the Peninsula himself to deliver the replacement ransom and found this among your father's things in Lisbon."

A large golden heart held a ruby that pulsed in the rays of the setting sun. Her own heart started to pound in tandem.

She pulled the other two rings and the blood-soaked letter out of her pocket, slipped off the heart ring and fumbled the puzzle together, two hands clasping a heart. "Filomena said she got her part of the ring from my father. She thought there were only two parts and he had the other. But he didn't. He'd given that part to my mother, and he'd kept the heart. I guess. Shall we ever know the whole story?"

"We'll ask Shaldon before he dies again."

"My poor mother." She shook her head. "Or mothers. You know, Bink, I'm the same as you. I'm a bastard too."

Moisture pricked her eyes and she blinked. "My father was a scoundrel. I couldn't bear to have you hand off our child and your own self to another woman. I would track you down and thrash you without mercy."

He squeezed her hand. "You won't have to."

She handed him the rings. "Shall we see if there really is a code here?'

"Let's look at those markings."

As they bent their heads together, his scent engulfed her, soap and clean linens, and a hint of the alcohol used on his wound.

"These marks on the heart don't look like much," he said. "Perhaps they're just from the jeweler's tongs gripping hot metal. I don't see any key here."

She pulled out the letter. "Filomena, Kincaid, Tellingford and I had a long chat." She put the paper aside and fingered the rings. "Tellingford thinks my father's man, Jock, had the key to whatever code my father was using, but he'd been coshed on the crossing, and couldn't remember father's last message. Filomena said my father would have made allowances for that possibility, and would have laid in another—or perhaps two more paths to the treasure."

"If there really is a treasure."

She looked at him through her lashes. "I didn't tell you... Jock had claimed my father left a great fortune for me. Forgive me."

He lifted her chin and studied her. "You had expectations of treasure, yet you married me anyway." A smile cracked his face.

"One doesn't pass up a house, an income, and a man who can kiss like you."

He leaned forward but she held up a finger and stopped him. "There *is* a treasure, at least, that much Jock did swear to." She chewed on her lip. "Though when Mama denied she'd ever been a spy and said the stories he'd told me about her weren't true, I doubted his treasure story also."

"He was speaking of Filomena."

"Yes. And why could he not just tell me the truth, directly?" She shook her head. "Because he too was a spy and a liar, and nothing is ever a straight path with them."

He drew her head to his chest where she heard his great heart beating fiercely.

"I'm glad you're not a spy, Bink. And I don't truly care about this hidden money."

"Not at all?"

"Well, perhaps I do. Perhaps a little. I suppose I won't entirely stop wondering."

"So perhaps we should look for one of the other crooked paths your father laid. He sent you Jock, who was no help, and the ring, which has proven ineffective, the letter to your mother, which holds no clues, and this."

He slid the wooden box closer.

She drew in a sharp breath, her chin lifting. "And there's also the message he wrote to me."

She unfastened the lid and drew out the yellowed paper, Bink's breath warming her ear.

"But it's not a letter," he said.

He'd read that also, when he'd searched her things. Of course he had.

Never mind. "It's a poem." She read the terse script aloud:

A sweet girl named Polly
Curled up with her dolly

And spent the whole morning in play.
She ought have been learning
From books, pages turning
At work at her letters all day.

A quill you must take
And write without break
Until all of your letters are true.
Be good, do not shout
And help Mama out
Whenever she's weary and blue.

And when it is night
Put all away right
And snuggle up tight in your bed.
Into dreams you will glide
On your back or your side
Sleeping happy, beloved, and fed.

If the tides they do shift
Know this box is my gift
And I think loving thoughts of my Polly.
With this chest's treasure thrive
For the rest of your life
And be healthy, long-lived and jolly.

His lips touched her neck. "Hmm. About as good as Byron, I'd say. I always liked a good rhyme. Perhaps I shall start calling you Polly. I'm already thinking loving thoughts of you."

She chuckled and reached for the ring. "What do you make of these marks?"

He squinted at the rings' backs. "How the devil did Agruen get any kind of code out of this?"

"See here," she said. "Perhaps this one mark signifies a letter, and here where there are two, another letter. Perhaps the code marks every word or every other word or some such." She took a pencil and slip of paper. "I'll guess and you write down the letters."

They worked away, without any sensible message revealing itself.

"Drat." She pounded the lid on the lap desk.

Bink picked up the poem. "'With this chest's treasure thrive'...that does seem to indicate a treasure in here...'for the rest of your life'. Hmm. The rhyme is off a bit there."

She picked up the box. "It's too light to be filled with pirates' gold."

He took it from her. "And too heavy to be a mere shell." He felt all around. Jiggled it. Moved the hinges. Emptied all her whatnots and clawed at the interior panels. "Nothing loose. Nothing hollow. There must have been another letter Jock lost, or that your mother destroyed."

She stood and paced. Her mother, both mothers, had destroyed plenty in her world. As had her father.

And to hell—or heaven—with them. She marched into the dressing room and came back with her mother's hairbrush.

She smashed the brush paddle down on the box. *Bam, bam, bam.* A crack formed in the wood along the dovetailing.

"You must finish it, my love." She handed Bink the brush. "I'm not strong enough."

"I'm injured."

"Even so you can apply more force. I'll put you to bed afterwards with more laudanum."

"No laudanum. But perhaps you'll join me in bed."

"Agreed. Hurry then."

He searched her eyes, frowning. "Are you sure, Paulette? It's what he left you. He made it himself, you said."

"I'm sure. And if this doesn't work, we'll take it down to the brick wall in Lady Hackwell's garden."

Bink pounded, and winced and she would have stopped him, but suddenly a huge crack appeared on the right side, along the stout joining of one of the seams. Bink ripped at it, examining it closer. "Look here," he said.

A slim hollow space had opened into the side panel. Her pulse ticked up, excitement simmering in her. "I see something white." She yanked out a hairpin and probed. A piece of tightly folded parchment slid closer. "Can you reach it?" she asked.

"Your fingers are slimmer."

She poked and coaxed, and finally got a grip on the paper, easing it out.

The tight writing set her chest pounding as though she'd run all the way from the village to Ferndale Cottage. "A note. For an account at Drummond's Bank. For a king's ransom."

Bink took the paper and bent over it, inhaling sharply.

"Quite literally." A smile creased his face. "In the name of Paulette Silva Heardwyn."

He studied the box, and reached for the poem, squinting over the words.

"Look here." He pointed at the second and third stanzas and laughed. "Break—out—right—side."

She shook her head. "Can it be? It might not be real...but...we must give it back, mustn't we?" She searched his face.

He chewed on his lip. "We truly don't need it." He stood and began to pace, looking much stronger. "Money, lost outside Talavera. We looked for missing money, and we found Josiah Dickson in a hovel with your father and Filomena."

She hurried over and reached for him, and he looked down at their hands locked together.

"Next thing I knew, I was taking a priest through the mountains. Only he wasn't a priest. He was my father, dressed as a padre. He must have been carrying the new ransom."

"You didn't know him?"

"I'd never met him."

She shook her head. "Shaldon is impossible."

"Aye, he is. My mother was Irish, you know," he said. "A spy, Shaldon says. For the Irish rebellion."

"You didn't know?"

"About her spying? No. Never."

"Well. We are well-matched, in that way also, I suppose."

His smile warmed her.

"He plans to acknowledge me. Now that I'm a propertied man, he wants me to stand for Parliament for one of his pocket boroughs."

"Truly?" She squeezed his hand. "Then, if you're to be a Member of Parliament, I suppose we must give the crown back this money."

Bink gazed back at the broken box. "It's your money, Paulette. All yours. And who's to say that was British money? Maybe it was French money your father took as a prize. In any case, you may decide. Keep it. Give it back. Give it away." He dropped a kiss on her forehead. "You choose, love."

Her heart swelled and thrashed around inside her, sparking tears. She clutched the blue skirts of her mother's gown and thought of Sela Heardwyn, locked away in the country, and so many women like her confined to their genteel poverty. She thought of Lady Hackwell and her children's home. Of the maimed soldiers who wandered the roads and begged on the streets. Of Jenny and all the other vulnerable girls.

"We shall keep it for now. And then, I think we must give it away, without anyone knowing the money came from us."

"Secret benefactors."

"Yes. Yes, that would make me happy. And you, Edward Bink Gibson, you make me happy."

"Do I then?" His lips, so soft, kissed around the edge of her cuts and bruises. "Perhaps we should marry again, on this side of the border. Just so you can make sure of keeping me."

She laughed. "The first banns have been posted. And we know that we suit."

"And will always."

She glanced at his side, where a white bandage showed under his shirt. "I should not bother your stitches."

"You won't."

"So much movement will pull—"

"Oh, love, let me show you a way." He took her hand and led her over to the bed where he started working the fastenings of her dress.

"I'm thinking you are only after my money."

The gleam in his eyes darkened. "Yes. I'm a fortune hunter." Her bodice loosened and fell. "And I've found my fortune."

She chuckled. "With this treasure you'll thrive."

"Yes." He nuzzled her neck. "And… into bed we will dive."

She tugged out his shirt tails and eased the shirt over his head. "No diving, husband. Not until you've healed."

He helped her step out of her dress and went to work on her stays. "Well then, with this treasure we'll bide." He sat down on the bed. "And into bed we will slide. And—"

She pressed her lips to his, and eased him down, kissing him for long moments before bracing herself above him. His eyes had gone dark and no blood stained his bandage.

"You're a treasure, Paulette."

"And you're my treasure." Her fingers shook as she fumbled with his trousers.

"And I'll bring you great pleasure."

He would. He did. She blinked back tears.

"What's this?" Bink swiped a thumb across her cheek.

She ran a hand through his flaming hair. "I'm happy, Bink."

"So am I, my jolly Polly. So am I."

The End

If you enjoyed this book, please consider writing a review at any of the major book retailers, Amazon, Kobo, Barnes & Noble, iBooks, or at Goodreads.com.

A Note from the Author

Bink Gibson made his first appearance in my 2014 novel, *Bella's Band*, and reemerged in the 2016 novella, *The Marquess and the Midwife*, both times as the sidekick of the Earl of Hackwell.

In 2017, he appeared as the hero of his own romantic adventure in *The Bastard's Iberian Bride*. In 2019, after consulting with my readers' group, I decided to give Bink and Paulette's story a new cover, and while I was at it, this new title: *Marrying Mr. Gibson*.

I hope you've enjoyed this love story, set in the turbulent post-war year of 1819. One of the major events of that year was the Peterloo Massacre, on August 16, 1819. I must beg the indulgence of historical purists, because that date was actually a Sunday, a bit off from the timeline of my story. As usual, all historical errors are mine alone.

The legalisms involving Scottish divorce were inspired by the colorful life of Henry Paget, 1st Marquess of Anglesey. If you're interested in learning more, worth reading is his biography, *One Leg*, by a recent Marquess of Anglesey, one of his descendents.

Thanks go to authors and beta readers Tari Lynn Porter-Jewett, Linda Phan, and Jenny Hansen; to my friends from East Valley Authors; and to my daughter, Alicia, for some marketing suggestions. Thanks also to Editor Tessa Shapcott, and to Dar Albert for cover design.

And, as ever, I'm grateful to my husband for his unfailing support and enduring patience.

I love hearing from readers! You can contact and follow me on Facebook, Twitter, and Goodreads, and at my website AlinaKField.com. For special notices about sales and other news, please consider signing up for my occasional newsletters at my website.

I promise I won't spam you or sell your email address!

Best regards, and happy reading!

Alina K. Field

Books by Alina K. Field

Sons of the Spy Lord Series

Marrying Mr. Gibson

Paulette Heardwyn rushes to visit her dying guardian,
set on learning the truth about her father. But the only man
with answers takes his secrets to the grave, leaving her
penniless—unless she marries his illegitimate son

The Viscount's Seduction

Lady Sirena Hollister has lost everything, even her fey
abilities. But when the fairies hand her a chance at a London
Season, her schemes for revenge stir up an unknown enemy,
and spark danger of a different sort, in the person of a
handsome Viscount.

The Rogue's Last Scandal

Falling—literally—into the arms of the *ton*'s most
outrageous rogue seems a risky path of escape, but Maria
Graciela Kingsley y Romero has no other choice. Only
England's greatest spy lord can help her, and he is not to be
found—so his son will have to do!

The Counterfeit Lady

Vowing she'll never submit to an arranged marriage, an
earl's daughter bolts for the seaside cottage that will
someday be hers. But she finds her quiet refuge occupied by
the last man she ever wants to see—an American artist,
who's also a thief. And, quite possibly one of her father's
spies.

Avenging the Earl's Lady

The long war is over, but honor requires vanquishing one
last enemy, and the Earl of Shaldon has no time for
romance. But when the lady he longs for interferes in his
plot, and his enemy strikes at her, nothing else matters but
avenging his lady.

Novellas and Holiday Stories

The Marquess and the Midwife
A Christmas Novella
Finalist, 2016 National Reader's Choice Award

Uncovering a lie drives a new marquess back from a self-imposed exile at Christmas to find the only woman he's ever loved. Finding her turns out to be easy, uncovering her stunning secrets, a bit harder. But winning her back will be the greatest challenge of all.

A Leap Into Love
A Sweet Regence Romance Novella, a sequel to
The Marquess and the Midwife

Can a gentleman be too charming?
The ladies of Upper Upton think so.
When the single ladies of the village conspire to teach their charmer a lesson that might bankrupt him, the town's loveliest young widow—who's sworn off marriage forever—steps up to warn him.

Liliana's Letter
Finalist, 2015 National Reader's Choice Award

The Matchmaker Meets the Matchbreaker

Liliana Ashford's future as a professional chaperone depends on her wealthy charge's successful marriage, but her own close encounter with a scoundrel years ago makes her determined to save the girl from the same kind of rogue.

The Ghost of Depford Hall
A short, sweet Halloween story, a sequel to
Liliana's Letter

It's her mother's last All Hallows' Eve.
When family, friends, and tenants gather, goblins, ghouls, and ghosts are banned from this All Hallows' Eve party.
Only, no one told the Ghost of Depford Hall!

Bella's Band
A 2015 RONE Award Finalist

Saddled with his brother's title and debts, nothing about this new life makes the Earl of Hackwell want to stay—until he meets a lady with a secret that can change everything.

Rosalyn's Ring
2014 Book Buyer's Best Winner, Novella Category

Done with grieving her losses, a late nobleman's daughter has fallen into a tidy spinster's life in London. But when one snowy Christmas Eve, a young woman needs rescue, she seizes the chance to do good—and to recover a family heirloom that ought to be hers.

Haunting Miss Fenwick
Available 10/23/19

Thrilled to finally have a permanent home, a Squire's daughter won't let a supernatural creature scare her away. While hunting the ghost she doesn't believe in, she stumbles upon a mysterious flesh and blood man who might be the key to all of her problems.

The Duke She Despised
In the Winter Wishes Holiday Regency Romance Anthology
Available 10/15/19

Hiding her true identity, a young vicar's widow takes a position as housekeeper in a remote Scottish castle at Christmas for a new duke who years ago sabotaged her chance for happiness. She quickly falls for the duke's charming but not very competent factor, not knowing that he's hiding something also—he's the duke she despised!

Find out more at
https://AlinaKField.com
and sign up for my monthly emails
for news about upcoming books and
sales.